REACHING OLYMPUS

TEACHING MYTHOLOGY THROUGH READER'S THEATER SCRIPT·STORIES

REACHING OLYMPUS

THE GREEK MYTHS
TALES OF TITANS, GODS, AND MORTALS

WRITTEN AND ILLUSTRATED BY ZACHARY HAMBY
EDITED BY RACHEL HAMBY

DEDICATION

For Jacob

"Let me not then die ingloriously and without a struggle, but let me first do some great thing that shall be told among men hereafter."

-Homer-

ISBN-10: 0982704933
ISBN-13: 978-0-9827049-3-6
LCCN: 2014903014

Reaching Olympus, The Greek Myths: Tales of Titans, Gods, and Mortals
Written and Illustrated by Zachary Hamby
Edited by Rachel Hamby
Published by Hamby Publishing in the United States of America

TABLE OF CONTENTS

INTRODUCTORY MATERIALS

Introduction to the Series   7

Using This Book in the Classroom   11

SCRIPT-STORIES: TALES OF TITANS, GODS, AND MORTALS

A God Is Born   13

Prometheus the Firebringer   23

Mighty Aphrodite   37

The Loves of the Gods   55

The Golden Touch   69

Phaethon's Ride   81

The Life (and Deaths) of Sisyphus   97

Heracles: The True Story   111

Atalanta's Race   127

Theseus: The Road to Athens   139

Lost in the Labyrinth   155

GAMES, PUZZLES, AND EXTRA STORIES

The Creation of the Universe   171

War of the Titans   173

Deucalion and the Great Flood   175

Mount Olympus Find-It Picture Puzzle   177

Mount Olympus Find-It Picture Puzzle Key   179

Tournament of the Gods   181

APPENDICES

Glossary of Important Names   189

Pronunciation Guide   195

About the Author   199

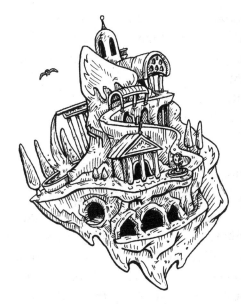

REACHING OLYMPUS:
AN INTRODUCTION TO THE SERIES

The faces of the souls of the Underworld could not have been more death-like. It was several years ago, but I remember it well. In a matter of weeks, I had gone from inexperienced student to full-time teacher. Smack dab in the midst of my student teaching experience, my cooperating teacher gave me some startling news. Because of a worsening medical condition, she would be leaving soon—then it would be all me. Even more startling: Four long years of college had not prepared me for the subject matter I would be required to teach—a class called World Short Stories and (gulp) Mythology. I remembered a few short stories from my survey literature courses, but with mythology, I was drawing a blank. In my cobwebbed memory there stood a woman with snake-hair and a psychedelic image of a wingéd horse—but that was it. Not to worry though. I had two whole weeks to prepare. After that I needed to fill a whole semester with mythological learning.

As any competent educator would, I turned to my textbook for aid. At first things looked promising. The book had a classy cover—black with the afore-mentioned wingéd horse on it. Bold gold letters tastefully titled it *Mythology*. Edith Hamilton—in the same lettering—was apparently the author. Yes, my judgment of the cover was encouraging, but what I found inside was anything but.

When I opened the text to read, I quickly realized I was doomed. Edith Hamilton had written her book in code. It was the same indecipherable language used by those who write literary criticism or owner manuals for electronic devices. Every sentence was a labyrinth, curving back in on itself, confusing the reader with many a subordinate clause and cutting him off completely from context with an outdated aphorism. If she wasn't randomly quoting Milton or Shakespeare, she was spending a paragraph differentiating between the poetic styles of Pindar and Ovid. It was as if Edith Hamilton was annoyed at having been born in the twentieth century and was using her writing style as some kind of literary time travel. Originally published in 1942, *Mythology* reflects the writing style of the day—a style that has grown increasingly more difficult for modern readers to comprehend. I knew if I could barely understand Hamilton's language, my students were going to be even more lost than I was.

Designed for average learners, Mythology was a junior-senior elective—the kind of class that was supposed to be entertaining and somewhat interesting. With Edith Hamilton tied around my neck, I was going down—and going down fast. It was at this point that the stupidly optimistic part of my brain cut in. "Maybe it won't be so bad," it said. "Don't underestimate your students." My ambitions renewed thanks to this still, small voice, and I laid Hamilton to the side, somehow sure that everything would turn out all right in the end. This was still more proof that I knew nothing about mythology.

Before I continue to tell how my tragic flaw of youthful optimism led to my ultimate downfall, I should take a minute to say a kind word about Edith Hamilton. In a time when interest in the classical writings of Greece and Rome was waning, Edith Hamilton revitalized this interest by writing several works that attempted to capture the creativity and majesty of Greco-Roman civilization. Hamilton's *Mythology* was one of the first books to take a comprehensive look at the Greco-Roman myths. The popularity of mythology today owes a great deal of debt to this book and its author. Fifty years after its publication, it is still the most commonly used mythology textbook in high school classrooms. Ironically, *Mythology* is no longer on an average high-schooler's reading level. As I mentioned earlier, Hamilton's writing style, with its ponderous vocabulary and sphinx-worthy inscrutability, further alienates any but the most intrepid of readers.

My first semester of teaching Mythology was a disaster. If I hadn't been so idealistic and gung-ho, I probably would have given up. Instead the new teacher within me stood up and said, "No! I'm going to do this, and we're going to make it fun! After all, Mythology is filled with all kinds of teenage interests: family murder, bestiality, incest, etc. It'll be just like watching MTV for them."

Utilizing every creative project idea under the sun, I threw myself into making the class work. We drew pictures, we read aloud, we watched related videos, wrote alternate endings to the stories—yet every time I kept coming up against the same brick wall: the text. It did not matter how enjoyable the activities were. Whenever we turned to the actual stories and cracked open that dreaded book, the life was sucked out of my students, and I was staring at their Underworld faces once again.

My last resort was boiling the stories down to outlines and writing these out on the whiteboard. Even that was better than actually reading them. At least the students would get the basic facts of the story. One student, possibly sensing I was seconds away from the breaking point, made the comment, "I didn't know this class would be a bunch of notes. I thought it would be fun."

Then I gave up.

When I look back on that semester, I realize that I failed a whole batch of students. They came and went thinking that studying mythology was a brainless exercise in rote memorization. Perhaps the failure of that first experience would not have been so stark if a success hadn't come along the next year.

The second time through the class, I was determined not to repeat the mistakes of the past. There must be some way of avoiding the text—somehow relating the stories without actually reading them. But then I thought, "Isn't this supposed to be an English class? If we don't actually read, can it be called English? What has this outdated text driven me to?"

When I looked into the stories, I could see excellent tales trapped behind stuffy prose. How could I get the students to see what I saw? How could I set those good stories free?

On a whim I decided to try my hand at rewriting one of the myths. I had dabbled in creative writing in college, so surely I could spin one of these tales better than Edith Hamilton had. The idea of dividing the story into parts struck me as a good one. Maybe that would foster more student involvement. A few hours later, I had created my first Reader's Theater script. (At the time I had no idea that there was an actual term for this type of thing or that there was sound educational research behind reading aloud.) Part of me was excited. The other part was skeptical. "These kids are high-schoolers," I said to myself. "They'll never go for this." I looked at some of the elements I had included in my script: overly-dramatic dialogue, sound effects, cheesy jokes. What was I thinking? Since I had already spent the time and energy, I decided to give it a shot.

There are those grand moments in education when something clicks, and those moments are the reason that teachers teach. My script clicked. It clicked quite well, in fact. The students loved reading aloud. They were thrilled beyond belief not to be reading silently or taking notes or even watching a video. They performed better than I ever dreamed possible. They did funny voices. They laughed at the cheesy jokes. They inhabited the characters. They even did the sound effects.

As I looked around the room, I noticed something that was a rarity: My students were having fun. Not only that, but they were getting all the information that Edith Hamilton could have offered them. When the script was done, I encountered a barrage of questions: "Why did Zeus act like that to Hera? What is an heir? Why did Aphrodite choose to marry Hephaestus? Did the Greeks have *any* respect for marriage?" Did my ears deceive me? Intelligent questions—questions about character motivation, vocabulary, and even historical context? I couldn't believe it.

I was also struck by another startling fact: The students were asking about these characters as if they were real people. They were able to treat the characters as real people because real people had inhabited their roles. Zeus was not some dusty god from 3,000 years ago. He was Joe in the second row doing a funny voice. Something had come from the abstract world of mythology and become real. And as for the quiz scores, my students might not remember the difference between Perseus and Theseus, but they definitely remembered the difference between Josh and Eric, the two students who played those roles. On top of all this, the class had changed from a group of isolated learners to a team that experiences, laughs, and learns together.

After the success of that first script, I realized I had created some kind of teaching drug. It was an incredible experience, one that I wanted to recreate over and over again. I wouldn't and couldn't go back to the old world of bland reading. So I didn't.

The great moments of Greek mythology flew from my keyboard, and I created script after script. Despite my overweening enthusiasm, I knew that too much of a good thing could definitely be bad, so I chose stories that would spread out the read-aloud experience. We would still use Edith Hamilton in moderation. After all, a few vegetables make you enjoy the sweet stuff all the more.

Over the course of that semester, I discovered a new enthusiasm in the students and myself. They enjoyed learning, and I enjoyed teaching. I had students arguing over who would read which parts—an unbelievable sight for juniors and seniors. Laughter was a constant in the classroom. As the Greeks would say, it was a golden age of learning.

Now I have the chance to share this technique with other teachers. With these script-stories, I hope my experiences will be recreated in other classrooms. Mythology should not be an old dead thing of the past, but a living, breathing, exciting experience.

USING THIS BOOK IN THE CLASSROOM

Script-stories (also known as Reader's Theater) are a highly motivational learning strategy that blends oral reading, literature, and drama. Unlike traditional theater, script-stories do not require costumes, make-up, props, stage sets, or memorization. Only the script and a healthy imagination are needed. As students read the script aloud, they interpret the emotions, beliefs, attitudes, and motives of the characters. A narrator conveys the story's setting and action and provides the commentary necessary for the transitions between scenes.

While Reader's Theater has been enormously successful with lower grade-levels, it is a great fit for older learners as well. Students of any age enjoy and appreciate the chance to *experience* a story rather than having it read to them. For years now script-stories have been the tool that I use to teach mythology to high-schoolers. I wouldn't have it any other way. Below are the answers to some of the most frequently asked questions concerning the use of script-stories in the classroom.

How do you stage these stories in the classroom? Hand out photocopies of the particular script for that day. (Note: It is perfectly legal for you to photocopy pages from this book. That is what it was designed for!) Certain copies of the scripts should be highlighted for particular characters, so that whichever students you pick to read parts will have their lines readily available. (This is not necessary, but it does make things run more smoothly.) Some teachers who use script-stories require their students to stand when reading their lines or even incorporate physical acting. As for the sound effects in the scripts *(fanfare)*, noisemakers can be distributed to the students and used when prompted. Otherwise, students can make the noises with their own voices.

How do you structure a class around script-stories? How often do you use them? Too much of a good thing can be bad. In my own classroom I do employ the script-stories frequently—in some units we read a story every day of the week—but I do supplement with other notes, texts, activities, and self-created worksheets. Some of these activities are included in the back of the book. For other examples of these activities, check out my website *www.mythologyteacher.com*.

How do you assess script-stories? A quick reading quiz after the completion of a script is an easy way to assess comprehension. In my own classroom I ask five questions that hit the high-points of the story. I never make the questions overly specific (for example, asking a student to remember a character's name like Agamemnon or Polydectes). Each script in this book comes with five recall questions for this purpose.

Another form of assessment is by fostering as much classroom discussion as possible. How well students discuss will tell you how well they have comprehended the story. The discussion questions included in this book have seen success in my own classroom.

I hope you find this book to be a great resource. It was designed with the intent of helping a much wider audience experience the timeless tales of world mythology in a new manner. Below I have listed some further notes concerning the script-stories. Thanks for purchasing this book. Please feel free to contact me if you have any questions.

Sincerely,

Zachary Hamby
mr.mythology@gmail.com
www.mythologyteacher.com

FURTHER NOTES FOR TEACHERS

UNIT PLAN Teaching one of these scripts a day and including some of the suggested activities (see individual teacher pages) should yield at least an 11-day unit.

INTENDED AUDIENCE: 6-12th grade

LENGTH: Script-stories range between 25-45 minutes in length

SCRIPT-STORY PROCESS

- Every student will need a copy of the script-story.
- Reading parts may be highlighted for greater reading ease.
- As the teacher, you are the casting director. Assign the parts as you deem best.
- Give your largest parts to your strongest readers but still try to draw out the reluctant participant.

- As the teacher, you should take the part of the narrator. Actively participating only makes it more fun for you and the students.
- Cut loose and have fun. Script-stories allow students to see their teacher in a whole new light.

POSSIBLE MODIFICATIONS

- Costumes, props, and even sets can be added to any script-story to make it more engaging.
- Requiring the students to stand while reading their parts creates a stronger dynamic between speaking roles.
- Encouraging students to write their own script-stories gets them thinking about the elements of storytelling and the use of dialogue.
- Assigning one student to be responsible for all the sound effects in a script-story can involve someone who is not a strong reader in the performance. Including certain tools that actually make the indicated sound effects (noise-makers, whistles, coconuts, etc.) is another excellent way to add interest.

A GOD IS BORN
TEACHER GUIDE

BACKGROUND

Everything has a beginning, right? According to the ancient Greeks, the gods did as well. They saw the divine through a very human lens and gave their immortal deities human characteristics and personalities. So naturally, the gods (just like humans) had births.

The births of many gods are recorded in mythology. Zeus' birth is famous for his father's reaction to it—Cronus, the titan father of the first gods, tries to devour all his children and only Zeus escapes alive. Aphrodite is born when drops of blood from a wounded immortal fall upon the sea foam. Athena is born directly from Zeus' head—a fitting start since she is the personification of wisdom. Hephaestus is born an ugly baby, and Hera, his mother, takes one look at him and casts him off Olympus. Zeus accidentally incinerates the pregnant mortal mother of Dionysus and transports the baby-god into his own body, eventually giving birth to him himself. And so the list of famous god-births goes on and on.

Like his many Olympian relatives, Hermes has a birth story as well. He is one of the youngest gods—the little, twerpy brother of his siblings. Only Dionysus is younger than he. In addition to a birth story, Hermes also has this tale about his "childhood." Even though no myth ever answers the question of how exactly gods grow up, it is interesting to see a god as a child. Known for his clever wit and ingenuity, Hermes immediately makes a name for himself—as a brilliant inventor, a sneaky thief, and a trouble-maker.

SUMMARY

Hermes, the newest god in the Greek pantheon, is born in a cave in the mountainous part of Greece called Arcadia. His mother is Maia, a nymph, and his father is Zeus himself. Baby Hermes immediately startles his mother by speaking to her, demonstrating his fully developed vocabulary, and announcing that he is off to make his way in the world. Stunned, Maia watches her newborn son leave their cave completely alone.

On his adventure Hermes meets an old shepherd named Battus. From the shepherd Hermes receives sheep gut, which he stretches over the hollow of a turtle shell to make a musical instrument called a lyre. Battus, completely baffled by Hermes' behavior, warns him he must avoid the cattle that graze across the valley, for they belong to the god Apollo. Baby Hermes takes this as a challenge and declares that he will abduct Apollo's herds in a way that will completely fool the god. He drives the cattle backward, which makes their tracks confusing, and hides them in a cave.

Hermes returns to his home, and Zeus soon arrives to meet his newborn son. Maia tells Zeus about Hermes' strange abilities, and as she does so, Apollo appears and angrily declares that his cattle have been stolen. Hermes' parents realize that it is he who has committed this crime. They force Hermes to tell them where he hid the cattle. To make amends with Apollo, Hermes gives his older brother the newly-created lyre. Apollo forgets his anger immediately.

In an effort to keep such a troublesome youngster out of mischief, Zeus makes Hermes the official messenger of Olympus and presents him with a magical staff.

ESSENTIAL QUESTIONS

- How important is being clever?
- How do incidents in childhood shape us into adults?
- How can talents be used for both good and evil?

ANTICIPATORY QUESTIONS

- Who was Hermes?
- How would a baby with god-like powers act?
- Have you ever invented something?
- Do your younger siblings ever play tricks on you?
- What is tough about being the youngest in a group of brothers and sisters?

CONNECT

Before They Were Gods Hermes has a myth about his "childhood," but many of the other gods don't have this type of story. Imagine there is a show called *Before They Were Gods*, which shows episodes from the gods' childhoods. Write a skit that shows an event from the younger years of one of the gods.

The Myth of Dionysus Read about the Greek god Dionysus. There are many myths about this god's early years. Since Dionysus is the newest of the gods, many of the Greeks do not accept him, and he must struggle to prove himself as a god worthy of Olympus. How are his experiences similar to those of Hermes? What is strange about the idea of a god "growing up" and having to prove himself?

TEACHABLE TERMS

- **Alliteration** Hermes' line about "walking wads of meat" on pg. 17 and Zeus' line on pg. 19 about "a bunch of brainless bovines" both make use of alliteration.
- **Oxymoron** This term, defined as "a self-contradictory statement or idea," could apply to the title of this script-story. Discuss why the title "A God Is Born" is somewhat self-contradictory.
- **Characterization** This story characterizes Baby Hermes as rude and arrogant. How is this different from a baby's expected behavior? How does this create humor?
- **Diction** How is Hermes' vocabulary advanced? How does his elevated diction add to the humor of the story?
- **Symbol** The staff that Zeus presents to Hermes on pg. 21 is called the caduceus. It has two snakes curling about its handle and a pair of eagle's wings at its crest. Over the centuries this staff had many symbolic meanings. In the modern world the staff has become a symbol for medicine.
- **Homophones** On pg. 21 humor is created from the mix-up between *liar* and *lyre*, two homophones or words that have the same pronunciation but different meanings.

RECALL QUESTIONS

1. What musical instrument does Hermes invent?
2. What two things does Hermes use to invent this instrument?
3. What does Hermes discover that startles Battus the shepherd?
4. What does Hermes steal from his brother Apollo?
5. What occupation does Zeus give to his young son?

A GOD IS BORN

CAST

MAIA	*Mother of Hermes*
HERMES	*Newborn God*
BATTUS	*Elderly Shepherd*
ZEUS	*Lord of the Gods*
APOLLO	*God of Light*

NARRATOR: In a cave in the mountainous region of Greece called Arcadia, something quite rare was happening—a god was being born. The god's mother was the beautiful nymph, Maia, and his father was none other than Zeus.

It was dawn, and a new immortal life had begun. Maia held up her newborn son.

MAIA: The youngest of the gods! My son! You are born!

HERMES: Yuck. Don't remind me. That was a horrible experience.

MAIA: *(startled)* Ah! You can speak!

HERMES: Obviously.

MAIA: *(confused)* Wouldn't you rather cry like a normal child?

HERMES: That's kiddie stuff, Mother. I can call you "Mother," can't I?

MAIA: Uh…

HERMES: Good! It's a pleasure to finally meet you face to face. I feel like we've grown very close these past nine months.

MAIA: Er…

HERMES: Now, if you don't mind, hurry up and name me. I've just been born into this big world, and I want to go out and do some exploring. If you don't name me first, I won't know when you're calling me home. Ha. Ha. Just a little joke there.

MAIA: I—I—I was planning to name you Hermes.

HERMES: Hmmm. Not the best name. But I'll make it great. Very well, Mother. I'm off.

NARRATOR: The child hopped from her arms but looked down in shock at his naked body.

HERMES: *(cry of shock)* Ah! Some clothes, please! You don't expect me to go around like this, do you? It's barbaric.

MAIA: Um…here!

NARRATOR: She wrapped his blanket about him.

HERMES: Not exactly fashionable. Oh well. Goodbye, Mother. Don't wait up.

NARRATOR: The baby let himself out. His mother sat in silence for several minutes.

MAIA: What just happened here?

NARRATOR: Baby Hermes strolled down the mountainside, clasping his chubby hands behind his back and inquisitively glancing here and there.

HERMES: Hmmm. This is a strange world.

NARRATOR: As he walked, he happened to find the shell of a dead tortoise lying across his path.

HERMES: This seems to be some kind of animal protective device. Hmmm. Interesting.

NARRATOR: He picked up the tortoise shell and placed it on his head. Leaning over a nearby pool, he admired his reflection.

HERMES: Ah! Intelligent *and* handsome.

NARRATOR: Soon Baby Hermes wandered into a field, where a shepherd was tending his flock. The old man looked down and beheld the strange child.

BATTUS: Bless me! It's a little baby.

HERMES: Watch it, old man, you are addressing a god!

BATTUS: *(baby-talk)* Aw. Awen't you jus' the cwutest thing?

HERMES: Sir, I see that you have some kind of speech impediment, but please—

BATTUS: Just look at these chubby-wubby cheeks!

HERMES: Unhand me!

BATTUS: And that is jus' the cutest lil' hat I've ever seen.

HERMES: Good grief! *(angrily)* I am one of the immortal gods! Fall upon your knees in fear of me, mortal!

NARRATOR: Baby Hermes gestured menacingly at the old man.

BATTUS: Awwww.

HERMES: *(sigh)* This is going nowhere.

NARRATOR: Hermes turned his attention to the sheep that the old man was tending.

HERMES: Tell me, unintelligent mortal, what are these fluffy quadrupeds that I see before me?

BATTUS: Oooh. Aren't you verbal? These are sheep. *(slowly)* Can you say *sheep*?

HERMES: I'm surprised you can.

NARRATOR: A pile of unsavory looking meat lay at the shepherd's feet.

HERMES: And what is that disgusting pile of stuff there?

BATTUS: Oh! What an observant little fellow you are! These are the remains of the old ram—his fleece, his meat, and his guts.

HERMES: Intriguing. Might I see those guts?

BATTUS: Huh?

NARRATOR: Hermes took the tortoise shell from his head and spread the stringy thread of the guts tightly across the hollow of the shell. He plucked it with his chubby fingers. *(musical note)*

HERMES: Voila!

BATTUS: Well, I'll be! That's a pretty neat trick, sonny!

HERMES: That's nothing. Watch this!

NARRATOR: There was a flurry of motion as Hermes went to work. When he was finished, six gut-strings stretched over the hollow of the turtle's shell. Hermes deftly plucked out a tune upon it. *(musical tune)* The shepherd watched all this in wonder.

BATTUS: I can't believe it! If I told the other shepherds about this, they'd call me a liar!

HERMES: Liar, huh? That's exactly what I was going to call this invention—the lyre!

BATTUS: This is amazing!

HERMES: So it is. If these creatures are called sheep, what are those creatures across the valley there?

BATTUS: Oh, those are moo-cows. But do not go there, little master. Those golden cows belong to the mighty god, Apollo. And no one dares pester them. They belong to the gods.

HERMES: I *am* one of the gods, you simpleton. No one tells me what I can and can't do. I am Hermes!

BATTUS: What an imagination you have, too! Wait a minute. Does your mommy know where you are?

HERMES: *(sigh)* If this is what mortals are like, I have no use for them.

NARRATOR: Hermes tucked his newly-invented lyre under his arm and marched away toward the herds of Apollo.

HERMES: Hmmm. No one dares to mess with Apollo's herds, huh? Well, they have not met Hermes!

NARRATOR: Hermes planted his plump legs firmly apart and stared at the cows imperiously.

HERMES: All right! Listen up, you walking wads of meat! There's a new god in town.

NARRATOR: The cows lazily raised their heads. *(confused mooing)*

HERMES: Now, yah! Yah! Get up there!

NARRATOR: As Battus the shepherd watched from across the valley, Baby Hermes took control of the golden herd. He drove them backward across the mountainside. This would make their tracks confusing if anyone came looking for them. He drove them all the way back to a well-hidden cave and barricaded them within.

HERMES: Not bad for a baby, huh? Let's see this Apollo fellow find his herd now! Ha!

NARRATOR: Battus was still in shock when Hermes returned back along the path. The baby god was picking his teeth with a stick.

HERMES: Hello, old man. I had to try one of those cows for myself. Not bad. Not bad. Their meat works better if you cook it though.

BATTUS: Cook it?

HERMES: *(sigh)* Here let me show you.

NARRATOR: The god gathered a pile of grass, snatched up two sticks, and rubbed them furiously together until they produced a spark. A fire blazed.

HERMES: Voila!

BATTUS: *(in fright)* Ah! Witchcraft!

NARRATOR: The old man ran and hid behind a rock.

HERMES: Oh please. It's just fire. I invented it to cook my meat.

BATTUS: You're no baby! Y-y-you're not natural!

NARRATOR: The infant stomped out the blaze and approached the cowering old man.

HERMES: You're finally catching on. Now listen to me and listen carefully. When Apollo comes looking for his herd, you will tell him that you saw nothing.

BATTUS: Please! Please just leave me in peace, demon-baby!

HERMES: Yes, "demon-baby" is right, and I will get you if you don't do what I tell you to!

BATTUS: I will! I will! Just leave me in peace!

HERMES: Remember your story! You saw nothing!

NARRATOR: Satisfied with this answer, Baby Hermes left the old man behind and returned to his mother's cave.

MAIA: My child! Where have you been?

HERMES: Out.

MAIA: Doing what?

HERMES: Sheesh. Can't I have a life? If you don't mind, Mother, I'm going to turn in.

NARRATOR: Baby Hermes climbed up into his bed, plucked a few melodies on his lyre, and fell asleep.

MAIA: This is most strange.

NARRATOR: It did not take long for Apollo to discover the theft of his golden cattle. Even though he was an intelligent god, he could not decipher the meaning of the herd's tracks. They led into the valley and then just disappeared! He found Battus the shepherd babbling to himself. The old man told him of a strange demon-baby who had stolen his cattle.

Meanwhile, Zeus decided to visit Arcadia to pay a visit to his newly born son.

ZEUS: Show me that newborn boy of mine!

MAIA: Zeus, we have to talk. I'm worried about Hermes.

ZEUS: Who is Hermes?

MAIA: Your son!

ZEUS: Oh yeah. I meant to be here yesterday to see his birth, but I just couldn't get away. Running the universe and everything, you know. Now what is wrong with the little tyke?

MAIA: He left yesterday, and I do not know where he went.

ZEUS: Left? What do you mean *left*?

MAIA: He got up, said, "Goodbye," and left. When he returned, he wouldn't tell me where he had been.

ZEUS: An advanced lad, isn't he? Usually they wait for the teenage years for this type of behavior.

MAIA: I'm worried that it means something horrible.

NARRATOR: Suddenly Apollo, blazing brightly with anger, burst into the cave.

APOLLO: Father Zeus! I've been looking all over for you! You will never believe what has happened!

ZEUS: (shocked) The titans have escaped from the Underworld?

APOLLO: No.

ZEUS: Giants are attacking Mount Olympus?

APOLLO: No. Worse! Someone has stolen my cattle!

ZEUS: What? You're this worked up over a bunch of brainless bovines? What is a god doing with a bunch of cows anyway?

APOLLO: Helios had a herd, and I wanted one as well.

ZEUS: You and that blasted God of the Sun! Always competing! Well, so what if someone has stolen your cows? It's not like you eat their meat anyway. We're gods. We eat nectar and drink ambrosia—or do we drink nectar and eat ambrosia? I can't ever remember.

APOLLO: That's not the point! Those cows are my pets, and I want them back!

ZEUS: Cows? As pets? Good grief.

APOLLO: You must help me find them.

ZEUS: Very well. But what god would be fool enough to mess with you?

APOLLO: That's just it. I interrogated an old shepherd who saw the whole thing. He told me that it was no god at all—but a talking baby!

ZEUS: A talking baby! Was this shepherd sober?

MAIA: Wait a minute, Zeus. You don't think…

ZEUS: You mean…the newborn boy? It couldn't be!

NARRATOR: Maia shrugged.

ZEUS: Hmmm. Maybe it's time I met my new son.

NARRATOR: Zeus, Maia, and Apollo made their way into the baby's nursery. Hermes was lying innocently within his cradle, serenely clutching his rattle in sleep.

MAIA: Hermes! You're in big trouble, young man! We want to know what you've been up to! What do you have to say for yourself?

HERMES: Goo goo! Gah gah!

NARRATOR: Hermes peered up with innocent eyes.

ZEUS: (sappy) Awww. That is soooo cute. (pause) Wait a minute. You said he can talk, right?

MAIA: He can! Hermes, cut it out!

ZEUS: Hermes, this is your father, Zeus, speaking to you now!

HERMES: Da-da!

ZEUS: *(sappy)* Awwww.

APOLLO: Zeus! My cattle!

ZEUS: Oh right! Now, Hermes, stop that! I know that you can talk.

MAIA: What did you do with this nice man's cattle?

APOLLO: Did you steal my cattle, you little brat?

HERMES: Who you calling a brat, golden boy?

ZEUS: Hermes! You should treat Apollo with respect. He is your half-brother!

HERMES: Big deal. If you're my dad, I have half-brothers all over the place!

MAIA: *(scolding)* Hermes!

ZEUS: No. He has a point there.

HERMES: Mother, what makes you think I could steal cattle? I'm a simple baby. I was just born yesterday.

MAIA: And you must think we were, too! The shepherd saw you! Now what did you do with Mr. Apollo's cattle?

HERMES: That's for me to know and you to find out.

APOLLO: *(angrily)* That's it! No chubby baby is going to make a fool out of me.

HERMES: Too late. Already did.

APOLLO: Why you—!

HERMES: *(teasing)* You can't hit a baby! Nah-nuh-nah-nuh-boo-boo!

MAIA: Please, Hermes! Act your age!

HERMES: I am!

APOLLO: Father! Do something! Make him give me my herd back! *(throwing a fit)* They're mine! They're mine!

HERMES: He's acting my age, too.

NARRATOR: A huge smile spread over Zeus' face.

ZEUS: *(loud happy laughter)* Ha! Ha! Ha!

APOLLO: Father, what has gotten into you? Cattle-rustling is no laughing matter.

ZEUS: Of course, it is, my son! This one-day-old child has gotten the better of us. He is still in diapers, and already he is a master thief.

HERMES: Actually, I don't have a diaper at all. Maybe I should check into one of those…

NARRATOR: Apollo's face began to turn red.

APOLLO: I will not be mocked by this child. Father, make him give me my herd back! I must be appeased!

HERMES: Here!

NARRATOR: The infant held up the lyre.

HERMES: It is not much, Brother Apollo. An elementary invention.

APOLLO: Ha! You offer me this dirty turtle shell?

HERMES: A lyre!

APOLLO: How dare you! It is obviously *you* who are the liar! I am the God of Truth.

HERMES: Sheesh. Are all the gods as stupid as you? The harp is called a lyre.

APOLLO: Another joke! And what are these disgusting things stretched across it?

HERMES: Sheep guts!

APOLLO: I am insulted!

HERMES: No! Look! Look!

NARRATOR: Hermes began strumming happily upon the lyre. *(happy music)*

HERMES: See? Harp make pretty music.

NARRATOR: Apollo's features quickly softened. He drew forward and took the lyre.

APOLLO: Amazing! This beautiful sound is produced from this crude apparatus?

HERMES: No fooling you, bro.

ZEUS: This child is full of many surprises!

HERMES: I am sorry that I stole your cows, Apollo—I guess. So this is my present to you.

NARRATOR: Apollo looked up happily.

APOLLO: Then I consider it a fair trade! This is the greatest wonder I've ever seen!

HERMES: And for you, Father, I have a little discovery I call "fire."

ZEUS: Sounds intriguing, my boy!

MAIA: Now wait a minute! Hermes, you may be able to buy off your father and your half-brother, but you can't fool me! You're in big trouble, mister! I won't have you sneaking out all the time and causing so much trouble.

ZEUS: Hmmm. You know, I've been thinking. Little Hermes here seems like he could get himself into endless amounts of trouble.

MAIA: You can say that again! He's only been alive one day, and I almost have an ulcer from worry!

ZEUS: I think I need to fix this problem.

HERMES: *(nervously)* Well, look at the sun! It's getting way past my naptime. Good night!

ZEUS: Hermes, how would you like it if I made you the official messenger of Olympus?

HERMES: *(in shock)* What? That's my punishment?

ZEUS: It's a way to put your *talents* to use. You can travel around the world and deliver my divine decrees.

HERMES: I *do* have quite a propensity for words. And I've always wanted to travel.

ZEUS: And plus, I will give you this magical staff.

NARRATOR: Zeus held out his hand, and a golden staff appeared within his grip. At its crest were a pair of eagle wings and, curled about its handle, two serpents. Hermes picked up his own rattle and chucked it away.

HERMES: Now that's a rattle! I'll take it!

ZEUS: Use your power wisely! Don't be causing mischief. We will give you enough work to keep you busy.

HERMES: I will serve you well, Father!

NARRATOR: He eyed his new staff greedily.

HERMES: My first task will be to track down that dumb shepherd, Battus, and turn him into a rock!

MAIA: Hermes!

HERMES: He won't mind. It won't be much of a change for him anyway.

MAIA: Hermes!

NARRATOR: Zeus placed a hand upon Apollo's shoulder.

ZEUS: Apollo, would you say that you and Hermes have made peace?

APOLLO: I would. *(to Hermes)* Thank you for the present, little brother. I will use it well.

ZEUS: Then let us ascend back to Olympus.

HERMES: Father, just let me say what a learning experience this whole day has been. I will never again use my talents for wrongdoing! I am a changed god!

ZEUS: Well, good. Farewell!

MAIA: Farewell!

HERMES: Farewell!

APOLLO: Farewell!

ZEUS: Wait a minute. Where is my thunderbolt? I had it just a minute ago. *(yelling)* Hermes!

NARRATOR: And so Hermes, the cleverest of the gods, joined the Olympians.

DISCUSSION QUESTIONS

- What is odd about the title "A God is Born"?
- What does this myth show about Hermes? What are his strengths and weaknesses?
- Do you think Hermes' new job will keep him out of trouble, as Zeus hopes? Explain.
- According to the myth, Hermes actually does return to Battus and turns the shepherd into stone. Does Battus deserve this punishment? Explain.
- How do you think gods age? The myths never give a good explanation.

PROMETHEUS THE FIREBRINGER
TEACHER GUIDE

BACKGROUND

Surprisingly, it is not the gods of Greek mythology that create the first human life. Instead a kindly titan named Prometheus first makes man. Rather than applauding this, Zeus and the other gods are hostile to mankind—grinning at the idea of their destruction and releasing evil and hardship upon them. In fact, Prometheus proves to be his creation's only ally. He steals fire from Olympus to help humans survive, and Zeus sentences him to eternal torment for this crime.

To the ancient Greeks Prometheus stood as a symbol of the struggle against tyranny. In the tragedy *Prometheus Bound* the playwright Aeschylus presents Prometheus as an idealistic hero who struggles against the all-powerful injustice of Zeus. The titan does not regret his actions but rather laments living in a world where helping others is considered treason.

In later centuries Prometheus became a symbol for human progress—waging a seemingly impossible battle against the forces of nature. Today Prometheus' spirit lives on, as we continue the struggle. We continue to seek for ways to undo and outwit nature. But should we play with the immortal fire of science? Will we go too far? Will we risk the wrath of the gods?

SUMMARY

War between the gods and the titans rages—threatening to destroy the heavens and the earth. At last the tide turns, and Zeus leads the gods to victory. After the battle he sentences the titans to eternal punishment. The massive titan Atlas is forced to bear the weight of the sky upon his shoulders, and the watery titan Ocean becomes a river that surrounds the entire earth. Zeus decides to spare two young titans who did not pick a side in the conflict— Prometheus, who possesses the ability to glimpse the future, and Epimetheus, his dimwitted brother.

The titan brothers go into the world to help it heal. From the mud of the earth Prometheus creates many creatures—all types of animals. As he creates them, he allows Epimetheus to decide what special abilities they will have. Finally, Prometheus makes a creation in the image of the gods and calls it *man*. When he goes to give it special abilities, he realizes that Epimetheus has given them all away. In order to make sure that the other animals do not gain the upper hand, Prometheus gives man a crafty mind.

News of Prometheus' new creation reaches Mount Olympus, and Zeus is not pleased. He dislikes the idea of anything being created without his permission, but he knows that winter will spell doom for the men that Prometheus has created. As Zeus predicted, cold weather and wild animals soon begin to kill off the newly-formed men. In desperation Prometheus realizes that there is only one thing that will save mankind— immortal fire that only the gods possess.

Prometheus travels to Olympus and requests the gift of fire for mankind, but Zeus flatly refuses. Prometheus steals fire from the forge of Hephaestus and, hiding it in a fennel stalk, smuggles it back to earth. When Zeus sees fires glowing upon the earth, he furiously summons Prometheus to him. The titan does not deny his crime, and Zeus sentences him to a grisly punishment: Prometheus will be chained to a mountainside, and each day an eagle will tear out his liver. Each night the liver will painfully reform within him only to be ripped out again the next day. Prometheus bemoans his fate—punished for helping his mortal children.

Zeus feels that Epimetheus and all mankind must be punished as well. He commands Hephaestus to create another kind of human—a female. The gods bestow all kinds of charms and gifts upon her to make her a "beautiful evil." The first woman, Pandora, is given to Epimetheus as a wife. With her comes a jar that she is instructed not to open.

Since Epimetheus is dimwitted and Pandora is extremely curious, she fools her husband and opens the jar, releasing all kinds of evils into the world—sickness, decay, death, and other hardships. Yet the last thing to exit the jar is a little bit of hope to make the evils of the world bearable.

ESSENTIAL QUESTIONS

- Are there forces in nature that should not be tampered with?
- Should we sacrifice ourselves for the good of others?
- How can curiosity cause trouble?

CONNECT

Frankenstein or the Modern Prometheus by **Mary Shelley** In the novel Dr. Frankenstein bestows life upon a creature made from dead body parts. Ultimately, he is cursed for doing so. The novel deals with some of the same themes as the myth of Prometheus: What are the dangers of playing God? Are there some aspects of nature that should not be tampered with?

ANTICIPATORY QUESTIONS

- What is Pandora's Box?

- According to Greek mythology, who created human beings?
- Who were the titans?
- Why was fire incredibly important to ancient peoples?

TEACHABLE TERMS

- **Character Type** Prometheus is an example of the self-sacrificing hero, who gives selflessly of himself for others. Think of other examples of this type of character.
- **Juxtaposition** Prometheus symbolizes forethought, the literal meaning of his name, while Epimetheus symbolizes afterthought, the literal meaning of his name. The contrast between them helps develop their characters.
- **Symbolism** Fire symbolizes several different things in this myth. First, it represents power because the gods horde it. Secondly, it represents human intelligence and ingenuity. The gift of fire allows humans to thrive and subdue the other animals.
- **Sexism** Zeus describes Pandora as a "beautiful evil" on pg. 33 and uses her as a weapon against Epimetheus and mankind. She is presented as conniving and incredibly curious—an insinuation that all women are like her. Considering that male writers crafted this tale, this is an example of sexist stereotyping.

RECALL QUESTIONS

1. Which god or titan created man?
2. Who is Epimetheus?
3. Why does Prometheus steal fire from the gods?
4. How will Prometheus be tortured each day?
5. What is the last thing to exit Pandora's jar?

PROMETHEUS THE FIREBRINGER

CAST

PROMETHEUS	*Peaceful Titan*
EPIMETHEUS	*Prometheus' Brother*
ZEUS	*Ruler of the Gods*
ATLAS	*Powerful Titan*
HADES	*Ruler of the Underworld*
HEPHAESTUS	*God of Fire and the Forge*
KRATOS	*God of Strength*
BIA	*God of Force*
HERMES	*Messenger God*
PANDORA	*First Woman*

NARRATOR: The newly-formed world now faced a cataclysmic conflict that could unmake it. The great war between the gods and the titans was about to begin.

Standing in their ranks were the gods, brimming with power—their weapons smoldering in their hands. Opposite them stood Cronus and his fellow titans—colossuses with all the powers of nature.

Then with wicked war cries the two sides ran forward and clashed together with such force that the atmosphere crackled with power. The unfathomable sea shrieked, the earth crashed and rumbled, the vast sky groaned, and massive Olympus shook down to its roots. *(sounds of battle)*

The battle reached fever pitch, but as of yet, one god, the mightiest among them, had not made his presence known. When he saw that the time was right, Zeus charged down from the sky—a whirlwind of holy flame—hurling thunderbolts one after another with deadly accuracy. *(sizzling of thunderbolts)* His bolts blasted the titans, consuming them with electric fire. The whole earth burned. The continents melted. The waters boiled. And then the battle was over.

The gods stood victorious. Terrified and defeated, Cronus fled to the far regions of the earth, and the remaining titans were seized by many strong arms. Zeus, triumphant, ascended to Olympus and seated himself on that high throne.

ZEUS: *(angrily)* You treacherous titans! You are defeated! And for your crimes against the gods, you will be eternally punished!

NARRATOR: He turned first to Atlas, a titan as massive as a mountain.

ZEUS: Atlas, with your strength you tried to bring the wide heavens down upon us gods. Now I condemn you to forever hold the horrible weight of the sky upon your shoulders!

ATLAS: *(groaning)* No. No.

NARRATOR: Next Zeus turned his eyes upon Ocean, a watery giant.

ZEUS: Ocean, you tried to drown us gods in your floods, but now we will put you to use. I command you to surround the world with your waters and define its boundaries. Never again will you rise against us.

NARRATOR: Then Zeus faced the rest of the defeated titans.

ZEUS: As for the rest of you, you will be bound forever in the deepest pits of Tartarus. Where is Hades?

NARRATOR: The Lord of the Underworld slunk forward from the crowd.

HADES: Yes, Zeus.

ZEUS: Take them into your depths and never allow them to escape.

HADES: With pleasure. *(pause)* But there are two missing—two titans who should be among these.

ZEUS: Do you speak of Prometheus and Epimetheus? They are here.

NARRATOR: A pair of young titan brothers stood before Zeus' throne.

ZEUS: I have not yet decided what to do with them.

HADES: *(greedily)* Give them to me! I will make them regret fighting against the gods!

ZEUS: Well, that's just it. They did not fight.

HADES: What does that matter? They're titans, and they deserve to be punished with the rest of their kin!

NARRATOR: Prometheus bowed his head before Zeus.

PROMETHEUS: Zeus, may I speak?

ZEUS: Quickly.

PROMETHEUS: It is true that I share blood with these titans, but I am not like them in nature. They rely only on their terrible strength instead of their minds. They have no use for ideas. They are brutes.

ATLAS: *(angrily)* You traitor!

(growling from the titans)

PROMETHEUS: While I am a titan by blood, I am a god at heart.

HADES: Once a titan, always a titan, I say! Send him with me, Zeus!

PROMETHEUS: I have no use for war as the other titans do. As you said, when the war raged, I did not give battle.

HADES: Ha! An enemy *and* a coward!

ZEUS: Why did you not fight?

PROMETHEUS: It's not that I am a coward. It's just that I have always possessed the ability to see beyond time—catching little glimpses of the future. I foresaw that the gods would be victorious.

ATLAS: And why didn't you share that information with the rest of us?

PROMETHEUS: I tried to! Don't you remember? But you were so sure that you would win.

ZEUS: You say that you can see the future? That could be quite useful. What about your brother here? What is his excuse?

EPIMETHEUS: Err…um…err…

PROMETHEUS: Please, Zeus. He is simple-minded. I have always cared for him. I don't know what would happen to him otherwise.

HADES: I've heard enough from these liars! Give them to me! Let me lock them in darkness forever!

ZEUS: No. Prometheus and Epimetheus may go free. They had no part in the war.

HADES: Zeus! I do not think it is wise to—

ZEUS: I have spoken! You have enough titans to torture.

PROMETHEUS: Thank you for sparing me, Zeus. I will go my way and live humbly. I shall never trouble you again.

ZEUS: See that you don't!

PROMETHEUS: Come on, Epi.

EPIMETHEUS: *(dimwitted voice)* Okay, Pro.

ATLAS: Prometheus! You have betrayed us for nothing! You have placed your trust in the gods! They will never forget you are a titan! One day you will join us in our torture. Then you'll learn—like we have—never trust a god!

NARRATOR: Prometheus turned his back on these words. He and his dimwitted brother departed Olympus.

HADES: Prometheus will betray you. I feel it in my bones.

ZEUS: Oh, don't worry. I will be keeping my eye on him. He might still be useful.

NARRATOR: The two titan brothers made their way into the world. It lay in ruins—scorched and smoking from the heavenly war.

EPIMETHEUS: Pro, what will happen to the other titans? Will they be sad forever?

PROMETHEUS: They chose war, and they will have to pay the consequences.

EPIMETHEUS: What will we do now, Pro?

PROMETHEUS: Now we shall explore the earth.

NARRATOR: The two titans traveled the broken world and helped it heal.

EPIMETHEUS: The world is getting better, but it is so empty.

PROMETHEUS: You are right.

NARRATOR: Prometheus scooped up a clump of dirt in his hand and molded it into a living being.

EPIMETHEUS: *(happily)* What is that, Pro?

PROMETHEUS: This is an animal. I have made its form, but it's up to you to decide what gifts it shall have.

EPIMETHEUS: Ummm. Make it fast!

PROMETHEUS: Very well.

NARRATOR: Prometheus ran his expert fingers over the animal—lengthening its feet and ears and giving it strong legs.

PROMETHEUS: We will call this one a bunny.

EPIMETHEUS: Ha! That's great!

NARRATOR: The rabbit leapt from Prometheus' arms.

EPIMETHEUS: Do another one! Another one!

PROMETHEUS: *(laughing)* All right! All right!

NARRATOR: The process was repeated time and time again. Prometheus shaped the animals, and Epimetheus decided their gifts. They made creatures that swam and scurried—creatures that traveled below the earth, upon it, and above it. Some animals were given claws and fur. Others had feathers or scales.

Under Prometheus' gentle touch, the world healed and bloomed with new life. Then at last the two titans sat back and admired their work.

PROMETHEUS: Nothing on Mount Olympus or all of heaven could rival this.

EPIMETHEUS: I like the animals best, Pro. Especially the bunnies. Could we make more bunnies, Pro?

PROMETHEUS: I think we have enough.

EPIMETHEUS: I like it here, Pro.

PROMETHEUS: Me too, Epi. This world *is* beautiful—but something is missing. Among all these creatures there is not one who has a hint of heaven—a divine spark.

EPIMETHEUS: The bunnies do, Pro.

PROMETHEUS: *(laughing)* Here let me show you what I'm talking about.

NARRATOR: Prometheus stooped down by the river's edge where the red clay was thick and deep. He began to mold some in his hand—sticking out his tongue a bit as he sculpted. When he was finished, he held his handiwork up for his brother to see.

EPIMETHEUS: It's a face, Pro! It's a face!

PROMETHEUS: Exactly. Now watch this.

NARRATOR: From the river's clay Prometheus shaped out the complete form of a god. He stepped back from his creation with a smile on his face.

PROMETHEUS: Animals always look earthward. But this creature will look up to the heavens—into the blue sky—and wonder.

NARRATOR: Prometheus noticed that his brother looked frightened.

PROMETHEUS: What's the matter?

EPIMETHEUS: It's a god, Pro. That is not good. The gods will not like you making one of them.

PROMETHEUS: This is not a god. It's man.

EPIMETHEUS: I don't like it, Pro.

PROMETHEUS: Nonsense. Now let's finish him. You've given all my other creatures gifts and probably saved the best for last. What gifts shall we give man?

EPIMETHEUS: Uh…I don't have any more, Pro.

PROMETHEUS: What?

EPIMETHEUS: I used them all—the claws, the sticky tongue, the sharp teeth, the prickly spines. I'm all out.

PROMETHEUS: Hmmm. Then this creature will be defenseless. He will do not have the tools of the other animals. I will have to give him the greatest weapon of all—a cunning mind.

NARRATOR: Prometheus bent down and breathed life into his creation. Its eyes opened, and it sat up.

EPIMETHEUS: This is not good.

NARRATOR: Prometheus did not stop with just one man. He fashioned many copies of his creation from the red clay—each one a bit different than the last.

Since the mind would be man's greatest weapon, Prometheus taught his creations sense and reason—as well as all the vast learning that he knew.

EPIMETHEUS: Why didn't the gods create man, Pro?

PROMETHEUS: Simple, Epi. They only care about themselves.

NARRATOR: News of man reached all the way to Mount Olympus.

ZEUS: What is this I hear? Prometheus has made a new creation. Something he calls "man."

HERMES: It's freaky! They look like us gods, but they're such crude imitations. It's laughable. They're not like animals either. They have no fur or claws or instincts. They're pathetic.

ZEUS: Then I say we send them a challenge. Isn't it about time for Demeter's mood to change?

HERMES: When isn't it changing?

ZEUS: A little winter will fix these humans.

NARRATOR: The seasons changed, and the balmy summer days were replaced with frigid ones. Prometheus soon discovered how weak his new creations were. When the berry bushes shriveled up, the men had nothing to eat. Wild wolves came down from the mountains to prey upon them. The cold caused them to grow still, their lips turned blue, and the life he had given them left them. There was nothing Prometheus could do to save them.

EPIMETHEUS: What is happening to them, Pro?

PROMETHEUS: They are dying.

EPIMETHEUS: Oh no.

NARRATOR: Prometheus knew what they needed to survive.

PROMETHEUS: They must have fire.

EPIMETHEUS: But only gods have fire, Pro. And they do not like to share!

NARRATOR: Epimetheus was right. Divine fire glowed in Hephaestus' forge and in the halls of Olympus but nowhere else in all the dark world. Fire was the gods' sacred treasure.

So Prometheus made the long trek up to the place where it was a danger for any titan to go—Mount Olympus. He humbly approached the throne of Zeus.

PROMETHEUS: Man must have fire, or he will soon be extinct.

ZEUS: Good. If man was not strong enough to live on his own, he should not live at all.

PROMETHEUS: I beg you! They are like my sons.

ZEUS: You made all these other beasts. Why didn't you give man warm fur or a coating of blubber?

PROMETHEUS: My brother gave away all the gifts to the other animals. There was nothing left for man.

ZEUS: Then your brother is truly a fool, and he has doomed man. It serves you right for creating something without my permission.

PROMETHEUS: *(coldly)* Your judgment is hard.

ZEUS: The hardest—and as inflexible as stone. Now go!

NARRATOR: Prometheus could not and would not allow his creations to die out. Deep down, he had expected this verdict from Zeus, and within his robe he carried a fennel stalk.

Leaving the throne room of Olympus, Prometheus made his way to the empty forge of Hephaestus. Using the fennel's hollow stem, he stole some of the gods' eternal fire for himself and smuggled his prize back to earth. He presented this treasure to man.

PROMETHEUS: Now take this treasure, which the gods selfishly hoarded. Once you have it, they can never take it back. Use it to prosper. Now that you have fire, you will live forever.

NARRATOR: The glow of fire dotted the landscape. With fire man could subdue the wild beasts. He could cook his meat. He could keep warm on the cold nights. Instead of dying out, as Zeus had planned, man flourished.

But Zeus' wrath had been stirred. Prometheus looked up to the height of Mount Olympus. A gray storm-cloud swirled there, and lightning silhouetted Zeus within it.

ZEUS: *(raging)* Prometheus! Prometheus!

EPIMETHEUS: What is happening, Pro?

PROMETHEUS: Stay here! Watch out for the humans!

EPIMETHEUS: This is not good.

NARRATOR: Zeus seethed as Prometheus climbed the high mountain once again.

ZEUS: *(seething)* You betrayed me! You lied to me!

PROMETHEUS: Yes, I stole your precious fire and gave it to man. I have saved them from being hurled into Hades.

ZEUS: It takes boldness to admit to such deception!

PROMETHEUS: I did what was right, and I do not regret it.

ZEUS: I should never have trusted you! Your titan blood has led you into evil!

PROMETHEUS: *(passionately)* Is it evil to have compassion? Is it evil to love something other than yourself?

ZEUS: It is evil to defy me.

PROMETHEUS: Fine. Do not listen to reason. Do what you will to me, but please do not punish my brother. He had nothing to do with it.

ZEUS: I will decide who shall be punished.

NARRATOR: Zeus summoned two of his mightiest henchmen.

ZEUS: Kratos! Bia!

NARRATOR: Kratos and Bia—strength and force—came forward and seized Prometheus.

ZEUS: *(to Kratos and Bia)* Take him to the very limits of the earth. Bind him with unbreakable steel chains to the highest peak. *(to Prometheus)* There you will be scorched by the sun's fire, and you will suffer unending torment. No punishment can be painful enough to match your crime—but this one will come close! These are the wages you'll be paid for your sin of loving the mortals. *(to Kratos and Bia)* Take him away!

KRATOS: Gladly!

BIA: *(happy grunting and laughing)* Errmmm.

ZEUS: Take Hephaestus with you. He shall forge the shackles.

NARRATOR: The henchmen dragged Prometheus away.

PROMETHEUS: This is not justice, Zeus.

ZEUS: This is *my* justice.

NARRATOR: Epimetheus saw his brother being dragged down the mountain and ran to him.

EPIMETHEUS: Pro, where are they taking you? What will I do?

PROMETHEUS: You will be fine. But never trust any god that comes from Olympus! Remember that!

EPIMETHEUS: I will remember, Pro.

NARRATOR: Reaching the very ends of the earth, the henchmen dragged Prometheus to the top of an icy crag of the Caucasus mountains.

KRATOS: Heh. Heh. I bet you wish you had a bit of that fire now, don't you?

BIA: *(chuckling)* Heh. Heh. Heh.

KRATOS: Where is that lame blacksmith? It's freezing up here.

HEPHAESTUS: Here I am, you dumb goon.

NARRATOR: Hephaestus had appeared on the heights of the mountain.

HEPHAESTUS: And be careful who you call *lame.*

KRATOS: And what are you going to do about it, cripple?

NARRATOR: Hephaestus leveled an enormous hammer at the smirking face of Kratos.

HEPHAESTUS: Do you *really* want to find out? Let's just say I wouldn't be the only cripple on Olympus anymore.

KRATOS: Get to work! And be quick about it! I want to see this mortal-lover writhe in agony!

BIA: *(growling)* Grrrrr.

HEPHAESTUS: Oh, Kratos. You've always had a heart of steel—not to mention rocks for brains. Prometheus here is nobler than you will ever be.

KRATOS: You're defending him? He stole the very flower of your craft—the spark of every art—and he threw it away on mortals—on trash!

HEPHAESTUS: Eh. I have lost nothing, and they have gained everything. With my flames humans will make wondrous things—things that the gods can only dream about and will never understand.

KRATOS: Bah! Why bother saying a kind word about this traitor?

HEPHAESTUS: I wouldn't expect a couple of meatheads like you to understand. You follow orders blindly. You delight in pain and torture. I cannot disobey Zeus' orders—but in this instance, how I wish I could! I wish I did not bear this burden.

KRATOS: No one is free from burdens—except Zeus.

HEPHAESTUS: You *almost* speak wisdom. Yes, Zeus is on the top, and all others must bear the weight of him.

NARRATOR: Kratos and Bia shoved Prometheus up against the cold crag.

KRATOS: Bind him! Make the chains tight! Leave no room for escape!

NARRATOR: Hephaestus faced Prometheus sadly.

HEPHAESTUS: Fire thief, I must bind you with these torturous chains. Forgive me. The mind of Zeus cannot be changed.

NARRATOR: Hephaestus began to hammer the steel fetters tightly across the titan. *(hammering sounds)* The chains dug into his flesh.

PROMETHEUS: *(cries of pain)* Argh! Ah!

HEPHAESTUS: Forgive me, noble titan! I feel your agony!

KRATOS: Be careful whom you cry for. We'll tell Zeus about your sympathy, and then you'll be crying for yourself!

NARRATOR: Hephaestus had finished his job. The titan's body was crisscrossed with unbreakable, tightly-cinched chains.

HEPHAESTUS: My part in this grisly deed is done. I will leave you vultures to your task.

NARRATOR: As the forge god departed, Kratos and Bia turned upon their captive.

KRATOS: Ha! Where are your precious humans now? No one can save you!

BIA: *(urgent grunting)* Ergh! Ergh!

NARRATOR: Bia pointed into the sky. An eagle was making its way through the mist toward the peak.

KRATOS: Oh yes! I'd almost forgotten! This is the best part! Every day Zeus' eagle shall descend from Olympus and tear out your liver—bit by bit. Then each night the organ will be painfully reformed within you. What do you say to that?

NARRATOR: Bound as he was, Prometheus cried out.

PROMETHEUS: Oh, Mother Earth! Look at me! Look at my suffering! I never thought I would end up like this—hanging here like a criminal, halfway between heaven and Hades. My only crime was helping those mortals that I loved. Why must a god suffer at the hands of other gods—just for doing good?

KRATOS: You are not one of the gods! You are a titan!

PROMETHEUS: The same blood runs through us all. Because of that, it is a sin to punish me in this way.

KRATOS: The eagle is here! Dinner time!

BIA: (*cruel laugh*) Heh. Heh.

PROMETHEUS: (*to himself*) If only I had gone to Hades with my brothers, then no one could mock me in my suffering. Instead I will be displayed like a scarecrow here in the wind to entertain my enemies.

(*eagle screech*)

NARRATOR: The eagle swooped in close. Prometheus' punishment was at hand. The titan's eyes gained a faraway look.

PROMETHEUS: (*strangely*) I see a vision! The future! One day, Zeus will have need of me. I will be the only one who can give him secret knowledge. And I will only help him if he frees me from these crushing fetters.

KRATOS: Zeus will never do that!

PROMETHEUS: Then Zeus will fall—just like his father before him.

NARRATOR: The eagle bared its talons and descended.
   All the world heard of Prometheus' punishment and wept for him. Many prayed that one day he would be released from his chains.
   With Prometheus bound Zeus began the next phase of his revenge.

ZEUS: Now I will punish that dimwitted brother of his. (*shouting*) Hephaestus! Ready your forge! You are to make a new creation to punish mankind. Since they are so fond of your fires, the same fires will forge their doom.

HEPHAESTUS: I have always tried to use my arts for good.

ZEUS: I say what is good! Now listen to my instructions and do not deviate from them.

NARRATOR: In the fires of his smithy, Hephaestus forged a creation similar to those of Prometheus—but still much different. Until then all mortals had been male. This one was a *she*. Zeus observed the maiden as she cooled in the forge.

ZEUS: Welcome to the world, my sweet weapon—my beautiful evil.

NARRATOR: The eyes of the female fluttered open.

ZEUS: Pandora I shall name you—"many gifts."

NARRATOR: When Pandora was completed, Zeus brought her before the other gods and goddesses, so that they might heap gifts upon her. Athena taught her how to weave and dressed her in a glorious gown. Aphrodite gave her unparalleled grace and the ability to break hearts. Finally, Hermes filled her to the brim with thieving morals, lies, and swindles.

ZEUS: Perfect! Beautiful on the outside. Evil on the inside. You all have done your job well. If I didn't know her true nature, I would be tempted to keep her for myself. But I will send her on her way—with one final gift.

NARRATOR: He motioned toward an enormous, tightly-sealed jar. (*rattling of* *crockery)* Something rattled violently within—trying to break free.

ZEUS: Hermes, take this bride to her new husband. And do not forget their wedding present.

NARRATOR: Since the sentencing of Prometheus, Epimetheus had lived alone and frightened in the hall that he and his brother had once shared. *(door knock)*

EPIMETHEUS: Hello?

NARRATOR: Epimetheus answered the door. A messenger with wings on his sandals was hovering there.

HERMES: I have a delivery for a Mr. Epimetheus. Are you Epimetheus?

EPIMETHEUS: Uhhh…

HERMES: Oh yeah. That's right. You're *slow*, aren't you?

EPIMETHEUS: *(affronted)* I am not!

HERMES: Did I say *slow*? I meant *witless*.

EPIMETHEUS: *(calming)* That's better! Are you a god from Olympus?

HERMES: No fooling you. I've come with a pair of parcels for you.

EPIMETHEUS: *(confused)* Parcels?

HERMES: *(sigh)* Here. Let me put this into language that even you can understand. *(as if talking to a child)* I've brought you two wonderful, shiny new presents!

EPIMETHEUS: Oh goody! *(catching himself)* I mean, no! I cannot accept them!

HERMES: Why not? It's not like I'm a stranger offering candy or anything. I have brought a friend for you!

EPIMETHEUS: A friend?

HERMES: *(slowly)* Yes. Friend. Good.

EPIMETHEUS: No, thank you. I do not need a friend.

HERMES: Are you sure? You are in this lonesome house—all alone—by yourself—with no one else to keep you company…

EPIMETHEUS: I guess I am alone.

HERMES: Exactly.

NARRATOR: Hermes stepped aside to reveal the glistening Pandora.

EPIMETHEUS: *(enraptured)* Wow! This is the package for me?

HERMES: Yep. And she's the whole package! Not just beauty but brains, too. There's a definite shortage of those around here. But that's not all. This doll comes with accessories!

NARRATOR: Hermes disappeared and returned lugging an enormous jar.

HERMES: *(grunting)* Here's the second part of the delivery. But listen to me—don't open it—under any circumstances. Got it?

EPIMETHEUS: Uh. Circumstances?

HERMES: *(annoyed)* Just don't open it, okay? Now, I'll leave you two little lovebirds alone. *(cruel chuckle)* This is too easy.

NARRATOR: As her new husband stared at her in wonder, Pandora smiled craftily. Ever since she laid eyes on the jar, her only desire had been to know what was inside it. Now she saw that Epimetheus would be no challenge for her cunning wits. She wasted no time.

PANDORA: Oh my! What a beautiful hall! Hey! I know! Why don't we open that jar?

EPIMETHEUS: No!

PANDORA: Aren't you the least bit curious to know what's inside?

EPIMETHEUS: The flying man said not to open it.

PANDORA: Do you think he really meant that?

EPIMETHEUS: (confused) Uh. I think so. He sounded like it.

PANDORA: But I bet it has a big surprise in it! You like surprises, don't you?

EPIMETHEUS: Yes, but you should not open that jar. It is a gift from the gods.

PANDORA: But I'm a gift from the gods, and I'm not bad. Am I?

EPIMETHEUS: Uh. No.

PANDORA: See?

EPIMETHEUS: But my brother, Pro, told me not to trust the gods.

PANDORA: Then that settles it! If the gods told us *not* to open it, then that means we *should* open it.

EPIMETHEUS: My head hurts.

PANDORA: Just one little peek won't hurt anything!

EPIMETHEUS: Okay. Just one peek.

NARRATOR: Pandora skipped over to the jar, untied the cords that bound it, and lifted its lid. (*shrieking of evil spirits*) Shrieking upward from the mouth of the jar came black, tentacle-like shadows that filled the room. It was all kinds of evil imaginable—sickness, decay, death, and hardships of every kind.

EPIMETHEUS: Close it! Close it!

NARRATOR: Pandora slammed the lid back onto the jar, but it was too late. The evils had escaped into the world. Even foolish Epimetheus realized that Pandora had cursed all mortals with this action.

EPIMETHEUS: This is not good.

PANDORA: What have we done?

NARRATOR: A tiny noise rattled within the jar.

PANDORA: Oh no. Not another one.

NARRATOR: One final tuft floated up out of the jar—a feathery wisp of hope. Zeus had sealed hope in the jar to make the troubles of the world bearable.

As the streaks of evil rose up into the sky, Prometheus spied them from his icy crag.

PROMETHEUS: Oh no. Zeus' revenge is complete. Now my creations are cursed. Even with the gift of fire, man's life will be filled with trouble—and eventually he will perish.

NARRATOR: The titan hung his head to weep, but something brushed across his face—a tiny puff floating upon the breeze. It was that little bit of hope. Somehow it strengthened his soul.

PROMETHEUS: Even Zeus could not doom man completely. No matter how miserable life may be, this bit of hope will survive.

NARRATOR: Away on the horizon Zeus' eagle appeared, winging its way toward Prometheus' peak—coming once again to perform its daily grisly deed.

PROMETHEUS: (*hopefully*) If man is above despair, so will I be. The hatred of Zeus may one day soften, and perhaps wisdom will enter his heart. Perhaps he will free me from these chains. Perhaps there is hope for us all.

DISCUSSION QUESTIONS

- *Prometheus* means "forethought," and *Epimetheus* means "afterthought." How is this reflected in their characters?
- Atlas warns Prometheus not to trust the gods. Was he right?
- What is explained by Epimetheus' distribution of various gifts to various animals?
- Is the mind mankind's greatest weapon? Explain.
- If Prometheus had a chance to do it all over again, would he steal fire for man? Explain.
- What is heroic and noble about Prometheus?
- Why is Zeus so severe with Prometheus?
- What type of leader is Zeus? Explain.
- Why are the gods so opposed to man having the gift of fire?
- Compare Hephaestus to Kratos. They are both servants of Zeus, but how do they approach their jobs differently?
- Are females naturally more curious than males? Explain.
- Is it fair that the first woman is labeled as a "beautiful evil"? Explain.
- Is hope a blessing—or a curse? Explain.
- If Zeus' plan is to release evil into the world, why does he bother creating an elaborate trick to accomplish this purpose?
- Why did Zeus include hope in his jar of evils? Is he going soft on mankind? Explain.
- What does the myth of Prometheus have to say about hope?

MIGHTY APHRODITE
TEACHER GUIDE

BACKGROUND

Appearance is everything—or at least that's how the saying goes. In ancient Greece physical beauty was highly prized. Just look at the statues produced by their culture. You'd be hard-pressed to find an "ugly duckling" among their subjects. What about in our own culture? Television, magazines, and billboards all flash images of physical perfection at us day after day. What are they trying to tell us? Is beauty really all that important?

Aphrodite, the Greek Goddess of Love, was the most beautiful of the goddesses. This was no mean feat as the Greek gods were all considered to be physically perfect (with one exception). Hephaestus, the maimed god of the forge, was the only ugly god. In order to be allowed to stay on Mount Olympus, he had to use his intelligence and skills to craft fabulous treasures for the gods. Ironically, he was also Aphrodite's husband.

Perhaps the Greeks were trying to make a point with this. "Beautiful" Aphrodite showed herself to be vain, capricious, and cruel, while "ugly" Hephaestus was intelligent, hard-working, and faithful. In the end, which one had the true beauty?

SUMMARY

Hera, the Queen of the Gods, has just finished boasting of her beauty, when a new goddess arrives on Mount Olympus. She is Aphrodite, a goddess born from the sea foam. All the gods are immediately smitten with her and vie for her affections. Crazed with jealousy, Hera demands that Aphrodite leave immediately, but Zeus intervenes, declaring that the goddess can stay. Hera agrees on one condition: Aphrodite must be married off to one of the gods. Hera also convinces Zeus to let her be the one to decide who that husband will be.

Soon after this event another god arrives on Olympus—a lame, ugly, blacksmith god named Hephaestus, who claims to be the abandoned son of Hera. After his birth Hera beheld his ugliness and tossed him off Olympus, a fall which resulted in his twisted leg. Hephaestus claims he has come to make peace and offers Hera a golden throne, but when she sits in it, the device traps her. The crippled god says he will only release Hera if she allows him to marry Aphrodite. Knowing how repulsed Aphrodite will be by this, Hera agrees. The most beautiful goddess and the ugly god are married to one another.

Vowing revenge for these events, Aphrodite begins an affair with Ares, the God of War, in order to hurt Hephaestus. When the smith-god learns of the affair, he makes a golden net, a booby trap that catches Aphrodite and Ares in each other's arms. Then Hephaestus summons all the gods to show them how his wife has betrayed him.

In order to punish the gods for mocking her, Aphrodite decides to use her love-powers to summon two murderous giants to Mount Olympus. The giants, Otus and Ephialtes, pile mountains on top of one another until they reach into the sky. As the giants invade Olympus, the gods do battle with them, but the giants manage to abduct the goddess Artemis and disappear back down their built-up pile of mountains. Although the giants think they have escaped, Zeus pelts them with thunderbolts until they fall back down to earth. There Artemis insults the giants until they both hurl their spears at her. When they do, the goddess leaps into the air, and the giants' spears pierce one another.

Once the threat of the giants is neutralized, Artemis angrily confronts Aphrodite, guessing correctly that it is she who is behind the giants' assault on Olympus. Aphrodite admits her guilt, and although the goddesses expect her to receive justice, all the gods take pity on her. She is allowed to stay on Olympus and be the new Goddess of Love and Beauty.

ESSENTIAL QUESTIONS

- How important is physical beauty?
- How does love sometimes cause trouble?

ANTICIPATORY QUESTIONS

- How was Aphrodite born?
- Does love ever cause problems?
- Do physically attractive people get away with things that others couldn't get away with?
- Are they treated differently in our society?

CONNECT

The Birth of Venus by Sandro Botticelli This painting depicts the birth of Venus (Aphrodite) as she springs from the sea foam. Is this how you imagined the birth of Aphrodite? Explain.

The Planets The Romans named several of the planets in our solar system after their most important gods, which were also the gods of the Greeks. Mercury (Hermes) was named after the swift messenger god because of its quick orbit. Venus (Aphrodite) was named after the love goddess because of how brightly the planet shone in the night sky. Mars (Ares) was named for the God of War because of its blood-red color. Jupiter (Zeus) was named after the Ruler of the Gods because of its superior size. Earth is the only planet in the solar system that is not named for a Roman god or goddess. Do you think the characteristics of the planets fit their namesakes? Explain.

TEACHABLE TERMS

- **Personification** Aphrodite is intended to be the personification of love. Is she? Or is she a better personification of something else? Explain.
- **Symbolism** On pg. 40 the script mentions that Aphrodite's carriage is pulled by a team of swans. In Greek mythology swans are symbolic of gracefulness and beauty.
- **Simile** On pg. 48 Hephaestus lays a trap for his prey "like a spider." This is an example of a simile.
- **Pun** On pg. 48 Ares says that Hephaestus is lame in every meaning of the word. This is a pun on two meanings of the word *lame*—"injured in the leg or foot" and "not impressive."
- **3rd Person** From their first appearance on pg. 49 Otus and Ephialtes refer to themselves in the 3rd person. What does this detail add to their characters?

RECALL QUESTIONS

1. Who gets to choose who Aphrodite's husband will be?
2. What gift does Hephaestus bring to Hera?
3. Hephaestus catches Aphrodite alone with what god?
4. How does Hephaestus capture Aphrodite and this god?
5. Who are Otus and Ephialtes?

MIGHTY APHRODITE

CAST

APHRODITE	*Goddess of Love and Beauty*
HERA	*Queen of Olympus*
ZEUS	*Lord of the Gods*
APOLLO	*God of Light and Truth*
ARTEMIS	*Goddess of the Moon*
HERMES	*Messenger God*
POSEIDON	*God of the Sea*
ARES	*God of War*
HEPHAESTUS	*God of the Forge*
OTUS	*Murderous Giant*
EPHIALTES	*Murderous Giant*

NARRATOR: Muse, tell me all about it—the latest gossip from Mount Olympus. Tell me the deeds done by the one called "Mighty Aphrodite," that beauty who arouses desperate love in gods and men—who brings out the best and also the worst in us all. Tell me of how she first arrived on that high seat of the gods, Mount Olympus—and how—as is her way—she almost brought it to destruction.

ZEUS: *(loudly)* Olympians! Today you will feast on nectar and sweet ambrosia. And why? Because I, Zeus, have made it possible.

NARRATOR: All the gods were feasting in the great hall of Mount Olympus.

ZEUS: Behold! The mighty thunderbolt! With this weapon I rule over you gods.

HERA: *(interrupting)* And don't forget it!

NARRATOR: Zeus grimaced at his wife, Hera, in annoyance.

ZEUS: Hera! Please! Who is the Lord of Olympus here? You or I? As I was saying… *(pause)* Wait. What was I saying?

NARRATOR: Hermes, the youngest of the gods, rolled his eyes at his Olympian father.

HERMES: Hey, pops, can we get on with the meal already? Some of us are starving.

HERA: *(angrily)* Silence, you mongrel! Do not interrupt the Lord of Olympus!

HERMES: *(sarcastically to Zeus)* What a lovely wife you have there, Dad. Remind us again why you married her.

ZEUS: Limited options.

HERA: What?

ZEUS: Nothing.

HERA: Now, I will speak. Behold! I am Hera, the Queen of Olympus. Zeus took me as his wife because of my superior beauty.

HERMES: (*sarcastically*) Really? We thought it was your sparkling personality.

HERA: (*ignoring him*) Let's face it. None of you hags can compare to the splendor that is…me. I caution all you goddesses—do not challenge my beauty—or I will destroy you!

ZEUS: Um. Nice speech, dear.

HERA: Thank you. I just wanted to make a few things clear around here. No one on Olympus is as beautiful as I.

HERMES: Uhhh…except maybe her.

NARRATOR: Hermes was pointing out the window. Approaching Olympus was a flying carriage drawn by six swans, flapping their white wings in perfect synch. Inside sat a glorious goddess with flowing hair. (*murmuring from the gods*)

HERA: (*gritting teeth*) Who—is—that?

HERMES: That's what I want to know, too! Whoever she is, she's foxy!

ZEUS: (*happily*) Well, now! This day is looking up!

NARRATOR: The heavenly carriage, delicately carved from a salmon-colored scallop shell, landed on the balcony of Mount Olympus. All the gods and goddesses crowded around to get a look at the lovely goddess who stepped forth. (*murmuring from all the gods*) All the gods were immediately love-struck with the drop-dead-gorgeous beauty.

APHRODITE: (*sweetly*) I beg your pardon. I hope I'm not interrupting anything.

HERA: (*rudely*) Actually, you are! We were—

ZEUS: (*happily*) Doing nothing! Absolutely nothing! Welcome, my beauty! Welcome to Olympus! Tell us your name. Obviously you must be one of us immortal gods.

NARRATOR: The goddess' face flushed pink with the cutest blush.

APHRODITE: I am called Aphrodite—"she who rises from the sea foam."

ZEUS: Charming! Please. Have a seat.

NARRATOR: Several of the gods moved eagerly forward to offer Aphrodite a seat.

APOLLO: Sit by me, my lady!

HERMES: No, please sit here!

APHRODITE: Why, thank you!

NARRATOR: Aphrodite seated herself and arranged her gown about her. A group of eager gods crowded in closely.

HERA: (*rudely*) So…"she who rises from the pond scum" is a bit vague. What exactly are you? A sea nymph? Or some other kind of salt water hussy?

APHRODITE: I am a goddess like you.

HERA: (*chuckle*) There is *no one* like me.

APHRODITE: I do not know where I came from. All I remember is that I rose from the sea and landed perfectly upon a scallop shell—the same shell that I now use as a carriage.

HERA: (*hatefully*) I have an idea. Why don't you climb back into that flying clam of yours and go back to the sea where you belong?

ZEUS: My dear! We must treat strangers with kindness.

HERA: Uh-huh. *Especially* strangers who look like she does.

ZEUS: Exactly. *(catching himself)* I mean—

APHRODITE: I do have this note that explains things a bit.

NARRATOR: Aphrodite held up a scroll.

HERMES: Stand back! I am the Messenger God. I shall handle this possibly dangerous note.

NARRATOR: Hermes took the scroll from the goddess.

HERMES: My sweet, I would hate it if you happened to paper-cut those beautiful fingers of yours.

APHRODITE: Oh. You're so brave.

HERMES: I am. Maybe later I could tell you more about my bravery—perhaps over a plate of reheated ambrosia?

APOLLO: Hermes, don't be stupid! She'll be too busy watching me practice my archery. *(to Aphrodite)* You know, Aphrodite, I am the God of Truth. I cannot tell a lie, and I say you are the most stunning female I've ever seen.

APHRODITE: Oh. Tee hee.

HERA: Just read the note already, so we can get this floozy on her way.

HERMES: It's from Zephyr, the West Wind. *(reading)* Greetings, kind and gracious Olympians—and Queen Hera. I am sending to you beautiful Aphrodite. I have cared for her many years, but now it is time for her to ascend to Olympus to be one of the gods.

HERA: *(angrily)* Aha! So Zephyr's responsible for sending her here! I'll find that old airbag and knock the wind out of him!

HERMES: *(reading)* Many years ago I witnessed Aphrodite's birth. She was born when enormous drops of blood fell out of the sky.

ZEUS: It was the blood of Uranus.

HERMES: *(giggles)* Ahem. Sorry.

ZEUS: Uranus was the first divine ruler of the heavens, but he was murdered by his son, Cronus—the father of us first gods. Read on, Hermes.

HERMES: *(reading)* Some of these blood drops landed upon the earth. A violent rumble was heard, and the earth opened up. From these fissures emerged horrible giants.

POSEIDON: Yeah. Yeah. Nobody cares about giants. Where did Aphrodite come from?

HERMES: *(reading)* But one drop of blood landed on the sea. A wave was just rising, and the foam was just perfect. The foam and the blood mingled, and Aphrodite sprang up from the waves.

POSEIDON: A perfect entrance for a perfect creature!

NARRATOR: Poseidon, the sea god, came forward and kissed Aphrodite's hand.

APOLLO: Back off, fish-breath.

POSEIDON: Who you calling "fish-breath," goldenrod?

ZEUS: Gentlemen, please! Hermes, does Zephyr say anything else?

HERMES: Hmmm. He does encourage Aphrodite to date a messenger god.

ZEUS: Give me the letter! Hmmm. That is the end.

APHRODITE: For many years I have lived on the island of Cyprus, where I first stepped ashore. But now I humbly ask to live here on Olympus with you gods.

ALL GODS: Of course!

HERA: (*simultaneously*) No!

ZEUS: Hera! Look how innocent and helpless she is! Just look at those big, sad eyes, that long flowing hair, those pouty, red lips… (*trails off*) What was I saying?

HERA: I don't buy this damsel-in-distress act.

NARRATOR: Aphrodite's lovely features wilted in sadness.

APHRODITE: (*sniffling*) How could you be so cruel?

HERA: It comes naturally.

NARRATOR: Several gods moved to comfort Aphrodite—offering her their handkerchiefs to wipe her tears.

HERA: Look! What a manipulator! She's only been here five minutes, and already she has you gods drooling all over yourselves.

POSEIDON: We aren't drooling! (*slurping sound*)

NARRATOR: Poseidon hastily wiped his mouth.

HERA: I didn't expect to hear sense from a bunch of gods. But what about the goddesses? Ladies, who else thinks we should send this hussy-in-a-half-shell back where she came from?

NARRATOR: Artemis, the huntress goddess, stepped forward and shook her bow.

ARTEMIS: Hera is right! I fear that Aphrodite's presence will cause trouble here.

APOLLO: How could a beautiful woman possibly cause trouble?

ARTEMIS: Ha! My brother, for the God of Light, you are terribly dim! Aphrodite's presence here will cause fighting between you gods. I have seen how men value women. That is why I have sworn never to marry and to remain a virgin huntress for all my days.

APHRODITE: I pity you—to live a life so empty of love.

ARTEMIS: I pity you—to live a life so full of it.

HERA: So it sounds like the goddesses have spoken. Aphrodite must go. Will none of you gods listen to reason?

NARRATOR: Ares, the God of War, stepped forward and eyed Aphrodite coolly.

ARES: I agree with the goddesses. This girl will cause nothing but trouble.

APOLLO: And why would that bother *you*, Ares?

NARRATOR: Ares smirked.

ARES: Causing trouble is *my* job.

HERA: What do you say, Zeus?

NARRATOR: But Zeus was busy chatting with Aphrodite.

ZEUS: *(to Aphrodite)* Have you ever seen a real thunderbolt before? I have one, you know.

HERA: Zeus!

ZEUS: *(in shock)* What? I'm not doing anything! I mean—did you say something, dear?

HERA: Grrr. I said that we goddesses must be heard!

ZEUS: *(annoyed)* Yes, yes, my dear. I know you must be heard—over and over again.

HERA: Aphrodite must go!

ZEUS: Go where? We can't just hurl her off Mount Olympus!

HERA: Why not? Cram her back into that tacky carriage and send her packing.

ZEUS: Aphrodite is welcome here!

HERA: A little too welcome!

ZEUS: *(shouting)* She can stay! That is final!

NARRATOR: Hera's eyes narrowed in catlike anger.

HERA: Fine. If she is to stay, she must be married off. Otherwise, she is a threat to all our marriages. My marriage is already threatened badly enough as it is. Matrimony is the only thing that can put an end to passion.

ZEUS: *(grumbling)* You can say that again.

ARTEMIS: But who would the husband be?

NARRATOR: The hands of several eager gods shot up at once. *(shouts of "Me!" from the gods)*

HERMES: Ooh! Ooh! Me! Me!

POSEIDON: I would happily marry the goddess.

HERA: Poseidon, did you forget that you already have a wife?

POSEIDON: *(sadly)* Oh yeah.

HERA: Zeus often forgets that, too.

APOLLO: I'm free!

HERMES: So am I!

ZEUS: Silence! None of you may have her.

HERA: Why? So you can keep her for yourself?

ZEUS: Hera! This is a serious decision, and I must deliberate about it. While I do, we should all give Aphrodite some privacy. That's an order!

NARRATOR: All the gods cleared the hall. Aphrodite and Hera alone remained.

APHRODITE: Thank you, noble queen, for allowing me to stay.

HERA: Cut the act, sister. I know why you're here. You thought you'd come and cozy up to Zeus and rule the heavens! Well, this mountain isn't big enough for the both of us!

APHRODITE: I don't know what you're talking about!

HERA: Yeah right. I've seen your kind here before—Olympus-climbers. I'm top dog here. Don't forget it.

NARRATOR: Aphrodite's look of sweetness vanished, and her innocent tone changed.

APHRODITE: You're a dog all right!

HERA: What did you say?

APHRODITE: You heard me. All right, so you see through me, but no one else does. I am the Goddess of Love, and no one can resist my powers. Soon I will have these gods eating out of the palm of my hand.

HERA: Soon you'll have a husband, and your romances will be over.

APHRODITE: Will they?

HERA: Why, you little tramp!

ZEUS: (*yelling from the other room*) Hera! I thought that I told you to give Aphrodite some peace.

HERA: (*hatefully*) I will give you peace—for now. But soon it will be war.

NARRATOR: Aphrodite spent the next day surrounded by a crowd of eligible gods.

APHRODITE: Apollo, which would you like more—a moonlit walk along the beach or a private dinner for two?

APOLLO: (*sappy*) It would not matter as long as I was with you.

APHRODITE: Tee hee. Good answer. What about you, Hermes?

HERMES: That depends. What *is* the dinner?

APHRODITE: (*disappointed*) Hmmm.

NARRATOR: Hera, observing this spectacle, burned with jealousy. She went to speak with her husband.

ZEUS: What now, Hera?

HERA: I have decided. I am the Goddess of Marriage, so I should be the one to say who marries Aphrodite.

ZEUS: Now, just a minute. I don't think—

HERA: Exactly. You don't think. That's why I want to be the one to choose.

ZEUS: Now see here!

HERA: You cannot make this decision yourself. If you do, the greatest gods in Olympus will be angered against you. Leave it to me, and I will bear their anger.

ZEUS: Hmmm. I didn't think of that. Very well.

NARRATOR: Later Zeus announced this to all the gods.

ZEUS: (*loudly*) It is decided. Hera, the Queen of Heaven, will decide whom the goddess Aphrodite shall marry.

APHRODITE: (*in shock*) What?

HERA: That's right, dear. *I* will be making this choice. It will be the biggest decision of *your* life. (*cruel chuckle*)

NARRATOR: The eligible gods, who had showered attention on Aphrodite, now begged Hera to choose them to be the goddess' husband.

HERMES: Hera, you know you've always been my favorite stepmother.

HERA: I'm your only stepmother. And the other day you called me a blood-sucking shrew right to my face.

HERMES: Uh, well. Erm…You should have heard the name Apollo called you. It was much worse.

APOLLO: What? Why you—!

HERA: What did you call me, Apollo?

APOLLO: (*stammering*) I—I—I…

HERMES: Ha! Mr. Truthful. He can't deny it!

NARRATOR: Hera smiled. She loved to see the gods turning on one another. But a sudden commotion interrupted their conversation. (*distant murmuring*)

HERA: What is that noise?

HERMES: Allow me to find out, noble queen!

NARRATOR: Hermes buzzed off and returned.

HERMES: The servants say another strange guest has arrived!

HERA: Hopefully, it's not another strumpet from the sea. Bring the visitor here before Zeus returns!

NARRATOR: The visitor was brought before the gods. But instead of being another shapely goddess, it was a squat, hairy god with a twisted leg. His wild mane and beard frayed out in all directions.

HERMES: Whoa. This guy is so ugly, he'd have to sneak up on a ham sandwich.

HERA: Who are you? Or *what* are you? You are too hideous to be a god.

HEPHAESTUS: I may not look it, but a god I am. Are you the Queen of Heaven?

HERA: I am she. Who addresses her?

HEPHAESTUS: Hephaestus. Don't you recognize me? You were once my mother.

(*gasping from all the immortals*)

HERA: Don't be ridiculous. I would never give birth to an ugly creature like you.

HEPHAESTUS: But you did, my mother. When I was born, you took one look at me and beheld my ugliness. Then you tossed me off this mountain before anyone else could see me.

HERA: Oh yes. It's coming back to me now.

HEPHAESTUS: That is why I walk with this limp. The fall twisted my leg. But I learned a valuable lesson. I learned not to rely on my physical appearance. Instead I developed my skills. I was taken in by the kindly Cyclopes, and they taught me their art—of the fire and the forge.

HERA: *(sarcastically)* Blah blah blah. How inspiring. You overcame your ugliness. That's quite an obstacle, I admit! So what do you want from me?

HEPHAESTUS: Nothing. I bring you a present—to make peace.

HERA: A present, eh? Why didn't you say so? Show it to me!

NARRATOR: Hephaestus smiled and clapped his large hands together. *(whirring sound)* A whirring sound filled the air, and three mechanical maidens—made all of bronze—clanked into the hall. Hoisted on their shoulders was a golden throne.

HEPHAESTUS: I have crafted a throne befitting the Queen of Heaven.

NARRATOR: When Hera beheld the throne, her eyes flashed with greed. But she tried to suppress her obvious love for the object.

HERA: *(shrewdly)* If I take this gift, I am not bound to give you anything in return, correct?

HEPHAESTUS: No. You are not bound to anything—yet.

HERA: Then fine! I accept it!

NARRATOR: The bronze assistants brought the throne forward, and Hera seated herself grandly within it.

HERA: See? I have proved you are not truly my son. No son of mine would be dim-witted enough to give such a gift without the guarantee of getting something in return. I have taken this throne, and I will give *you* nothing! *(evil laugh)*

HEPHAESTUS: I expected as much. You have never given me anything in my life—not respect or love. So now I will take what I deserve.

NARRATOR: Bronze chains shot out from the arms of the throne, binding Hera firmly. *(whirring sounds, cries of wonder from all the gods)*

HERA: *(enraged)* Ah! Release me! How dare you! When Zeus hears of this—

HEPHAESTUS: I doubt he will mind much.

NARRATOR: Hera raged and raged, but the throne held her fast. None of the gods could free her of its metallic grip—and none of them really wanted to either.

At last Zeus returned to Olympus, and when the other gods informed him of the situation, all he did was bellow with laughter.

ZEUS: *(loud laughter)* I am glad to meet you, Hephaestus! You have done something that I was never able to do. You tamed the Queen of Olympus!

HERA: *(psychotically)* Zeus! Command him to release me—at once!

ZEUS: *(sigh)* All right, dear. *(halfheartedly)* Hephaestus, will you please release Hera?

HEPHAESTUS: No.

ZEUS: Oh well. I tried, dear. I really did.

HEPHAESTUS: Unless…

HERA: Speak, you deformed freak! Speak!

HEPHAESTUS: Unless she agrees to make me the husband of Aphrodite.

(uproar from all the gods)

NARRATOR: A look of revulsion passed over Aphrodite's face.

APHRODITE: *(cry of disgust)* Ugh!

POSEIDON: Never!

APOLLO: Now this joke is going too far!

NARRATOR: Hera began to smile.

HERA: *(chuckling)* Now why didn't I think of that? They say opposites attract. Why shouldn't the most alluring of goddesses be married to the most repulsive god?

APHRODITE: For my beauty to be coupled with his hideousness—it's unholy! You must truly hate me, Hera, if you would give me such a fate.

HERA: You're catching on. Hephaestus, I agree to your bargain. Release me, and you shall have Aphrodite!

NARRATOR: Aphrodite bowed low before Zeus.

APHRODITE: Zeus, no! Please don't let this happen to me. I'm so attractive—and he's so...so—just look at him! *(weeping)*

ZEUS: I am sorry. This is Hera's choice to make.

HERA: Release me from this contraption!

NARRATOR: Hephaestus clapped his hands, and the mechanical throne released its captive. Hera stood, rubbing her chafed wrists, and drew near the weeping Aphrodite.

HERA: You belong to Hephaestus now.

APHRODITE: I will never forgive any of you for this. You've ruined my life. I hate you all.

HERA: That's the point, dear. But you'll get used to the bitterness. What good is eternal life if you don't have hatred to carry you through it?

NARRATOR: Zeus patted the lame smith-god on his crooked back.

ZEUS: You are quite the inventor, my boy. You must stay here on Olympus and share your craft with us. Let me show you around.

NARRATOR: One by one, the other gods departed, leaving Aphrodite alone in the great hall.

APHRODITE: They have underestimated me. I will make them all regret how they have treated me. I will make them burn with passion and choke on their misery. And Zeus, most of all, will desire my love. But he shall never have it. Instead he will seek elsewhere for love—all over the world—and never be satisfied. That will be my punishment.

NARRATOR: So it came to pass that the most beautiful goddess of Olympus was wedded to the ugliest.

HEPHAESTUS: I will work hard for you, Aphrodite. Perhaps through my devotion you will come to love me.

APHRODITE: *(coldly)* Never.

HEPHAESTUS: Well, the heart is a fickle thing. Yours may change in time.

NARRATOR: One day while Hephaestus labored in his newly-constructed forge on

Mount Olympus, he was visited by Helios, the God of the Sun. He informed Hephaestus that Aphrodite had taken up company with Ares, the shifty God of War. Every day after Hephaestus left for his forge, the two lovers would meet in Aphrodite's chambers.

HEPHAESTUS: So she has betrayed me. No one makes a fool out of Hephaestus.

NARRATOR: In his forge Hephaestus began to craft a golden net with fibers finer than a spider's web. And like a spider he laid a trap to catch his prey.

The next morning Hephaestus bade Aphrodite goodbye, pretending to leave for the forge as usual. Instead he snuck into the next-door chamber and watched her chamber through a peephole. Soon he saw Ares enter. The God of War and the Goddess of Love sat down next to each other upon the couch and embraced.

ARES: Good morning, my love. So are you ready to go through with your plan of revenge?

APHRODITE: Yes, all the gods will pay dearly. Do you think anyone suspects anything?

ARES: Like who? That crippled husband of yours? Ha! He is lame in every meaning of the word. He doesn't even know that we meet here every morning.

APHRODITE: *(laughing)* True! Remember when I first came to Olympus, and you said I was nothing but trouble? You were right.

NARRATOR: Hephaestus had heard enough. He sprung his trap. The golden net descended from the ceiling and bound up the two lovers. *(whirring sound)*

ARES AND APHRODITE: Ah! *(cry)*

NARRATOR: Then Hephaestus strolled casually into the chamber. Ares and Aphrodite now hung suspended in midair, trapped together in the golden net.

HEPHAESTUS: *(happily)* Hi, honey. I'm home!

APHRODITE: *(in shock)* Hephaestus! Dear! I can explain!

HEPHAESTUS: Can you? Hurry up! Our guests will be here any minute!

APHRODITE: Guests?

HEPHAESTUS: All of Olympus will be here shortly. You are quite a *catch*, my dear, and I want to show you off.

NARRATOR: Hephaestus had secretly summoned the other gods, and soon they arrived. *(laughing from the gods)* They hooted with laughter at the sight of Ares and Aphrodite literally caught in a loving embrace.

ARTEMIS: Even I, the Goddess of the Hunt, am impressed! I've never trapped a tart before! *(laughing)*

ARES: Release me! This is humiliating!

HERMES: Hey! Don't be complaining. Want to switch places? I wouldn't mind being cuddled up with Aphrodite! Ha!

APOLLO: Truthfully, neither would I.

HEPHAESTUS: Knowing my wife, I am sure you will both have your chance.

NARRATOR: Aphrodite seethed with anger.

APHRODITE: Hephaestus, didn't you humiliate me enough when you forced me to marry you? You disgust me!

HEPHAESTUS: Ditto. Zeus, is this the wife you have given me? Is there not a better one I could have? Maybe one who is not quite so free with her love?

ZEUS: You made your choice. You received Aphrodite and became the envy of all the gods.

HEPHAESTUS: I was a fool. Now I envy the god who has a faithful wife.

HERMES: Well, if you really want to get rid of her, I could take her off your hands…

HEPHAESTUS: No, I will keep her, but hopefully she has learned not to betray me.

HERA: Fat chance. I have a saying—"Once a harlot, always a harlot."

NARRATOR: Finally the gods tired of their merriment, and Hephaestus released Ares and Aphrodite from his golden net. The situation passed. Little did they know that the full fury of Aphrodite had been unleashed.

APHRODITE: Soon Olympus will realize that they should not have angered me—but by then it will be too late.

NARRATOR: Two murderous giants named Otus and Ephialtes lived upon the earth. Born from the same divine blood that had given birth to Aphrodite, they were wild brutes who stood fifty-feet high and had the strength to move mountains.

APHRODITE: Zeus may wield the thunderbolt, but I have a greater weapon—uncontrollable desire. I will bewitch Zeus with love for some mortal maiden, and while he is away, I will summon Otus and Ephialtes to Olympus. It will be perfect chaos.

NARRATOR: Aphrodite summoned the spirit of maddening desire, a scarlet vapor that hung in the air.

APHRODITE: Wild desire, find the hearts of Otus and Ephialtes. Drive them into a frenzy for the love of two goddesses, the two whom I hate the most—Artemis and Hera.

NARRATOR: At the goddess' command the vapor sank earthward. It found the two murderous giants and invaded their minds. They trembled and turned their eyes toward heaven.

OTUS: Argh! Otus must have a goddess!

EPHIALTES: Wife! Must have wife!

NARRATOR: The two giants began to rip mountains up from their roots and stack them up on top of one another. (*booming of mountains being piled up*)

OTUS: Rip up the mountains!

EPHIALTES: Pile them up to Olympus!

APHRODITE: That's it! Come on! Hera and Artemis await you here! Drag them off Olympus and make them your wives. Then we will see who has the shameful husband! (*wicked laugh*)

NARRATOR: The giants' tower grew higher and higher into the air. At last the monsters neared the threshold of Olympus.

APHRODITE: Yes! The door is open, and the master is away. Come on in!

NARRATOR: The rampaging giants topped Mount Olympus. *(shouts of fright)* The gods were in a panic at the sight of the twin colossuses.

OTUS: Raar! We want wives! Take us to the ones called Hera and Artemis.

HERA: Uh-oh. I'm out of here.

ARTEMIS: Hermes, go fetch Zeus!

HERMES: I'm on it!

NARRATOR: The giants began to smash the massive columns of the great Olympian hall one by one. *(tremendous crash)* Chunks of the lofty roof broke loose and fell—shattering upon the marbled floors.

OTUS: Raar! Wives! Now! Or Otus will destroy Mount Olympus!

ARTEMIS: We must stand our ground. *(pause)* Ares, what are you doing?

NARRATOR: Ares was cowering behind a large vase.

ARTEMIS: Stand and fight with the rest of us!

ARES: Are you nuts? I could get killed doing that!

ARTEMIS: Be a man! You're supposed to be the God of War!

OTUS: God of War, huh?

NARRATOR: Otus sprang forward and seized Ares up by the arm.

ARES: Ah-eeeee! *(cry of fright)*

EPHIALTES: Ephialtes saw him first!

NARRATOR: Ephialtes grabbed Ares by the other arm and pulled roughly in the opposite direction.

ARES: Argh! Ah! *(cries of pain)*

NARRATOR: The bickering giants nearly pulled Ares in two.

OTUS: Otus wants to kill the God of War!

EPHIALTES: No! Ephialtes shall!

ARES: Gentlemen, please! You've got me pegged all wrong. I'm not the God of War.

EPHIALTES: Then what god are you?

ARES: Uh…I'm the God of…Flowers!

EPHIALTES: Then we'll pot you, flower-boy!

NARRATOR: Ephialtes grabbed up a vase and painfully stuffed the war god into it.

ARES: *(cries of pain)* Oof! Argh! Ah!

NARRATOR: Ephialtes tucked the vase under his arm.

OTUS: Now where are your pretty goddesses—the ones called Hera and Artemis?

NARRATOR: The huntress goddess stepped forward.

ARTEMIS: I am Artemis! Spare these others, and I will go with you willingly.

EPHIALTES: Oooh! She *is* pretty!

APOLLO: Artemis! No!

ARTEMIS: It is my choice to make. These brutes will destroy Olympus if they are not satisfied.

OTUS: Where is wife for Otus? Otus needs one as well.

ARTEMIS: I will marry you both.

OTUS: Fair enough.

NARRATOR: Otus snatched up Artemis. Apollo ran forward to protect his sister.

OTUS: Not so fast!

ARTEMIS: Ahh! *(cry of pain)* Stop, Apollo! He'll squeeze me in half.

OTUS: Otus will take this one and the flower god. Goodbye, god-lings.

NARRATOR: The gods watched in horror as the giants and their captive disappeared over the side of Olympus.

The giants returned to their mountain pile and began their descent. As the giants climbed down, they grumbled at one another.

EPHIALTES: Let Ephialtes hold her! She is Ephialtes' wife, too!

OTUS: Let go! Let go!

NARRATOR: Their argument was interrupted when a blast of lightning struck the mountain beside them. *(shazam!)*

OTUS: Uh-oh. Lightning god. Not good.

NARRATOR: Above them Zeus stood on the heights of Mount Olympus—thunderbolts sizzling in his grip. *(shazam!)* Another bolt struck, blowing loose the outcropping of rock that the giants clung to. They fell through the sky.

OTUS AND EPHIALTES: Argh! *(fading away)*

NARRATOR: With a tremendous crash Otus and Ephialtes finally struck the earth—spraying rocky debris for miles. *(tremendous crash)* The giants rose from the deep craters they had created in the ground.

EPHIALTES: Where is Otus?

OTUS: Over here. Where is wife?

ARTEMIS: Here I am.

NARRATOR: Artemis, standing upon a hillside between the two rising giants, stared at them imperiously.

ARTEMIS: But I will never be your wife. I will die first.

OTUS: Grrrr. That can be arranged.

NARRATOR: Both of the giants seized up their massive spears and prepared to hurl them at Artemis. They did not notice that they each stood in the line of the other's throw.

ARTEMIS: Now die!

NARRATOR: The giants hurled their spears toward the goddess, and Artemis, transforming into a deer, leapt high—avoiding their throws. *(sounds of two spears entering two bodies)* The spear of each giant had found its mark in the stomach of his brother.

OTUS AND EPHIALTES: *(dying sounds)*

ARTEMIS: Perfect shot, boys.

NARRATOR: Artemis surveyed the dead bodies of the giants with a sneer.

ARTEMIS: I guess this means the honeymoon's over.

NARRATOR: A searing light descended from Olympus, and Artemis shielded her eyes. Apollo's golden chariot shone before her.

APOLLO: Sister, you are safe! But where is Ares?

NARRATOR: Artemis motioned to a fallen vase lying near the slain giants.

ARES: *(groaning)* Errggh.

ARTEMIS: I say we leave him in there for a while. It might teach him some manners.

APOLLO: You speak the truth.

NARRATOR: The twin gods returned to Olympus and announced the death of the giants.

ARTEMIS: I have one question: How did two dumb brutes come up with the idea of kidnapping us goddesses? It's almost as if someone put the idea in their heads. Maybe a goddess of love?

NARRATOR: All eyes turned toward Aphrodite.

APHRODITE: *(sadly)* Oh, you have caught me. I only wanted to teach you all a lesson.

NARRATOR: Aphrodite put a perfect little pout on her face.

ARTEMIS: Well, here on Olympus once someone has betrayed us, there are no second chances.

ZEUS: Well…I doubt Aphrodite meant any harm.

ARTEMIS: Are you serious?

APHRODITE: I never dreamed the whole thing would go this far. I am deeply sorry.

ZEUS: *(happily)* Very well! All is forgiven!

HERMES: It was an honest mistake. It could have happened to anyone.

ARTEMIS: Really? Anyone would have invited a pair of murderous giants into Olympus? Apollo! Help me out here!

APOLLO: I was angry before, Artemis, but when I look at her, I just can't stay mad.

ARTEMIS: *(cry of disgust)* I can't believe this!

APHRODITE: Awww. You all are the sweetest. Thank you.

NARRATOR: Aphrodite turned toward Artemis and smirked.

APHRODITE: *(quietly)* See, my dear? That's the power of love.

NARRATOR: That very day Aphrodite was inducted as the Goddess of Love and Beauty, and Mount Olympus was never the same again.

DISCUSSION QUESTIONS

- Is Aphrodite a good personification of love? Explain.

- Does love often cause trouble? Explain.
- Should Aphrodite be allowed to stay on Mount Olympus? Explain.
- Do beautiful people sometimes receive special treatment? Explain.
- Rather than having strength herself, Aphrodite can control others. Does this make her more or less powerful? Explain.
- How is the importance of physical appearance different for Hephaestus and Aphrodite?
- Do Hephaestus and Aphrodite make a good match? Explain.
- Is Hephaestus a likeable character? Explain.

THE LOVES OF THE GODS
TEACHER GUIDE

BACKGROUND

Many myths explain the why's of nature: why the seasons change, why the sun travels across the sky, why sounds echo, why the designs on a peacock's tail-feathers resemble an eye. Ancient people asked these questions, and because science was still in a primitive stage, they used myths to answer their queries.

Nature is unpredictable. The same natural forces that create peaceful, sunny afternoons can produce earthquakes, hurricanes, tornadoes, and floods just as easily. The Greeks equated nature with the gods; therefore, the gods must be just as unpredictable as nature. They believed that the gods must have moods like humans—otherwise, what would explain the inconsistent nature of the world?

In the myths the Greek gods are rarely (if ever) worthy of worship. Their antics seem more like the actions of spoiled children than all-powerful deities. Emotions are not a bad thing among mortals, but the mood swings of gods have the ability to ruin lives and destroy civilizations. These gods with human shortcomings helped the Greeks explain an unpredictable world.

SUMMARY

Prometheus the titan spends his days chained to a mountain by the edge of the world. Zeus chained him there because the titan gave the gods' immortal fire to man. Every day an eagle comes and rips out Prometheus' liver, and each night the organ is painfully reformed within him. This is the titan's eternal punishment.

One day a cow makes its way down the path that leads to Prometheus' mountain. He calls out to the cow, and it answers with a human voice. It is actually a mortal maiden who has been transformed by Zeus. The titan asks the cow-maiden to share her story, and she does.

Once she was Princess Io, and Zeus came to her and offered to make her his mistress. The star-struck girl agreed, and Zeus whisked her off to a faraway meadow. In order to prevent his jealous wife, Hera, from seeing his actions, Zeus shrouded the meadow with fog. Watching from Olympus, Hera saw this fog and grew suspicious. She appeared on earth to catch Zeus red-handed. She demanded that Zeus lift the fog, and when he did, he stood beside a beautiful white heifer (Io in disguise). Zeus tried to act like nothing was going on, but wise Hera saw through his deceptions. She demanded that Zeus give her the cow as a present. Zeus had no choice but to turn his lover over to his suspicious wife.

Once Zeus was gone, Hera summoned her one-hundred-eyed watchman, Argus, to watch over the cow until she could plan a suitable punishment for her. Io was frantic with fright, realizing she could never escape from a watchman like Argus.

Meanwhile, Zeus arrived back to Olympus and commanded the god Hermes to rescue Io from her captor. In order to do this, Hermes appeared before the Argus disguised as a mortal pipe-player. Hermes played his pipe music for Argus, hoping it would make him fall asleep, but while many of Argus' eyes slept, one always stayed open. At last Hermes decided to tell him a story. The following is the story that he told:

Long ago, Hermes said, the world did not have seasons. The harvest goddess, Demeter kept the earth in eternal summer. But one day while Demeter's daughter, Persephone, gathered flowers in the meadow, Hades, the

Lord of the Underworld, spied her there. He roared up through the earth in his chariot and abducted her. No one knew what had happened to the goddess. Demeter wandered the earth, looking for her daughter. Because of her sadness, the world grew cold, and all crops died. Finally, Helios the sun god told her that Hades had abducted her daughter. Demeter appealed to Zeus, and he demanded that Hades give Persephone back. Hades agreed, but because Persephone had eaten of the food of the Underworld (a few pomegranate seeds), she was required to return to Hades for a portion of the year. Now every year Demeter grows sad when her daughter is away, giving the earth the seasons of fall and winter.

When Hermes finished his story, the Argus was completely asleep. He used this opportunity to cut off the creature's head. He told Io to flee and Zeus would come to her and transform her back into her original form. After Hermes and Io were gone, Hera returned and found Argus murdered. To honor her watchman, she placed his hundred eyes on the tail-feathers of her favorite bird, the peacock. She also summoned a gadfly (horsefly) to continually sting Io.

When Io finishes her story, Prometheus declares that the maiden will soon find happiness. Zeus will return her to her true form, and she will bear mighty sons. One of Io's descendants will be Heracles, who will also one day free Prometheus from his chains.

ESSENTIAL QUESTIONS

- How do myths explain nature?
- How can hasty decisions lead to long-term problems?

ANTICIPATORY QUESTIONS

- What do the patterns on peacock feathers resemble?

- Can you picture a creature with a hundred eyes? What would it look like?
- How are the Greek gods immature?

CONNECT

Greek gods or Hollywood celebrities? The Greeks enjoyed hearing about the many affairs and scandals of the gods. In many ways, this parallels the modern obsession with celebrities. Instead of ascending Olympus, modern men and women flock to Hollywood to achieve "immortality." What do you think of this comparison?

TEACHABLE TERMS

- **Frame story** A frame story is an opening story that has a different story imbedded within it. A **story-within-a-story** is the imbedded story, which often tells of past events or makes the events of the frame story clearer. This myth begins with a frame story and features two stories-within-a-story.
- **Idiom** On pg. 58 Hera saying, "pulled the wool over my eyes," is an example of an idiom.
- **Tone** Io says, "Moo," several different times (such as pg. 60), but in each instance, a different tone is implied.
- **Onomatopoeia** On pg. 67 the sound effect (*snicker-snack*) is an example of onomatopoeia. Two other examples, "Blip" and "buzzing," appear in the narration on the same page

RECALL QUESTIONS

1. Who transforms Io into a cow?
2. What is Argus?
3. How does Hermes put Argus to sleep?
4. How does Hera memorialize Argus?
5. What does Hera send to torture Io?

THE LOVES OF THE GODS

CAST

PROMETHEUS	*Chained Titan*
ZEUS	*Lord of the Gods*
HERA	*Queen of Heaven*
IO	*Mortal Princess*
HERMES	*Messenger of the Gods*
ARGUS	*Henchman of Hera*
HELIOS	*God of the Sun*
HADES	*Lord of the Underworld*
DEMETER	*Goddess of the Harvest*
PERSEPHONE	*Goddess of Springtime*

NARRATOR: It was a typical day for Prometheus the titan. The eagle that came every morning to rip out his immortal liver had not yet arrived. Over time, he had grown somewhat numb to the pain. The steel fetters that held him fast to the rock prevented any resistance, and after the daily grisly deed was done, he would writhe in constant agony until the orange of the sun touched the line of the sea. Then, by some otherworldly force, a new pain would begin as the organ reformed within him.

This was his life—waiting and watching the landscape below him—but today something was different. A white speck was making its way down the coastline path that wound past his rocky perch. As it drew closer, he saw that it was a white heifer—perfectly formed.

PROMETHEUS: Hello, my animal sister.

IO: Hello.

NARRATOR: He was rather surprised that it responded. Of course, being a titan, he could communicate with any beast, but this one had answered with the voice of a human.

PROMETHEUS: *(thoughtfully)* You are no beast. Are you under some hex from the gods?

IO: I am. How did you know?

PROMETHEUS: Zeus gives blessings grudgingly and curses easily. I myself am under one of Zeus' curses.

IO: I see that. You seem so kind. What did you do to deserve such a punishment?

PROMETHEUS: Ah, I offended Zeus by giving men his immortal fire. I have been trapped here ever since.

IO: That doesn't seem fair.

PROMETHEUS: Eh, I have gotten used to it. Besides, I always know that my crime was worth its penalty. Tell me, what has happened to you?

IO: I wasn't always like this. I used to be a princess—in Thebes.

PROMETHEUS: Well, the day is hot, and you could surely use a rest. I am interested to hear how a maiden came to be transformed as you have been.

IO: *(sadly)* It's a sad story. I have never told it to anyone. You are the first person who has cared enough to listen. I doubt I can get through it without tears.

PROMETHEUS: Speak. I will share your tears then. I have much to weep over myself.

IO: It all started with Zeus. I was a naïve girl—easily infatuated with the thought of a handsome god loving *me*. I was sucked in by the excitement of it all, I guess.

NARRATOR: And so Io began her tale, and the imprisoned titan listened intently as she recounted it. It had begun many years before, when Zeus had appeared to Io in a restless dream and requested to be her lover.

ZEUS: Fair princess, I am Zeus, Lord of the Gods. I have seen your charms from above. The arrows of desire have pierced me. Will you consent to be mine? I will make you happier than any woman upon the earth.

NARRATOR: Io found this quite shocking, and her heart beat desirously. To be the lover of a god—what prestige! She had no idea what gifts the immortals bestowed upon those they loved, but she was sure it was something undreamt of.

IO: I agree, my lord. Tee hee. *(giggling)*

NARRATOR: And so the affair was begun. As the sun rose, Zeus spirited her away to a faraway meadow and appeared to her in all his glory.

ZEUS: Long have I waited for this, my sweet. But, first, let me overcast the sky so that my wife's spying eye cannot see us.

IO: *(nervously)* Your wife?

ZEUS: *(confidently)* Don't worry about her. She's a hideous old thing. I'm only concerned with *you* right now.

NARRATOR: With a wave of his mighty hand, mist filled the meadow—until the sun was all but obstructed. He smiled upon this with satisfaction and swept the maiden quickly into his arms.

Within the hanging gardens of Olympus, Hera strolled casually. Her husband had left the palace early that day. "I have business among the mortals," he had said. But she had her suspicions.

HERA: *(to herself)* I must have Iris follow him. That fool thinks he's pulled the wool over my eyes. If only I were a bit mightier, I would punish him *permanently* for his unfaithfulness.

NARRATOR: As she said these words, her gaze happened to stray over the balcony to the world below.

HERA: Hmmm. What is this?

NARRATOR: A haze lay over one portion of the countryside. Nothing could be seen beneath it.

HERA: Ha! I knew it! You arrogant fool!

NARRATOR: Swift as an arrow, Hera vaulted over the railing of the balcony and shot down through the atmosphere toward the hideaway of her amorous husband. The fog beat at her vision, and she slammed to the ground with an earth-shaking jolt.

ZEUS: Gaea save us all! It's my wife!

IO: *(frightened)* Oh no!

HERA: *(screaming)* Where are you, you dolt? I know you're around here somewhere—hiding in the smoke with your mortal hussy!

IO: What will she do to me?

ZEUS: Shhhh. Be still. I will transform you until she has left.

IO: But…

ZEUS: Trust me.

NARRATOR: The Queen of Heaven began swiping at the cloud around her—growing angrier by the second.

HERA: *(raging)* I know you're here! Show yourself! Be a man!

NARRATOR: The haze was at once whisked away revealing Zeus standing beside a pristinely white, though somewhat scared, heifer.

ZEUS: *(acting surprised)* Hera? What a surprise!

HERA: *(calmly)* Zeus, what are you doing?

ZEUS: Me? Oh, nothing. I was just admiring this gorgeous cow here.

HERA: Oh really. And what about this atmospheric disturbance? Clouds aren't commonly found on the ground! You weren't trying to block someone's view, were you?

ZEUS: Atmospheric disturbance? Oh, you mean the fog. That must be my fault. I've had a headache today. Whenever I have one of those, for some reason, the weather seems to change. *(nervous laugh)* Ahem. Yes. That's it.

NARRATOR: Hera eyed her husband suspiciously.

HERA: Uh-huh. And why exactly are you so interested in this cow? I missed that part.

NARRATOR: Zeus looked nervously to his transformed lover and began to stammer.

ZEUS: Well, you know, it's a beautiful specimen…and, uh…

HERA: Fine eyes? Large udders?

ZEUS: No, no, you see, I was looking at it because, because… *(sudden idea)* it's a present!

HERA: For whom?

ZEUS: For you, of course!

IO: Moo?

ZEUS: I knew how you—love—cows…

NARRATOR: His wife's frown quickly transformed into a smile.

HERA: *(fake happiness)* Well, why didn't you say so, husband? And here I was thinking that it was one of your little hussies—transformed in a lame attempt to fool me. Whew. What a relief.

ZEUS: Nope. None of that here.

NARRATOR: Hera stepped forward and began to stroke the shaking haunches of the princess.

HERA: Thank you so much. I know exactly what I will do with it, too.

ZEUS: And what's that, my dear?

HERA: *(slyly)* I will butcher it at once, of course.

ZEUS: *(shocked)* What? Butcher it?

IO: *(shocked)* Moo?

HERA: Of course, dear. What else would I do with this? I can't have a smelly old cow stinking up my chambers, can I?

ZEUS: I meant for you to keep it—as a pet, you know. But I'll need to take it and have it groomed first, of course.

NARRATOR: The goddess stepped between Zeus and his lover.

HERA: I think it's been *groomed* enough. Very well. I will not butcher it *yet*. I'll keep it, but it's such a fine cow. I'm afraid someone will steal it. Aphrodite might want a cow of her own and try to steal mine! I'll have to put a guard on it.

ZEUS: A guard? No, no, dear. No one would try to steal this beast away. Even if they did, I would replace it immediately—with an even finer one.

HERA: I could not bear it, Zeus. I love *this* cow. In fact, I think I will name her. I'll name her Whitey. Do you like that name, Whitey?

IO: *(negative)* Moo.

HERA: See? We're inseparable. Thank you so much, my husband. This is the best gift a wife could ask for.

NARRATOR: She smiled good-naturedly at Zeus, who began to say something but stopped.

ZEUS: Well—I guess I'll be going—now that you have your—your—

NARRATOR: He waved a hand at Io, who looked back at him helplessly.

HERA: *(cheerfully)* Goodbye!

ZEUS: Hmmmm.

NARRATOR: The Lord of Olympus turned—his shoulders slumped in regret—and disappeared in a puff of smoke. Smirking to herself, Hera spun around to face her bovine prisoner.

HERA: *(gloating)* So…you thought you would get away with this, didn't you? What a pathetic disguise. I mean, *really*. I'll teach you the hard way to stay away from my husband.

NARRATOR: Io cowered in fright.

HERA: I cannot undo Zeus' transformation, or I would choose a much worse form for you. So I will put a guard on you to make sure no one come near until I can think of a suitable end for a cow such as yourself.

NARRATOR: Hera cupped her hands around her mouth and bellowed toward the sky.

HERA: *(yelling)* Iris! Goddess of the Rainbow! Send that good-for-nothing Argus down here at once. I need his services.

NARRATOR: The air was silent for a moment, and then a faraway sizzling sound could be heard. Spreading across the sky, a magnificent rainbow headed directly for their location. The meadow filled with color, and a towering form was shadowed within.

HERA: Argus!

NARRATOR: The shimmering light disappeared, and Argus appeared. Muscle on top of muscle padded his gargantuan body, and upon his brow were a hundred eyes—all blinking and staring in different directions.

HERA: Over here! I have a job for you.

ARGUS: *(dumb voice)* Yes, my queen.

HERA: Argus, please look at me when I speaking to you.

ARGUS: *(defensively)* Argus *is* looking at his queen.

HERA: *(grumbling)* I hate that. I can never tell. *(pause)* Anyway, this heifer here is one of Zeus' hussies. Watch her. Keep her guarded—until I can dream up a fitting punishment for her.

ARGUS: Duh. Yes, melady.

HERA: *(evilly)* I was thinking she'd make some nice steaks—or maybe some beef jerky.

ARGUS: *(licking lips)* Mmmm. Sounds good!

HERA: Watch her! Let no one near her! And whatever you do, don't fall asleep on the job!

ARGUS: Do not worry. Argus' eyes sleep one at a time. That way Argus is always seeing, and eyes still get rest.

HERA: *(sarcastically)* Fascinating. Apparently, being a freak of nature has its advantages. Well, I'm off. There are three other wenches I have to deal with today. My husband has been a busy man. Remember your job. If you fail me, I'll put each of those eyes out myself.

ARGUS: *(whimper)*

IO: *(whimpering)* Moo.

NARRATOR: Hera raised her arms above her and with a flash of flame disappeared. Io's monstrous guardian turned to her.

ARGUS: Moo cow, do not be afraid. Argus will not eat you. Argus is vegetarian.

IO: *(relieved)* Moooo.

NARRATOR: And so Argus of the hundred eyes seated himself upon the grass beside the white heifer. Io—though her mind reeled with tormenting thoughts—made the best of the situation and began to graze upon the turf. Every move she made, her watcher's gaze followed. So they spent the day—guard and guardian.

Up on Olympus, a frustrated Zeus had frantically called his son Hermes to him.

ZEUS: Hermes, I have a mission for you.

HERMES: In trouble with Hera again?

ZEUS: You have no idea. That woman won't give up. Of course, I can't really blame her. It *is* adultery. I just can't help myself, y'know. I have *needs*.

HERMES: You don't have to explain yourself to me, Father. I'm thankful for your adultery. Otherwise, I wouldn't be here—or Apollo for that matter—or Artemis—or Dionysus—or about half of the mortal world…

ZEUS: *(irritated)* I get the point. Anyway, Hera has taken captive one of my lovers, a white heifer.

HERMES: *(nudgingly)* A cow? Why, you old bull-god, you…

ZEUS: *(angrily)* She wasn't a cow to begin with! She was a gorgeous princess!

HERMES: Hey, I'm not judging you.

ZEUS: *As I was saying,* the Argus is watching her—and that's a problem. You must trick him and steal Princess Io back for me.

HERMES: Argus is the guy with the excellent vision, right?

ZEUS: Yes, I'm afraid so.

HERMES: So—let me get this straight. You want me to sneak up on a creature that can see in every direction and steal one of your mortal merry-makers out from under his very nose?

ZEUS: You got it.

HERMES: *(sigh)* I guess being the cleverest god really is a curse, isn't it?

NARRATOR: Hermes flew from the mountain—wracking his brain frantically, trying to come up with a scheme and achieve the impossible.

HERMES: He can't keep all those eyes open all the time. There's got to be some way to lull him to sleep.

NARRATOR: He dug in the satchel slung at his side and produced a set of reed pipes.

HERMES: These should do nicely. I haven't found a being yet who doesn't think pipe playing is the most boring thing on earth.

NARRATOR: Beating his way down through banks of clouds, the golden form of Hermes started to change—becoming common, coarse, and badly dressed. A ragged tunic and a large floppy hat replaced his Olympian garb. He touched down not far away from the Argus and his bovine captive. *(pipe music)*

ARGUS: *(speaking to Io)* And then, moo cow, that is when mighty queen take Argus in and give Argus job. *(pause)* Argus hears music.

IO: *(surprised)* Moo?

NARRATOR: The eyes of the monster tracked to the path where a scraggly-looking man was frolicking forth—playing jubilantly upon his instrument.

ARGUS: Stop! Who are you, pipe-man?

NARRATOR: Hermes stopped in his tracks and addressed one hundred inquisitive glances.

HERMES: *(happily)* I am a shepherd, of course. See my ridiculous clothes and my dirty hands? I will admit at the moment I am rather sheep-less, but today is my day for pipe-playing instead. Mondays, sheep-watching. Tuesdays, pipe-playing.

ARGUS: *(happily)* Music is very pretty. Can pipe-man play more?

HERMES: Certainly, my good monstrosity. Care if I pull up a rock?

NARRATOR: The shepherd god jauntily perched himself upon a nearby boulder.

HERMES: My, my. What a wonderful heifer! Say...I'm not interrupting anything, am I?

ARGUS: *(excitedly)* Play! Play for Argus! But no funny business! Argus sees everything.

HERMES: Obviously. That's a face only a mother could love—maybe not even her.

NARRATOR: Hermes winked at the confused cow and began to produce a trilling melody from his pipes—one that recalled a brook babbling far away. The soothing sound filled the air, and after several minutes, many of Argus' eyelids began to droop. Almost all closed in slumber, but one—one in front—refused to sleep. Hermes played on. *(pipe music)*

An hour later, his fingers cramping from their activity, the god realized it was no use. The final eye refused to close—even while all the others slept peacefully. He stopped. When he did, every eye of Argus flicked back open.

ARGUS: Why the pipe-man stop playing?

HERMES: My fingers are killing me. I need to give them a break. Are you sure you don't want to lie down—take a nap? Maybe have some warm milk? I can ask the cow to loan you some.

ARGUS: Argus will *not* go to sleep! Argus said he would guard moo cow, and he will.

HERMES: Very well. How about a story? Would you like to hear a story?

ARGUS: Hmmmm. What is story about?

NARRATOR: Thinking, the god glanced at the sunlit meadow for inspiration. The flowers around were in full bloom.

HERMES: Spring. That's what it's about! Spring! *(speaking very slowly in a soothing voice)* It happened a very, very, very, very long time ago—in a place far, far, far away.

NARRATOR: The god lapsed into his tale as the Argus listened intently.

HERMES: Many years ago the seasons were not as they are today. It was always spring. The sun shone, and the ground yielded. Demeter, the Goddess of the Harvest, was eternally happy—teaching mortal man to farm and to grow. She bore her brother Zeus a beautiful daughter, Persephone, the Goddess of Spring.

DEMETER: Wouldn't you say my daughter is the most gorgeous sight you have ever seen?

HERMES: She would say. Demeter was a very proud mother and thought that nothing could ruin her happiness. But she had not counted on the eye of Hades—the Lord of the Underworld—landing upon Persephone as she picked flowers one day. Hades was a god of few words. Living below with the dead had made him morose and withdrawn. His skin was sickly pale, and his fingernails were in bad need of cutting.

HADES: *(mumbling, nearly incoherent)* What a beautiful maiden. I must have her as my own.

HERMES: Roaring up from a crack in the ground, his black chariot—pulled by skeletal horses—thundered into the meadow where the young Goddess of Spring was frolicking.

PERSEPHONE: *(innocently)* Who are you?

HADES: *(muttering)* I—I—am—Hades—would—you—hmmmm...

PERSEPHONE: I'm sorry, but I'm not supposed to talk to strangers.

HADES: But—I—

HERMES: Definitely lacking in social skills, Hades began to sweat. Most of the people he dealt with on a daily basis were *dead*. He desperately wanted to tell this stunning goddess just how stunning she actually was, but all he could do was grunt inarticulately.

HADES: Um—would—you—mind—(cough)—errrr...

PERSEPHONE: I'm afraid I don't understand.

HADES: (angrily) Oh, never mind!

HERMES: Spurring his steeds forward, Hades swept the terrified goddess into his chariot.

PERSEPHONE: (screaming) Help! Mother! Mother! Heeeeeeeeeeelp!

HERMES: The ground once again opened, swallowing its deathless master, and the cries of Persephone were sealed up within the earth.

PERSEPHONE: Let...go! Let go of me, you brute! What kind of freak kidnaps a defenseless girl?

HADES: I only—want—you—to—(cough) love me.

PERSEPHONE: Are you insane? You just grabbed me!

HADES: Sorry, I panicked. I just get so nervous around girls.

PERSEPHONE: So you just abduct them instead?

HADES: No—I mean, yes. This whole dating thing is so hard to figure out.

PERSEPHONE: Let me give you a little hint! This is *not* the way to do it! Heeeeeelp!

HERMES: Back above the earth, the Goddess of the Harvest was discovering that her daughter had vanished.

DEMETER: (calling out) Persephone! Where are you? Oh, I told you not to wander away!

HERMES: Demeter soon realized that she had, in fact, disappeared without a trace. The goddess began to wail.

DEMETER: (in anguish) My daughter! My daughter! Woe! (pause) I will search until I learn what has befallen her.

HERMES: But then a sudden thought came to her: What would happen to the earth with no one to tend it? It would wither without her powers to make its fields prosper.

DEMETER: Let it die. What has it done for me? It has taken my only love and hidden her from me.

HERMES: So the world wilted. Crops failed. The sky produced no rain. The sun scorched the land barren. And Demeter wandered, in the guise of a simple maid, searching for her beloved daughter.

At last, Helios, the sun himself, saw that creation would soon die if someone did not intervene. He called down from his fiery chariot to Demeter below.

HELIOS: Demeter! You must cease your wandering! Tend to the earth, or it will die—along with all that live upon it!

DEMETER: I will not allow a plant to grow or a flower to bud until I have my daughter again.

HELIOS: Persephone? Do you not know? Hades has taken her into the Underworld. He has made her his queen there.

DEMETER: *(gasping)* My baby? Abducted?

HELIOS: I saw it with my very eyes. Go to Zeus and tell him your complaint. He is the only one strong enough to force Hades into giving her back.

DEMETER: *(gratefully)* Thank you, Helios. I will.

HERMES: Demeter cried out immediately to immortal Zeus, begging him to remember his sister and the daughter that he had fathered by her. Zeus heard her cry and immediately dispatched the devilishly handsome and infinitely intelligent god Hermes to fetch the Goddess of Spring back from the Underworld. As the gorgeous god flew into the bowels of the earth, he began to notice why they called them "the bowels" of the earth. Ranks of decaying bodies waited in endless lines, foul rivers crisscrossed across stinking plains, and the air smelled of rotting flesh. No wonder Hades had to abduct his dates.

Soon Hermes came to the palace of Hades and appeared before the grim god seated on his throne of death. Beside him sat the emotionless Persephone—her youthful colors muted with a veil of black.

HADES: *(mumbling)* What are you doing here, Hermes?

HERMES: Hello, uncle. I bring orders from Dad.

HADES: Orders? What do you mean *orders?* He rules above the earth. I rule below it.

HERMES: Interesting distinction, but what I've come about is definitely an above-earth matter.

HADES: *(angrily)* Hmph. Well, I—

HERMES: You know, nobody's trying to point fingers here, but abducting a young goddess in broad daylight, right out in the open, isn't really the brightest idea.

HADES: I take what I want!

HERMES: Uh-huh. Well, you see. This lovely lady happens to be the daughter of Demeter. *(sarcastically)* And for some strange reason she's a bit depressed about her daughter getting sucked down into Hades.

HADES: Maybe she should watch her more closely.

HERMES: You're not listening. Long story short, she's so miserable that the earth is dying, people are starving, yaddah, yaddah, yaddah.

HADES: Why should I care?

HERMES: Think about it. Everybody's *dying*. This place is crowded as it is. Do you really want to be swamped with all that extra work?

HADES: *(sheepishly)* No, not really.

HERMES: Plus, I have this personal message from Zeus Almighty. *(narrating)* The dashing messenger god unrolled a parchment.

(speaking) Ahem. He says—"Don't make me come down there."

HADES: (angrily) Fine! You may take her back to her mother! I didn't want a queen anyway. It's not fair! (weeping)

HERMES: (consoling) Oh, calm down! There'll be more girls to abduct. There are plenty of maidens in the meadow.

PERSEPHONE: (emotionlessly) Am I free to go? Ever since I ate those pomegranate seeds yesterday, my heart has grown so cold. I think the sun will be the only thing to warm it once again.

HERMES: Uh-oh. Did you say pomegranate seeds?

PERSEPHONE: Yes. Why?

HERMES: How many?

PERSEPHONE: Four.

HERMES: Whoops. Well, I don't know if anyone told you this rule, but if you eat the food of the Underworld, you are bound to it.

HADES: (excitedly) Aha! I had forgotten that rule. Oh, well. Too bad. Guess you'll have to stay here and be my queen after all.

HERMES: Wait a minute. If she's only eaten some tiny seeds, then she doesn't have to stay here all the time.

HADES: What?

HERMES: She may leave, but since she has eaten *four* seeds, she shall return here for *four* months out of the year.

HADES: No! I won't allow her to leave.

HERMES: (cautioning) Remember the note.

HADES: (pouting) Fine. Go. I'll see you in eight months, I guess.

HERMES: (narrating) Persephone smiled and leaned in close to the Lord of Death.

PERSEPHONE: It's weird, but I kind of like it here. And underneath it all, you're kind of cute—in a creepy kind of way.

HADES: (stunned) You really think so?

HERMES: (narrating) Hades leaned in for a kiss, but the Goddess of Spring took his hand.

PERSEPHONE: Let's work up to that, okay? (pause) I'll go visit Mother, but I'll be back.

HERMES: (speaking) If you don't, he'll probably come and get you.

HADES: (laugh) True. Goodbye, my love.

PERSEPHONE: Goodbye.

HERMES: (narrating) And so every year Persephone returns to her mother, the Goddess of the Harvest, and there are eight months of plenty. But when she once again goes away to be with her subterranean husband, Demeter mourns, and the earth grows barren until her daughter's return. And that's why we must put up with fall and winter each year.

ARGUS: (loud snoring) Zzzzz.

NARRATOR: Hermes stopped his story. All of the Argus' eyes were closed in slumber. Violent snoring was escaping his huge nostrils.

HERMES: I knew that one would put you to sleep. And now that you are easy pickings…

NARRATOR: The mischievous god drew a shining sword from the pouch slung at his side.

HERMES: Sucker!

NARRATOR: With a quick slice he severed the monster's head from his body. *(snicker-snack)* The hundred eyes had enough time to open before they became dim with death. With its deformed head rolling helplessly in the grass, the body slumped forward.

IO: *(excited)* Moo!

HERMES: You're free! Run while you still can! It won't take my stereotypically evil step-mother long to figure out what's happened.

NARRATOR: The transformed maiden looked to the messenger god questioningly. Was he not going to turn her back into her normal self?

HERMES: *(sadly)* Only Zeus can undo what he has done! Run! And when there is no harm of his wife finding him out, he will come to you and transform you once again!

NARRATOR: The animal turned and galloped away.

HERMES: *(loud yawn)* Wow. I almost put *myself* to sleep with that one.

NARRATOR: There was a blip, and Hermes dissolved. Seconds later the fabric of the universe was again disturbed. Hera appeared.

HERA: What the—?

NARRATOR: With suppressed rage she knelt by the carcass of her favorite henchman.

HERA: *(angrily)* Argus! What measly peon of Zeus has done this to you?

NARRATOR: She picked up the severed head into her arms and cradled it *almost* lovingly.

HERA: My faithful servant, let your hundred eyes never be forgotten. I will place them upon the feathers of my peacocks. There they will watch out over the world for eternity, and all will remember your greatness.

NARRATOR: With a sniff she wiped the sadness from her face and dropped the head to the ground.

HERA: *(seething)* So, the harlot has found a way to escape I see! Run, cow! Run!

NARRATOR: The Queen of Heaven snapped her fingers, and a faint buzzing grew closer. A tiny gadfly landed in her palm.

HERA: Pursue her. Never give her rest. Drive her on through country after country. Make her regret her lust. Let her seek death.

NARRATOR: The fly took to the air, and Hera, with a cruel smile of satisfaction on her lips, watched it wing itself away.

IO: And so I have wandered these many years—stung by the fly of Hera. Misery has been my life.

NARRATOR: The transformed maiden finished telling her tale to Prometheus. There was a pause as the chained titan took it all in.

PROMETHEUS: You have been wronged most severely. Your punishment is equal to my own. But I can tell you to take heart. As you spoke, I heard the future in your words. I have seen down the corridors of time. The day is not far off when Zeus will come to you and make you whole once again.

IO: *(excitedly)* Really? Wonderful!

PROMETHEUS: Then this curse will be lifted. From him you will bear mighty sons—sons to bring you joy in the later years of your life. You will be repaid all this misery through that happiness.

IO: This gives me hope!

PROMETHEUS: It is hope for me as well! From your line will come a mighty hero, the greatest hero, and he will be the one who will free me from my eternal punishment. Heracles, they will call him.

IO: *(relieved)* Finally! We both have been so wronged by the gods. Justice will be served at last.

PROMETHEUS: Indeed. Goodbye, Io. Journey well.

IO: Goodbye.

NARRATOR: Leaving the chained form upon the rock, the white heifer continued on her path with a newfound spring in her step. Relief was in sight. Prometheus smiled as he watched her leave. Beyond her he saw the eagle approaching—coming to mutilate him once again. But the glorious day was nearing when he too would be freed from his torment and released from his immortal chains.

DISCUSSION QUESTIONS

- What does this myth explain about nature?
- What does this myth explain about certain types of animals?
- Why is it not wise for Io to begin an affair with Zeus?
- Why does Hera punish Io instead of Zeus? Is this fair? Explain.
- In this story how are the gods shown in an unflattering light? Explain.
- Should Prometheus be released from his eternal torture? Explain.

THE GOLDEN TOUCH
TEACHER GUIDE

BACKGROUND

Wishing for things rarely gets results, and even when our wishes are granted, they often do not bring us the happiness we expected. Oscar Wilde said, "There are only two tragedies in life: One is not getting what one wants, and the other is getting it." The myth of King Midas illustrates this point.

Because of his greed, Midas wishes for the notorious Golden Touch, but he soon realizes that this magical power makes his life unbearable, and he must undo the wish. There are many lessons imbedded in the myth: Be careful what you wish for. Wealth doesn't solve all problems and often creates more than it solves. The best things in life are free. As obvious as these lessons seem to us, we get the impression that Midas is the only one who doesn't learn from his story. He is as much a fool at the end of his story as at the beginning. Because of this, Midas' misfortunes have always read more like comedy than tragedy.

On another note you will not find Plautus the wise slave in the original version of the myth. He was added to contrast Midas' foolishness. He is named for Plautus the Roman playwright, who (like the Greeks before him) often used the stock character of the wily slave who gets the better of his foolish master.

SUMMARY

Midas is the foolish king of Phrygia, who spends his days thinking up new ways of making himself richer. Plautus is his slave, who must suffer through the stupid schemes of his master.

One day, Silenus, a drunken satyr, wanders into Midas' garden. Midas intends to send the satyr packing, but Plautus points out that Silenus is the foster-father of Dionysus, the God of Wine. Hearing this news, Midas hatches a scheme: If he returns the bewildered satyr back to Dionysus, the god might give him a reward.

Welcoming the satyr into his home, Midas summons Dionysus. The God of Wine appears and is relieved that his foster-father is safe and sound. Midas (not very discreetly) asks for a reward of some kind. Dionysus agrees to grant Midas one wish but tries to warn the king that he should weigh his decision very carefully. Midas rashly asks for the power of turning anything he touches into gold. Dionysus grants this request, telling Midas how the wish might be undone if it goes awry. After Dionysus and Silenus disappear, Midas uses his new magical touch to turn item after item into solid gold. Plautus sees the foolishness in his master's wish.

Midas' happiness is short-lived, for he soon finds that food also turns to gold when he touches it and wine assumes a molten-gold form in his throat. The king sees he will starve if the wish is not reversed.

Plautus convinces Midas that they must travel to the River Pactolus, the waters that Dionysus said would reverse the wish. Once arriving there, Midas washes in the river. The power of the Golden Touch leaves the king and turns the riverbed to gold.

Soon after this the sound of nearby lyre-playing draws the king's attention. A music contest is occurring between Apollo, the God of Music, and Pan, the satyr God of Shepherds. Sighting Midas, the gods ask him to judge their contest. Midas foolishly agrees to this and even more foolishly chooses Pan over Apollo. Apollo punishes Midas by giving him the ears of a donkey.

Midas, now completely humiliated, decides to hide his new donkey ears beneath a turban. He tries to swear Plautus to secrecy concerning them, but the slave refuses unless Midas grants his freedom. Midas reluctantly agrees. Plautus, now sworn to secrecy, digs a hole by the side of the river and whispers his master's secret into it. Later reeds grow up from where Plautus planted this secret, and when the wind moves through them, they whisper the story of how Midas gained the ears of a donkey.

ESSENTIAL QUESTIONS

- Is greed good?
- Can money buy happiness?
- What would the consequences be if everyone received everything they wished for?

ANTICIPATORY QUESTIONS

- What is the Midas Touch?
- Can you name some stories that deal with magical wishes?
- Have you ever wished for something?
- Have you ever gotten your wish only to discover the result wasn't what you expected?

CONNECT

"The Monkey's Paw" In this 1902 short story by W. W. Jacobs, the paw of a dead monkey, brought back to England from India, turns out to be a talisman that will grant three wishes. The main characters find that the monkey's paw is cursed, and each wish has horrific results.

A Midsummer Night's Dream Shakespeare's fantastical comedy features a character named Nick Bottom, who is just as foolish as Midas and suffers a similar fate.

TEACHABLE TERMS

- **Cause and Effect** Midas does not think about the ramifications of his wish. Because of this, how does he suffer? What can others learn from this?
- **Humor** How is this myth told humorously? What elements tell you that it is intended to be humorous?
- **Verbal Irony** The slave Plautus continually uses verbal irony (in the form of sarcasm) to undermine his foolish master, such as his reply of "Blasphemy" to Midas' comment on pg. 71, calling Midas "Your Ignorance" on pg. 72, and "Your Freakishness" on pg. 76.
- **Symbol** For many ancient cultures, the donkey was the symbol of foolishness. *Ass*, an alternate term for donkey, has evolved to mean "a foolish person." This is why Midas is given the ears of a donkey. Does the donkey seem like a good symbol for foolishness? Can you think of a better one?
- **Juxtaposition/Characterization** What are some of the details that characterize King Midas? How are these characteristics juxtaposed with those of Plautus the slave?
- **Allusion** This script makes many allusions to other Greek myths and characters, including Orpheus (pg. 72), Nestor (pg. 72), Tantalus (pg. 72), and Patroclus (pg. 77).

RECALL QUESTIONS

1. What type of creature is Silenus?
2. Dionysus is the god of what?
3. How can Midas undo his wish?
4. Why does Midas receive donkey ears?
5. Even though Plautus never tells Midas' secret, how is Midas' story told?

THE GOLDEN TOUCH

CAST

MIDAS	*King of Phrygia*
PLAUTUS	*Slave to Midas*
SILENUS	*Portly, Old Satyr*
VOICE	*Female Voice*
DIONYSUS	*God of Wine*
APOLLO	*God of Music and Light*
PAN	*Satyr, God of Shepherds*

NARRATOR: There once lived a very rich and very foolish king in Phrygia named Midas. He spent his days hatching ridiculous schemes to make himself even richer than he already was. For most of these schemes, he enlisted the help of his infinitely intelligent and mostly-faithful slave, Plautus.

MIDAS: Plautus, I simply *must* have more money!

PLAUTUS: Master, why do you want more money? You have a humongous palace, a four-acre rose garden, and more fountains than you can shake a stick at.

MIDAS: *(sadly)* Yes, but there are kings out there who have bigger palaces, bigger rose gardens, and more fountains than you can shake an even bigger stick at.

PLAUTUS: *(sigh)* I heard a new philosophy about wealth just the other day—apparently, you have to *spend* money to *make* money.

MIDAS: Ha! That's the stupidest thing I've ever heard. You might as well say, "It's better to give than receive."

PLAUTUS: *(sarcastically)* Blasphemy.

MIDAS: Think of all the richest kings in Greece. What do they have that I don't have?

PLAUTUS: Power. Respect. Good looks. Talent.

MIDAS: *(angrily)* Okay. That's enough.

PLAUTUS: *(continuing)* Intelligence. A filled-out beard—not that patchy peach fuzz you have.

MIDAS: Enough!

PLAUTUS: *(continuing)* People skills. A fashion sense. Gods-for-parents.

MIDAS: Wait! That's it!

PLAUTUS: What? A fashion sense?

MIDAS: No, you fool! All the greatest kings have been descended from the gods! All I need to do is prove I'm a descendant of the gods.

PLAUTUS: And you'll automatically be richer?

MIDAS: Exactly. I'm bound to be.

PLAUTUS: Forget it! Don't you remember that rumor about your mother?

MIDAS: *(angrily)* It was a lie! My mother never wore men's sandals in her life!

PLAUTUS: No, Your Denseness—the rumor *you* tried to start about your mother.

MIDAS: It wasn't so far-fetched. Lots of kings are descendants of goddesses.

PLAUTUS: Not from Athena they aren't. Maybe if you hadn't claimed the almighty virgin goddess as your mother, it would have gone over better.

MIDAS: I get all the A-goddesses mixed up. I meant to say Aphrodite.

PLAUTUS: Well, there would have been no problem believing that one.

MIDAS: Maybe this time I could say I'm the son of Zeus?

PLAUTUS: Yes, but who isn't?

MIDAS: What about Apollo?

PLAUTUS: Too good-looking. Not believable. How about Hephaestus? *(pause)* But, you know, the trick isn't to fool other mortals. You'd have to get the gods to believe they accidentally sired you. Then they'd start heaping all that goodwill on you.

MIDAS: How hard could it be to trick a god?

PLAUTUS: Wouldn't try it. Remember my former master, Tantalus? He thought he'd get in good with the gods if he murdered his own son and served him up as a stew.

MIDAS: Brilliant! Why didn't I think of that? If only I had a son!

PLAUTUS: It didn't work. The gods cursed him forever.

MIDAS: Why'd he waste a perfectly good son on the deal then?

PLAUTUS: Bad communication. He asked me what the gods liked to eat, and I told him nectar. He thought I said Nestor. So then he figured if they liked to chew on an old guy like Nestor, they'd really go for some young and juicy flesh.

NARRATOR: The conversation between master and slave was interrupted by a commotion in the rose garden outside the palace—loud, drunken bellowing accompanied by horrible lyre music.

SILENUS: *(loud bellowing)*

MIDAS: What's that racket?

PLAUTUS: I hope it isn't Orpheus the musician again! Talk about a downer. I was depressed for weeks after his last visit.

NARRATOR: They rushed out into the garden. A pot-bellied satyr with a scraggly white beard was stumbling up the rosebush-lined path.

MIDAS: A goat-man!

PLAUTUS: Please, Your Ignorance. They prefer the term *satyr*.

MIDAS: Whatever he is, he better not have snacked on my prize roses!

NARRATOR: The satyr let out a huge belch—petals flitting forth from his mouth like a fountain.

SILENUS: (*loud belch*) Belch!

MIDAS: Ah! My babies! (*angrily*) You—you—

PLAUTUS: Wait a minute, master.

NARRATOR: Plautus pulled a scroll from his tunic.

PLAUTUS: Yes! I knew it! He's right here in *Who's Who of Olympus*.

NARRATOR: Midas looked up in shock at the satyr, who was taking yet another snack among the bushes.

MIDAS: That *thing*? They make filthy goat-men gods now?

PLAUTUS: Not a god. His name is Silenus. He's the tutor and foster-father of—let me see here—Dionysus!

MIDAS: (*trying to remember*) Dionysus. Dionysus. Is he the one with the limp?

PLAUTUS: No, the God of Wine. He's new. The Greeks just invented him a few months ago.

MIDAS: God of Wine, eh? Not the best god to forge a connection with, but oh well. (*kindly*) Salerno! Hello, Salerno!

PLAUTUS: (*whispering*) Silenus!

NARRATOR: The old satyr rose from the bushes and smiled drunkenly at the king.

SILENUS: (*drunkenly*) Greetings, sir. Could you tell me where I am—standing now—here?

MIDAS: You are in the gardens of Midas, my friend. Those are also my roses that you've made quite a mess of, too.

SILENUS: Wha? What did you—(*gurgling sound*)—say your name was being?

MIDAS: (*loudly*) Midas! King of Phrygia!

SILENUS: No thank you! I am lost. I was just snacking on some of your beautiful tulips here.

MIDAS: (*angrily*) My tulips! That's it! Get him inside before he makes a real mess.

NARRATOR: Silenus doubled over in the pathway and regurgitated his botanical breakfast.

SILENUS: (*puking sound*) Blarg!

PLAUTUS: Too late.

MIDAS: Master Saleeno, may we offer you some food? Something to drink?

NARRATOR: At the mention of drink the satyr jerked to attention.

SILENUS: I thought you'd never ask, meboy! Lead the way to the pitcher! I'm quite parched.

NARRATOR: Once the satyr was seated at the royal table partaking of even more wine, Plautus whispered to his master.

PLAUTUS: This may work to our advantage. If Silenus is lost, there might be some reward for finding him.

MIDAS: Don't be stupid. Who would pay money to find an old goat like him?

PLAUTUS: Maybe his foster-son? Dionysus?

MIDAS: Ah, yes. The God of Goats.

PLAUTUS: No! Wine!

MIDAS: That's what I meant. So how should we contact this god?

PLAUTUS: We need a priest.

MIDAS: Where are *we* going to find a priest to Dioneesia?

PLAUTUS: Orpheus the musician is one of Dionysus' followers. Don't you remember when he visited here?

MIDAS: Do I ever! I couldn't get those sappy songs out of my head for weeks.

PLAUTUS: Exactly.

MIDAS: Weren't they all about death and despair and despairing over death?

PLAUTUS: Mainly. But there was one—a chant for summoning Dionysus. Let's see if I can remember it.

NARRATOR: Plautus scribbled furiously on a roll of parchment. Midas picked it up and raised his eyebrows in surprise.

MIDAS: Plautus, I had no idea you could write.

PLAUTUS: I had no idea *you* could read. Just say the words!

MIDAS: Ivy-wreathed god of ripest grape
God of curly hair and shaven nape
Shrouded in thy purple cape
Now appear to me, a humble ape!

NARRATOR: A rumbling shook the palace. The large, decorative wine bowl in the midst of the table began to vibrate, and a god-like figure rose from the dark liquid within.

DIONYSUS: *(grandly)* Behold! I am Dionysus!

SILENUS: *(really drunk)* Whoa! What a trick! Do it again!

DIONYSUS: Silenus! I've been looking everywhere for you. When did you wander off?

SILENUS: I'm not sure, meboy. But these folks here found me and offered me food and drink. But I only took them up on the drink. *(drunken laugh)* Ha!

NARRATOR: Dionysus turned toward Midas, who began bowing copiously to the newly-appeared god.

MIDAS: It's true, Your Most Holiness. I am Midas—a kind, but poor, king.

DIONYSUS: Poor? Are you kidding? Look at this fancy table—and this pillared hall. Not to mention this golden wine bowl I'm currently swimming in.

MIDAS: Well, yes. I admit this hall is nice, but the rest of my home is very meager indeed. I'm a poor country king.

NARRATOR: Dionysus turned to Plautus.

DIONYSUS: Who are you?

PLAUTUS: His slave, Your Highness.

DIONYSUS: One of how many?

PLAUTUS: Twenty.

DIONYSUS: Ha! I knew it. I assume, Midas, that you are fishing for some kind of reward.

MIDAS: Heh. Heh. I would hate to ask for one, but I have so many children—so many mouths to feed—and my wife is in poor health.

DIONYSUS: Where is she then?

PLAUTUS: Dead.

MIDAS: Heh. Heh. Dead. The poorest health a body can be in, right?

DIONYSUS: (sigh) Very well. Even though you're the biggest buffoon I've ever met, and I sincerely doubt you have any true financial need, I *am* grateful that you have found my old foster-father here. So I will grant you one wish.

MIDAS: Oh, thank you for this one wish, most noble god of—of—

PLAUTUS: (whispering) Wine!

MIDAS: (whispering) I'm not wishing for wine! I have my own vineyard!

DIONYSUS: This is a major decision, I know. If you need time to—

MIDAS: (interrupting) I wish everything I touch would turn to gold!

DIONYSUS: —think about it.

PLAUTUS: Zeus save us all!

DIONYSUS: Interesting. All right, Midas. You have made your one and only wish. (chanting) By the waters of the River Styx
And the power of Dionysus
The touch of gold I give to thee,
King of mortals, Midas.
If this wish time causes you to regret
The waters of swift Pactolus may undo it yet.
(speaking) It is granted. Now, we will take our leave. Come, Silenus.

SILENUS: (snoring) Zzzzzzzzzzzzzz.

NARRATOR: The god grabbed the old satyr by the scruff, and both disappeared down into the depths of the wine bowl.

PLAUTUS: What a waste! Of all the stupid wishes you could have made, why did it have to be that one?

NARRATOR: But Midas did not hear his slave. He was staring in wonder at his hand, which had now taken on a golden sheen.

MIDAS: Don't you know what this means? I can have all the gold I desire! Imagine it! Golden floors! Golden walls! Golden everything!

NARRATOR: The king laid his hand upon the table, and it instantly transformed into gold. (cha-ching!)

MIDAS: Fantastic!

NARRATOR: He ran from object to object in the palace, touching it gleefully like a child. (cha-ching!) He whooped when each object assumed a golden shine. Plautus followed him about the palace, shaking his head in disbelief.

PLAUTUS: Please, Your Giddiness. Let's save *some* of the furniture. Do you really need a solid-gold couch? Besides, the cooks have set the table for dinner.

MIDAS: Don't be stupid! I can't think about food right now. There's so much gold to make! *(crazy laugh)*

PLAUTUS: But you'll need food to keep your strength up. It's going to be a long night of gold-making!

MIDAS: Oh fine. What a dumb kill-joy you are, Plautus! Can't you let an old king have a bit of fun?

NARRATOR: He jauntily pulled a chair up to the feast, grabbed an apple from the spread, and sank his teeth into it—or tried to.

MIDAS: Ahhhhhh! My toof! My toof!

PLAUTUS: See? You've cursed yourself, you soft-headed fool!

NARRATOR: Midas picked his tooth up from the table from where it had fallen and inserted it tenderly back into his gums.

MIDAS: No. Look. There. Good as new.

NARRATOR: He flashed Plautus a smile. A golden tooth gleamed out amid the others.

MIDAS: There's no problem at all. *You* can feed me.

PLAUTUS: *(sarcastically)* What a pleasure, Your Freakishness.

MIDAS: Give me some of that wine.

NARRATOR: Plautus tipped the cup to the king's lips. The king immediately fell from his chair and rolled about on the floor, grasping his throat in pain.

MIDAS: Ahhhhhhh! My throat! My throat!

PLAUTUS: What is it?

NARRATOR: The king wrapped his arms around his stomach.

MIDAS: My bowels! My bowels!

NARRATOR: Plautus looked down at the wine still left it in the cup. It was still liquid—yet gold in color and steaming.

PLAUTUS: Molten gold!

NARRATOR: Several excruciating hours later the molten gold finally passed through the king's system.

MIDAS: This is all *your* fault, Plautus! You should have stopped me from making such a foolish wish! Now I'm going to starve to death!

PLAUTUS: But look at it this way. You'll be the richest dead guy around.

MIDAS: You have to help me! There has to be a way to get rid of this curse!

NARRATOR: The slave pulled out his scroll once again and examined it.

PLAUTUS: Apparently, only the same god can remove a curse once it has been given.

MIDAS: What if Dio-what's-his-name won't return?

PLAUTUS: Then I suggest not picking your nose—or anything else for that matter.

NARRATOR: In a panic Midas climbed up onto the table and peered down into the wine bowl.

MIDAS: It's me—Midas. I need your help once again.

NARRATOR: A chipper, female voice replied.

VOICE: We're sorry. Dionysus is not available right now. If you would like to leave a message—

MIDAS: No! There has to be some way to undo this!

PLAUTUS: Don't you remember what Dionysus said when he cast the spell?

MIDAS: Hocus pocus something…

PLAUTUS: No, the last line! What was it? The waters of swift Pactolus may undo it yet.

MIDAS: Patroclus! Of course! The beloved friend of Achilles. But he's dead, isn't he? And what waters would he have anyway?

PLAUTUS: Not Patroclus! Pactolus! It's a river. Don't they teach you kings geography? Maybe if you wash yourself in that river, you will lose the Golden Touch.

MIDAS: What? Who said I wanted to lose it?

PLAUTUS: You can't be serious.

MIDAS: Maybe I could just have it on the weekend. It's really actually useful at times.

PLAUTUS: Master, give it up.

MIDAS: Very well.

NARRATOR: So king and slave made preparation to journey upland to the River Pactolus. After mounting two different donkeys, which both immediately turned to gold, Midas decided the best solution was to walk to the River Pactolus. The king and his slave made the journey easily—leaving a trail of golden grass in their wake.

MIDAS: I wish I'd never met Diomedes and that stupid old goat-man, what's-his-name. I wish I'd made a better wish.

PLAUTUS: There's the river, master. Wash in there, and we'll see if my theory is right.

MIDAS: Life's funny, you know. One minute you have the Golden Touch. The next minute you don't.

NARRATOR: The king knelt by the swift waters.

MIDAS: Goodbye, obscene amounts of gold.

NARRATOR: He plunged his hand into the water, which began to bubble and foam. When he jerked his hand out, the bottom of the river was shining. The rocks below had all been turned to gold.

PLAUTUS: Now try it, master. Touch something.

NARRATOR: Midas touched his hand to the grass. Nothing. It stayed grass—regular, green grass.

MIDAS: (laughing) Who knew that the sight of plain old grass could make a man so happy?

PLAUTUS: Perhaps, master, the wealth of the world is not in gold. It's in nature—the beauty that the gods have created—the trees, the rivers, the sky.

MIDAS: (*pausing to think*) No. It's pretty much gold. But thanks for trying to make me feel better.

PLAUTUS: (*sigh*)

NARRATOR: As soon as they turned to go, a sudden burst of pipe-playing erupted from a stand of nearby trees. (*sound of pipe-playing*)

MIDAS: Oh no. Surely, that's not old goat-breath again, is it?

PLAUTUS: No. I don't think so. This music sounds *good*. Perhaps we should investigate.

MIDAS: Hmph. Just because you've cured me of my curse doesn't mean you're making all the decisions now. I'm still the master, and you're the slave.

PLAUTUS: Yes, master. So are we investigating or what?

MIDAS: If you think it's a good idea—sure.

NARRATOR: The king and his slave walked toward the sound of the magnificent pipe-playing. In the midst of the stand of trees, there was a satyr playing his reed pipes, and directly across from him was the golden form of a god.

MIDAS: It's them again! Run for it!

PLAUTUS: No, no.

NARRATOR: Plautus produced his scroll.

PLAUTUS: It's Pan, the God of Shepherds, and Apollo, God of Music.

MIDAS: Oh! Celebrities! Which one's Apollo—the pretty boy or the goat-man? (*loudly*) Yoo-hoo! Hello, immortals. It's me—King Midas. Perhaps you've heard of me? The Midas Touch?

NARRATOR: The immortals stopped their pipe-playing.

PAN: Mortal, we are happy to see you. We were just having a contest.

MIDAS: What kind of contest, pray tell?

APOLLO: (*sarcastically*) An archery contest. What does it look like? A pipe-playing contest, you moron!

MIDAS: Ah. Fascinating. And how can I assist you?

PAN: We're in need of a judge.

MIDAS: And you were hoping I might be able to find you one.

APOLLO: No, fool. We want *you* to be the judge. Now sit down and shut up while we play.

NARRATOR: The gods returned to their music. (*sounds of frenzied pipe-playing*)

MIDAS: Well, that Apollo certainly is full of himself, isn't he? Pretty rude, if you ask me. I have half a mind to choose the goat-legged fellow.

PLAUTUS: Master, you *would have* half a mind if you did that. Apollo would be furious!

MIDAS: Bah. He's all talk.

PLAUTUS: I've heard stories of his anger. He's pretty trigger-happy with his bow and arrows.

MIDAS: I'm not afraid of him. Besides, goat-breath is doing much better anyhow.

PLAUTUS: Apollo is the God of Music! He's the master of all instruments!

MIDAS: Exactly. He needs to be brought down a peg or two. Ahem! Gentlemen, please. There is no need to play any longer. I have made my decision.

NARRATOR: The immortals lowered their pipes expectantly.

APOLLO: Let me warn you, Midas, offending me would have—

MIDAS: (*proudly*) I choose Pam!

APOLLO: —grave consequences.

PLAUTUS: (*whispering*) His name is Pan. Oh forget it.

APOLLO: (*angrily*) What? You can't be serious! You choose this mangy, little goat-man over me?

PAN: Um. We actually prefer the term *satyr*.

MIDAS: (*cockily*) You heard me, golden boy!

APOLLO: You ignoramus! I'll show you how the gods punish fools!

NARRATOR: The fiery anger of Apollo blazed forth in a blinding flash of light. (*shazam!*)

APOLLO: There! Now all the world will know what a complete donkey-brain you are!

NARRATOR: The god disappeared.

MIDAS: Plautus, you were right about his fiery temper. But I'm alive! He didn't strike me down or anything!

NARRATOR: The slave sadly guided Midas' hands to his head. Two gigantic donkey ears had sprouted there.

MIDAS: (*shocked*) No! It can't be!

PLAUTUS: I'm afraid so, master. Donkey ears.

MIDAS: Oh! Woe is me! Hee-haw! Hee-haw!

NARRATOR: Midas covered his mouth in shock. Pan approached the king apologetically.

PAN: Tough break, Midas. Look on the bright side. It's not the end of the world. I'm a little goat-man, and even *I* can still scare up a date or two on the weekends.

NARRATOR: He bowed and frolicked away, trilling on his reed pipes.

MIDAS: We've got to hide this somehow. I'll be the laughing stock of the kingdom. Maybe if I wear a very tall hat. What do you think?

PLAUTUS: We could wrap those ears up in a turban, I guess.

MIDAS: Perfect. Then no one will ever know—except you, and *you'll* never tell a living soul.

PLAUTUS: Wait a minute. Why shouldn't I?

MIDAS: Because you love your kindly old master—who has never beaten you—unless it was for a really good reason.

PLAUTUS: Ha! Give me my freedom. *Then* I swear I will never tell another living soul.

MIDAS: Your freedom? But, Plautus! What would I do? You know I can't function without you!

PLAUTUS: I didn't say I was leaving. You can put me on your staff—complete with a salary and everything.

MIDAS: *(shocked)* A salary! Why you—! *(pause)* All right. You'll have your freedom.

PLAUTUS: Excellent. Now if you'll excuse me, before we head back, I'd like to have one more look at that golden river.

MIDAS: Fine. Just hurry. I'm starting to attract flies.

NARRATOR: As he left the king, the slave placed a hand over his mouth to stifle the chuckles bubbling up inside him. He walked to the river and hunched down on its banks. He made a little hole in the earth there and leaned his lips down to it. Into that hole he whispered Midas' story—every last bit. He ended with the juiciest part.

PLAUTUS: Midas has the ears of a donkey.

NARRATOR: Then after he had whispered these words, he covered them over with dirt, stood, and returned to where Midas waited.

PLAUTUS: Back to Phrygia! First things first—we need to see a hatter. Otherwise, you'll look completely asinine.

MIDAS: How true! Hee-haw. Hee-haw.

NARRATOR: Plautus never told another living soul the story of his former master. Yet from the hole he dug on the banks of that river, there grew a cluster of reeds, and whenever the wind blew through their stems, they would whisper his words. Those who journeyed to see the river with the golden bottom heard this story carried in the night air, and through this, Midas gained his long-desired fame—as the most foolish of kings.

DISCUSSION QUESTIONS

- If you were granted one wish, what would it be? Explain.
- In this type of story, where a wish is granted by a supernatural force, the wish rarely has the desired result. Why do you think this is so? What are these stories trying to say about wishing for things or getting what you wish for? Explain.
- A *farce* is a story told with broad comedic strokes. A *satire* is typically a deadpan comedy meant to elicit a change in opinion among its viewers. A *parody* is a comedy where the style (and sometimes content) of source material is lampooned. Which type of comedy do you think this story is? Explain.
- In Nathaniel Hawthorne's version of the Midas myth, the king has a daughter, whom he inadvertently turns to gold. What does this detail add to the story? Explain.
- The slave Plautus is not part of the original Midas story. What does he add to the narrative? Explain.

PHAETHON'S RIDE
TEACHER GUIDE

BACKGROUND

Children sired (and then abandoned) by the gods form a common theme in Greek mythology. These typically male heroes learn from their mortal mothers the truth about their immortal fathers. From this point on their lives become a quest to prove their identity. Their lives seem to say, "Look what I did! I *must* be the son of a god!" So it went for Perseus, Heracles, Theseus, and others. But what happens when a hero fails? The myth of Phaethon answers that question.

Phaethon's ride helped the Greeks explain many puzzling things about the world: Why certain regions of the world are desert, why the sun sometimes hides his face, and why from time to time a star is seen falling from the sky. It also helped them demonstrate the concept of hubris or "overweening pride"—a dangerous character flaw, especially when directed toward the gods. Phaethon foolishly believes that he is qualified to do the job of his immortal father, Helios. It is a mistake that costs him his life.

It is a myth that is still relevant today. It asks many questions: How far will we go to prove ourselves? Why do we not listen to sound advice? Why do we give into peer pressure? How can one mistake have a far-reaching impact on us and others? There is still much to learn from the failure of Phaethon.

SUMMARY

Phaethon's mother, Clymene, has always told him that his father is Helios, the God of the Sun, but no one in his village believes him. In fact, several of the other boys, including a bully named Epaphus, accuse him of being a liar. In order to prove to these boys that he is truly the son of a god, Phaethon decides to leave his mother and sister, Phoebe, to journey across the world to the palace of Helios. There he will confront his father and find a way to prove his true parentage.

Phaethon reaches the palace of the sun and reunites with his father. Helios is so overjoyed to see his son that he foolishly swears on the River Styx to grant him any request that he might have. Phaethon knows that every day Helios drives his sun chariot across the sky, giving light to the world. Phaethon asks to perform this task. Then when his peers see him in the chariot of the sun, they will know that he was telling the truth about his father.

Helios is horrified at this suggestion and tries to talk his son out of his request. Not even Zeus is skillful enough to do what Helios does. The fiery horses are willful, the constellations of the heavens are ferocious, and the path across the sky is treacherous. In spite of his father's protests, Phaethon remains adamant. Since he has sworn on the River Styx, Helios has no choice. He reluctantly allows Phaethon to board the chariot and places the crown of light onto his head.

Phaethon's ride begins, and the boy soon learns that his father was right. The constellations of the heavens attack Phaethon, and the horses run out of control. The sun chariot bumps the sky and then swoops low over the earth. The seas boil, and the deserts of the earth are formed by the searing heat. At last Gaea, the earth herself, cries out that something must be done. Zeus aims a thunderbolt at the sun chariot and blasts Phaethon out of the sky. As the boy falls to his death, engulfed in flame, he resembles a falling star.

The sun does not shine for days as Helios grieves the loss of his son. Phoebe journeys to find her brother's body and buries it. Because of her grief, she transforms into a poplar tree, whose amber "tears" of sap reflect the light of the sun.

ESSENTIAL QUESTIONS

- How can one mistake completely alter (or even end) a person's life?
- Why should we listen to sound advice?
- Should we worry what other people think of us?

CONNECT

Ovid's *Metamorphoses* The account of Phaethon's ride in this epic poem is deservedly the most famous. Ovid's eye for detail and knack for storytelling bring the tale to life. Compare the tale from Book II of *Metamorphoses* with the version of the myth presented here.

ANTICIPATORY QUESTIONS

- Who is Helios?
- What exactly did the ancient Greeks think the sun was?
- What are some of the most famous constellations?
- Have you ever done something unsafe to prove yourself to someone else?

TEACHABLE TERMS

- **Anti-hero** Since he makes such poor decisions, Phaethon is an example of an anti-hero, a protagonist who does *not* possess conventional heroic qualities. Compare and contrast Phaethon's qualities with other heroes. How is he different?

- **Hubris** "Excessive pride and overconfidence" is the definition of the Greek concept of hubris. Often characters demonstrate this character flaw when they placed themselves on the same level as the gods. How is Phaethon guilty of hubris?
- **Metamorphosis** A common theme in Greek mythology is metamorphosis or transformation. Sometimes characters that undergo intense experiences (good or bad) change shape. Phoebe's transformation on pg. 94 is an example of metamorphosis. Think about what this adds to the story. Why is this such a common occurrence in myth?
- **Didactic** The myth of Phaethon is somewhat didactic as it is intended to teach a lesson. Think about what lessons this myth can teach about life.
- **Denotation-Connotation** Autumn calls Springtime a *prima donna* on pg. 87. The denotation for this term is the leading lady in an opera ("first lady"), but the connotation of the term is someone who is an arrogant show-off.
- **Setting** Although this myth takes place in ancient Greece with the involvement of supernatural gods and beasts, could the same story be told in the modern world with a "real-life" spin? How could one modify the setting but retain the same plot structure? Is anything lost from the story when the setting is changed?

RECALL QUESTIONS

1. What does Phaethon want to prove to everyone?
2. Why must Helios honor his son's request?
3. What are two ways the earth is changed because of Phaethon's ride?
4. What kinds of beasts attack Phaethon?
5. How is Phoebe, Phaethon's sister, transformed?

PHAETHON'S RIDE

CAST

PHAETHON	*Mortal Son of Helios*
EPAPHUS	*Mortal Son of Zeus*
BOY	*Friend of Epaphus*
PHOEBE	*Sister of Phaethon*
CLYMENE	*Mother of Phaethon*
HELIOS	*God of the Sun*
EOS	*Goddess of the Dawn*
AUTUMN	*Season of Autumn*
WINTER	*Season of Winter*
ZEUS	*Lord of the Gods*
GAEA	*Mother Earth*
POSEIDON	*God of the Sea*
DEMETER	*Goddess of the Harvest*
ARTEMIS	*Goddess of Wild Creatures*
HERMES	*Messenger God*

NARRATOR: In a land near the mighty Nile River, there lived a young man named Phaethon, who had never known his father.

He had *seen* his father many times—every day, in fact—but to see and to know are two different things. Phaethon's father was none other than Helios, the God of the Sun, who drives his fiery chariot across the sky each day. His mother had always told him so.

CLYMENE: For the five-hundredth time— your father is the sun!

PHAETHON: But Mother! How can I be sure?

CLYMENE: Just look at your golden hair. It's the exact color of sunshine! What other proof do you need?

PHAETHON: None of the other boys believe me. They say I'm a fatherless freak.

CLYMENE: Sticks and stones. Ignore them.

PHAETHON: That's easy for you to say.

NARRATOR: One day as Phaethon made his way home, he saw a group of boys engaged in a wrestling match. He tried to walk by unnoticed, but a bully named Epaphus noticed him.

EPAPHUS: Look! It's Mr. Sunshine! *(shouting)* Hey, Phaethon! It's a real scorcher today. Why don't you tell your "daddy" to cool it off a bit? *(cruel laugh)*

(laughter of the boys)

NARRATOR: Phaethon lowered his head and continued walking.

EPAPHUS: Hey! Get back here!

PHAETHON: *(hatefully)* What do you want?

EPAPHUS: I don't like your tone! Are you looking for a fight, sunbeam?

BOY: Teach him some manners, Epaphus!

EPAPHUS: I'll rearrange your face! Zeus the Bull-God is my father, and bull-power beats pansy sunshine any day.

(shouts of agreement from the boys)

PHAETHON: A bull-god, huh? Does that mean your mom's a cow?

EPAPHUS: *(enraged)* What did you say?

PHAETHON: You heard me, barn-boy!

EPAPHUS: Argh!

NARRATOR: Epaphus roared toward Phaethon, and the two boys fought furiously. *(sounds of a scuffle)*

BOY: Get him, Epaphus! That's it! Get him!

PHAETHON: Ah! *(grunting)*

NARRATOR: Epaphus pulled a sudden wrestling move—throwing Phaethon roughly to the ground. *(thudding noise)*

PHAETHON: Oof! *(choking sounds)*

EPAPHUS: There! Now maybe you'll watch what you say about my mother—and stop telling lies about your father!

PHAETHON: *(through tears)* My father *is* Helios! When he hears about this, he'll—he'll—

EPAPHUS: He'll do what? Give me a sunburn? Ha!

BOY: Grow up, Phaethon! Why do you believe that stupid story about your father anyway?

PHAETHON: It's not a story! It's the truth!

EPAPHUS: Yeah right! My mother has always told me that Zeus is *my* father, but—*(pause)* well, actually that's believable. I am pretty god-like. Ha!

PHAETHON: Helios is my father—and I'll prove it to you all!

EPAPHUS: Fine! Go ahead and believe in your mommy's bedtime stories.

NARRATOR: Phaethon's sister, Phoebe, happened to be coming along the path just then.

PHOEBE: *(in shock)* Hey! What's going on here?

EPAPHUS: We were just teaching your brother a lesson about keeping his mouth shut.

PHOEBE: Leave him alone. Get out of here!

EPAPHUS: *(smug laugh)* Sure thing, girly.

NARRATOR: The crowd of boys began to scatter.

PHOEBE: Are you all right? That bully Epaphus just picks on you because he has never had a father.

PHAETHON: Neither do we.

PHOEBE: Of course, we do! Helios is our father.

PHAETHON: Yeah right! Just like Epaphus is the son of Zeus and Lycus is the son of Poseidon! Those are just lies that mothers tell their sons when they can't bear to tell them the truth. But I'm ready to grow up now. I'm ready to know the truth.

NARRATOR: Phoebe helped her brother home.

CLYMENE: What has happened? Phaethon! Have you been in a fight?

PHAETHON: You could call it that. It was more like a beating.

CLYMENE: Was it that Epaphus bully again? Why if your father knew about this, he'd—

PHOEBE: Mother, this isn't really the best time for that right now.

PHAETHON: Actually it's the perfect time. I think it's time you told Phoebe and me the truth. Who is our *real* father?

CLYMENE: (*offended*) I've never kept the truth from you. Your father is the God of the Sun.

PHAETHON: No, I mean the *real* truth.

CLYMENE: (*passionately*) You have my word! If I am lying, may I never again see the light of day!

NARRATOR: With tears in her eyes, Clymene turned away to the window. Far away in the distance the sun was beginning to set. Phaethon neared his mother and placed a reassuring arm around her.

PHAETHON: I'm sorry. I believe you. But you have to admit. It is kind of far-fetched. How did you meet a sun god anyway?

CLYMENE: Well, I was sunning myself on my roof one day, and Helios spied me from his chariot in sky. The next thing I know the world was plunged into darkness. He had left the sky and was there beside me.

PHAETHON: (*in shock*) He caused an eclipse just to get to *you*?

CLYMENE: (*offended*) I was beautiful like Phoebe once. It was very romantic. He swept me into his arms—

PHOEBE: Mother, please! We get the picture!

PHAETHON: Okay. So Helios *is* our father. But you saying so doesn't fix anything. I wish he were here like other fathers. I want a father I can see!

CLYMENE: Look into the sky! There he is!

PHAETHON: But he doesn't know me!

CLYMENE: Sure he does. He can see everything and has been watching you your entire life.

PHAETHON: Seeing isn't knowing. I want him to be a *real* father.

CLYMENE: He's too busy to be a real father. Each day he spends driving his splendid chariot across the sky, reining in the steeds of fire. Then at night, when he settles to earth in the west, he boards his magical barge. And while he sleeps, it transports him and his noble steeds back over the sea to his palace at the very eastern edge of the world. Now do you see why he can't be with us?

PHAETHON: Not even for one day?

CLYMENE: He can't just plunge the world into darkness on a whim.

PHAETHON: He did for you.

CLYMENE: You cannot be selfish about this. Your father is a god, and he has his responsibilities.

PHAETHON: And I am apparently not one of them.

CLYMENE: Phaethon!

PHAETHON: I heard a story once about how a god swore upon the River Styx, and that meant that whatever he said must be true. Perhaps if you swore on the River Styx—in front of the other boys—that Helios was my father…

CLYMENE: Phaethon! That is a dangerous, binding oath. Besides only the gods can swear on the River Styx.

PHAETHON: If only the other boys could see it for themselves! Then they'd have to believe me!

CLYMENE: You just said seeing isn't the same as knowing.

PHAETHON: It would be in this case. I'm just so sick of being teased day after day!

PHOEBE: If you are so curious about our father perhaps you should go meet him yourself.

CLYMENE: *(shocked)* Phoebe! He's just a boy!

PHAETHON: That's a perfect idea!

CLYMENE: It's out of the question! You're too young! It's too far for a boy to travel!

PHAETHON: I'm almost a man now, Mother! And besides, if Helios *is* my father,

that means I'm destined to be a great hero. All the sons of gods are.

PHOEBE: Phaethon is older now. We both are.

CLYMENE: Oh my! I do not like this idea.

PHAETHON: Mother, do not deny me the chance to meet my father. I have a feeling that once I meet him, I will discover my destiny.

NARRATOR: Eventually Phaethon persuaded his mother to let him make the journey to Helios' palace. In the gloom of the early morning his sister and mother bade him goodbye.

PHOEBE: I've always watched out for you, but this is a quest you have to complete on your own. Be careful.

PHAETHON: I will.

NARRATOR: Phaethon traveled eastward— far beyond his own country. As he journeyed, he schemed how he would make Epaphus and the others eat their words.

PHAETHON: *(to himself)* Perhaps Father would surprise the other boys by swooping down from the sky in his fiery chariot. *(pause)* Of course, that would make them burst into flame. Hmmm. Not a bad idea. But then I wouldn't be able to rub it in their face. Their faces would have melted off. Ha! *(pause)* Maybe he would just write my name in the clouds.

NARRATOR: Finally, one night, Phaethon came to the edge of the world. On the beach of the endless sea sat the Palace of the Sun. It was a wonder to behold, for the great god-craftsman Hephaestus had fashioned it himself.

PHAETHON: (*in awe*) Amazing!

NARRATOR: Light emanated from it, and the palace's many columns gleamed with gold. Ivory-crowned rooftops shone like glass, and the doors were bright with silver. Phaethon gasped as he beheld the lifelike pictures carved there.

PHAETHON: (*gasp*) Look at these carvings!

NARRATOR: In the center was the earth, Gaea herself, surrounded by the mighty river, Ocean. Beautiful sea nymphs broke the waves—their sea-weed hair flowing behind them. On land there were men and wild creatures, moving through the plains and woods, going about their daily business. Over all this rose the dark dome of heaven and nestled within it the twelve signs of the Zodiac. The heavens were dark, awaiting the coming of the day.

Although the images were breathtaking, Phaethon saw that they were all motionless— all lifeless without the sun to guide them, to sustain them.

PHAETHON: Nothing lives without the sun. Even the fish in the depths of the seas need its light.

NARRATOR: With a trembling hand the boy touched the palace doors, and they swung silently inward. Phaethon entered the palace of the sun. Torches burned in the dark hall. Along the walls were alcoves, and giant statues stood within—their hands folded across their chests.

PHAETHON: Hello? Is anyone here?

NARRATOR: One of the closest figures suddenly jumped to life.

EOS: (*in shock*) What? What time is it? Is it morning already? I didn't oversleep, did I?

PHAETHON: No, it is still night! I did not mean to wake you!

EOS: The point is that you *did* wake me! Now I'll never get back to sleep! And if I don't get my sleep, I'm just no good in the morning!

NARRATOR: Her cries caused several of the other figures to stir and wipe their groggy eyes. One serene woman, who bore clusters of grapes upon her temples, smiled at Phaethon.

AUTUMN: Pay no attention to Eos. She is Aurora, the dawn. She is always irritable this time of evening. She's definitely more of a morning person. (*giggle*)

PHAETHON: Who are all of you?

AUTUMN: Well, I am Autumn.

NARRATOR: She pointed to a shivering old man on her right. Icicles dripped from his nose and chin.

AUTUMN: And there is my successor, Winter.

WINTER: (*shivering*) N-n-n-nice t-t-to m-m-meet y-y-you…

NARRATOR: Autumn then motioned to a young man, who wore flowers in his hair. He was lovingly admiring his reflection in the golden walls.

AUTUMN: And that is Springtime. But don't bother addressing him. He won't hear you. He's a bit of a prima donna—completely self-absorbed.

PHAETHON: Where is Summer?

AUTUMN: Out and about, of course. This is his time.

NARRATOR: Many other figures, ranging from young to old, lined the walls.

PHAETHON: And who are the others?

AUTUMN: Those are the Hours, the Days, the Months, the Years, and the Centuries.

PHAETHON: They don't have names?

AUTUMN: Yes, but who can remember them all? The hours turn into days, and days into months, and months into years. You know time. It all runs together.

PHAETHON: Why is it so dark in here?

AUTUMN: Helios, the lord of this palace, is not at home. Once he returns from across the sea, he will fill this home with his light once again.

EOS: Don't remind me! Try getting any sleep with the sun blaring in your eyes! *(sigh)* Now can we cut the chit-chat? Autumn, tell that mortal to go away and leave us in peace!

PHAETHON: No! Wait! I have business here!

EOS: Business hours are over! Come back and complain some other time!

WINTER: T-t-that's all we g-g-get here is c-c-complaints. Summer is t-t-too hot! Winter is t-t-too cold!

EOS: Time is too short! Blah. Blah. Blah.

PHAETHON: I have come to meet my father, Helios.

EOS: Helios? Ha! That's a laugh! Helios doesn't have children!

(laughter from the others)

NARRATOR: Winter laughed so hard that he shook the icicles off his frosty head. Even Springtime chuckled a bit.

PHAETHON: Is that so hard to believe?

EOS: Yes! Helios is a workaholic. He never takes a day off! I should know! Every morning, I have to get up at the crack of *myself!* Just once I'd like to have a day off! But noooo…

NARRATOR: A sudden light poured into the room. Helios had returned.

EOS: Oh great! I'll never get to sleep now!

NARRATOR: The blazing sun god appeared and seated himself on his massive throne at the far end of the hall.

AUTUMN: Go on. You have nothing to fear.

NARRATOR: Phaethon could not directly face the blinding light, but he moved toward the throne.

PHAETHON: Hello? I am Phaethon! I have come to see Helios, God of the Sun.

HELIOS: *(surprised)* Phaethon?

NARRATOR: When Helios beheld the mortal boy, he instantly recognized him as his son.

HELIOS: Oh! Let me remove my crown of light.

NARRATOR: The light faded, and for the first time, Phaethon saw the true face of his father.

HELIOS: You have traveled all this way—by yourself?

PHAETHON: Forgive me if I am wrong, but my mother says that you are my father. I've come to find out if this is true.

HELIOS: Your mother has told you the truth.

PHAETHON: Now the uncertainty is over!

NARRATOR: Phaethon and his father spent many happy hours in conversation. At first the boy was serenely happy, but then thoughts of Epaphus and the other bullies crept back into his mind.

HELIOS: What is the matter, son?

PHAETHON: You have told me that you are my father. But no one back home will believe me if I don't have some proof. They will still laugh at me.

HELIOS: If they are really your friends, they will not tease you. If they are your enemies, nothing will convince them.

PHAETHON: But if they see it, they will believe it!

HELIOS: What does their opinion matter? I am your father. That is the truth. Let no one doubt it.

PHAETHON: I wish it were that easy. *(pause)* If only you were like other fathers...

HELIOS: My greatest wish is to see you happy.

PHAETHON: Then you'll promise to help me? Will you swear on the River Styx to grant me any wish?

HELIOS: Son, that is not something that a god does lightly.

PHAETHON: It is something that he would do if he truly loved his son.

NARRATOR: The mighty brow of Helios furrowed in thought.

HELIOS: Very well. I swear by the River Styx that I will grant you whatever you wish.

PHAETHON: Then it's settled! Let me drive your chariot across the sky all by myself.

HELIOS: *(in shock)* What? Ask for anything but that! That is the one thing I must refuse you!

PHAETHON: No! You promised! You swore! You can't refuse me!

HELIOS: I did not know what you would ask! My love for you has made me foolish! Please make another wish.

NARRATOR: Phaethon folded his arms.

PHAETHON: That is my *only* wish. It will be the final proof! If I am truly your son, then I am mighty enough to do what you do!

HELIOS: It's not that simple. I am immortal, and you are not.

PHAETHON: That doesn't matter. The other sons of gods do mighty deeds!

HELIOS: *(angrily)* But what you ask is too dangerous. My chariot is not meant to be driven by a mortal—much less a mortal boy.

PHAETHON: *(offended)* A boy? I'm almost a man!

HELIOS: Boy or man—it wouldn't matter! No other god can take my place in the fiery chariot. Not even *Zeus* could manage it! And who is mightier than Zeus?

PHAETHON: Then it will be all the more impressive when *I* achieve it.

HELIOS: Listen! You have no idea what you are asking! At the beginning of my course, the way is so steep that my horses can hardly make it. At the height, we are so high that even *I* get dizzy when I look down at the earth spinning below me. Then the descent is just as steep, and the horses must be held firmly, or they will charge directly into the sea. Meanwhile, all the heavens are revolving, spinning around me. If I find driving my chariot to be a challenge, how could *you* do it?

PHAETHON: I can do all that you do—for you are my father!

HELIOS: That's not all. Even if you could keep the chariot steady—and by some miracle, on course—you have to make it past the beast-like constellations. Each time I go by they try to attack me.

PHAETHON: *(incredulously)* Stars? Seriously? I think I can handle stars.

HELIOS: They are more than stars! They are beasts—Taurus the charging bull, Leo the hungry lion, Scorpio the poisonous scorpion, and Cancer the vicious crab—just to name a few.

PHAETHON: Eh. They don't sound so bad.

HELIOS: If you want proof that I'm your father, just look at my face and see how much I care for you. Ask for anything—except to drive my chariot.

PHAETHON: I've made my wish, Father. Don't worry! I can do it!

NARRATOR: Helios was helpless. All through the night he tried to dissuade his son, but Phaethon would not back down, and Helios could not go back on his word.

EOS: Well, now that you two chatterboxes have kept me up *all night*—it's finally time for the dawn!

HELIOS: This will be the darkest day of my life.

PHAETHON: And the greatest of mine!

NARRATOR: With a heavy heart, Helios led the boy to where his flaming chariot was kept. It too was fashioned by the magnificent skill of Hephaestus. It was made of gold and silver and studded with precious jewels. *(neighing of horses)* Phaethon's eyes were filled with wonder as he beheld Helios' winged horses and their fiery manes.

EOS: Selene the Moon, the sister of Helios, has finished her circuit through the sky. Helios, it your turn to depart.

NARRATOR: The Goddess of the Dawn threw open the gates of the morning. A purple light began to flow from her—filling the air. The stars began to flee from the sky.

EOS: The dawn waits for no one!

HELIOS: Just a second!

NARRATOR: Helios turned to his son.

HELIOS: There is still time. Take my advice—not my chariot—and stay here while I go across the sky.

PHAETHON: It is my time now, Father.

HELIOS: Very well. Let me spread this ointment on your face. It will protect you from burns. I will set my fiery crown upon your head to light the world.

NARRATOR: Helios smeared his son's face with the ointment and sadly placed the crown upon his head. Phaethon's face glowed almost as brightly as the crown.

PHAETHON: I will wear it proudly!

HELIOS: Now, listen to me. Go easy with the whip and hard on the reins. The horses need to be held in—not encouraged. Do not cut a straight line through the heavens. The true path lies in a great curve. If you go too high, you will bump the stars. If you dip too low, you will scorch the earth. And remember to watch for the constellation beasts! That's all the advice I can give you.

NARRATOR: Phaethon jumped into the chariot.

PHAETHON: I am ready, Father.

EOS: Now, Helios! Now!

HELIOS: (sadly) Goodbye, my son.

NARRATOR: Phaethon took the reins into his hands.

PHAETHON: Let the day begin! Yah! Yah!

(neighing of horses)

NARRATOR: Phaethon urged the horses forward. The chariot shot upward into the sky like a comet. (whooshing of the chariot, neighing of horses)

HELIOS: Keep to the path! Hold the reins tightly!

PHAETHON: Goodbye, Father! Yah! Yah!

NARRATOR: Helios watched his son fade into the distance.

EOS: All right! I'm going back to bed!

NARRATOR: Racing up through the sky, Phaethon soon found himself in trouble. Handling the horses was harder than he first imagined.

PHAETHON: Uhhh...steady! Steady! Whoa! Whoa, fellas!

NARRATOR: Phaethon looked down. The earth was spinning away below him.

PHAETHON: Ah! Okay, don't look down!

NARRATOR: The horses sensed that the chariot was lighter without Helios in it. They ran out of control. (neighing)

PHAETHON: No! Wait! Nooo!

NARRATOR: As he rose in the sky, Phaethon saw the stars there. Ursa Major, the Great Bear, was lying in wait—along with her cub, Ursa Minor.

(growling of a bear)

PHAETHON: Ah! Noooo!

NARRATOR: The bear lunged, and Phaethon tugged violently at the reins. The beast missed gobbling up the chariot and its driver—but only barely. *(bear snarl)*

PHAETHON: That was close!

(hissing of a scorpion)

NARRATOR: Scorpio appeared out of the sky and struck at Phaethon with its deadly tail. *(hissing of a scorpion)* Phaethon ducked down into the chariot as the spiked tail swung overhead. *(whooshing sound)*

PHAETHON: *(cry of fright)* I wish Helios had laughed in my face when I called him, "Father." Then I could have gone home and been a nobody the rest of my life.

NARRATOR: Cancer the crab loomed ahead—its pinchers primed for attack.

PHAETHON: Gulp.

(snapping claws)

NARRATOR: To avoid the snapping of the crab's claws, Phaethon fell backward and tumbled from the chariot. He clung to the railing for dear life—his body dangling out over the expanse of the world.

PHAETHON: No! Ah! *(screaming)*

NARRATOR: Only with great effort did he pull himself back into the chariot, but he had dropped the reins. Now the horses were bolting wherever they wished. *(wild neighing of horses)* They charged upward and bumped the stars. Then they plunged down toward the earth.

PHAETHON: What have I done? The clouds are boiling! The mountains are burning! Meadows, crops, and trees have burst into flames! Whole cities are burning! Everything will burn!

NARRATOR: Then a startling realization hit him.

PHAETHON: And *I* will burn as well.

NARRATOR: The people of earth, staring up into the heavens with terror, feared that the end of the world had come. The sun was making erratic loops in the sky. All of Phaethon's hometown had congregated to see the phenomenon.

BOY: Look at the sun! What's it doing?

CLYMENE: What has gotten into Helios?

NARRATOR: The sun swooped low—blazingly close.

PHOEBE: Look, Mother! It's not Helios driving the chariot! It's Phaethon!

(murmuring among the townspeople)

EPAPHUS: Phaethon! Then Helios really was his father!

PHOEBE: Yes! And look what you've driven him to! He's driving that chariot to prove the truth to you fools! The world is going to be destroyed because of your stupid bullying!

EPAPHUS: I—I—I…

CLYMENE: Get down! Here it comes again!

NARRATOR: The chariot swooped low again, and the heat of its closeness blasted the town. When it finished its sweep, Epaphus and the other boys rose from the ground.

EPAPHUS: Do you smell something burning?

BOY: (cry of shock) Ah! Your hair is on fire!

EPAPHUS: So is yours!

BOY: (cry of shock) Ah!

NARRATOR: The boys ran toward the village well—their hair blazing. Clymene pulled Phoebe close to her.

CLYMENE: You must go to Helios and beg him to put an end to this madness! Save your brother—if you can!

PHOEBE: I will, Mother.

PHAETHON: (far away yelling) Ahhh!

NARRATOR: Meanwhile, the chariot barreled on. Sparks shot up from its wheels, and the golden carriage burned white hot. Under the heat of the low-flying chariot, pastures were scorched into deserts. The Sahara became a wasteland and is one still. The chariot passed low over the land of Ethiopia, and its people were burned from the heat. To this day, they are dark in skin.

Great rivers evaporated into steam, and the ocean boiled—killing the life within it. (hissing of steam) Poseidon rose up from the hissing waves and called out to Olympus.

POSEIDON: Zeus! Put an end to this!

NARRATOR: Gaea, Mother Earth, could no longer bear the pain either.

GAEA: Zeus! Is this what I deserve—after bearing crops for mortals year after year? If the seas dry up, and the lands perish, and the heavens cave in, we all shall be lost. Save what is left.

NARRATOR: Zeus heard their cries and called an emergency meeting of the gods.

ZEUS: Something must be done!

DEMETER: I'll say! My crops are burning in the fields!

ARTEMIS: The habitats of my wild animals have all burned away!

HERMES: Hmmm. I have no complaints! I like it nice and toasty!

ALL GODS: Hermes!

ARTEMIS: Father, don't listen to that little pyromaniac! Something must be done!

DEMETER: Yes, brother. As the Lord of the Gods it is your job to fix this!

ZEUS: Fine! Summon Helios!

NARRATOR: Helios soon appeared before them.

ZEUS: Helios, who is this mortal driving your chariot?

HELIOS: Forgive me! He's my son! I made him a promise on the River Styx that I'd grant him any wish.

HERMES: Well, that wasn't a very *bright* move for a sun god, was it?

HELIOS: Now all the world suffers because of my foolish fatherly love!

ZEUS: Then you see that I have no choice! Phaethon must die—or the earth will pass away. Now who will be the one to deal the deadly stroke?

NARRATOR: There was an awkward silence in the Olympian hall.

ZEUS: Fine. *I* will be the one to stop him.

NARRATOR: As Helios turned his head, Zeus reached up into the clouds and summoned the sizzling force of lightning. (*sizzling sound*)

ZEUS: Ahh! (*battlecry*)

NARRATOR: Zeus hurled his thunderbolt downward. Phaethon never saw it coming. (*shazam!*) The bolt struck the sun chariot, and the boy flew loose from it into the open air.

PHAETHON: Ahhhhhh! (*fading away*)

NARRATOR: The wreckage of the chariot filled the air—broken spokes, gilded axle, severed reins. The sun's light was snuffed out, and the world was plunged into darkness. The fiery horses ran free like fireflies through the blackness. And Phaethon fell—silently—like a flickering star.

From where Phoebe stood upon the earth, she saw her brother's fall.

PHOEBE: No! Phaethon!

NARRATOR: A trail of sparks hung in the air where Phaethon had fallen. Phoebe followed this path for many miles. It led to the banks of a great river. Here Phaethon had landed. The water nymphs who lived there had lifted the boy's broken body from the waves and buried him in the soft, riverside earth.

PHOEBE: (*crying*) It is my fault. I should have never told him to go.

NARRATOR: Phoebe found a large stone and laid it over her brother's grave. Into the stone she carved an epitaph.

PHOEBE: (*reading*) Here lies Phaethon. He drove the chariot of the sun. Great was his failure. Grandly was it done.

NARRATOR: Phoebe stood on the bank of the river and wept for her departed brother.

PHOEBE: (*sadly*) Do not worry, Phaethon. I will never leave you.

NARRATOR: For days, Helios mourned his son, and he did not shine. Those in the world wondered if the sun would ever rise again. But at last Helios returned to the skies—his chariot forged anew—and light filled the world once again.

When the sun's rays fell upon the grave of Phaethon, the weeping Phoebe was gone—vanished. In her place, there grew a poplar tree. Tears of amber sap fell from its mournful branches, and as they did, reflected back the light of the morning sun.

DISCUSSION QUESTIONS

- Should you care what other people think about you? Explain.
- Is it hard for people to listen to their parents? Explain.
- Who is *most* to blame for Phaethon's tragic ride—Epaphus and the other bullies, Helios, Phoebe, or Phaethon himself? Explain.
- What is the best way to respond to bullying? Explain.
- What natural phenomena are explained through the myth of Phaethon? Explain.
- The names *Phaethon* and *Phoebe* mean "shining" and "bright one" respectively.

Are these names appropriate for the characters?

- What part does peer pressure and bullying play in Phaethon's ride?
- Is Phaethon right—is seeing different from knowing? Do we have to experience some things ourselves in order to know them? How can some of these experiences cost us more than we're willing to pay?
- Do you think Phaethon should have gone to meet his father? Explain.
- What would be a situation in the modern world that might parallel Phaethon's ride?
- Does someone telling you *not* to do something make you want to do it?
- Is Phaethon a hero or an anti-hero? Explain.
- What does Phoebe's transformation add to the story?
- Is Helios a good father?
- Phaethon's actions affected not only his well-being but also the well-being of others. What can we learn from this?

THE LIFE (AND DEATHS) OF SISYPHUS
TEACHER GUIDE

BACKGROUND

Death and the struggle against death form the central ideas of this myth. Like us the Greeks fantasized about what it would be like to escape dying. To them death was personified in Thanatos, the Greek version of the Grim Reaper. Although it was Hermes' job to guide departed souls down into the Underworld, Thanatos was the actual Angel of Death who separated souls from their bodies. And, like all the Greek gods, he was capable of being tricked.

Enter the mortal Sisyphus, who is the ultimate trickster. No one is as wily as he—not even Odysseus. (In fact, there was a rumor that Sisyphus was the true father of Odysseus—through a trick, of course.) In this myth Sisyphus manages to do the impossible and outwit Death—twice!

The Greeks viewed the burial of the dead as one of man's most sacred duties. The eyes of the body were closed and a coin was placed inside the mouth. (This is the coin that all souls must pay the boatman Charon in the Underworld, so that he will ferry them across the River Styx.) If a body was not buried properly, its soul could never find rest in the Underworld. These lost souls would have to wait a hundred years on the banks of the River Styx before being allowed to pass over into the land of the dead.

Sisyphus' temporary triumphs over death highlight the power of human intelligence. But in the end Sisyphus is returned to Tartarus for his punishment. The final verdict: No one can escape death. Still the myth tantalizes us with the question, "Could we someday grow smart enough to conquer death?"

SUMMARY

Sisyphus, a clever king, witnesses Zeus (in the form of an eagle) abducting a maiden and transporting her to a nearby island. When the maiden's river-god father arrives, Sisyphus tells him where Zeus has taken his daughter. Zeus soon finds out that Sisyphus relayed this information and declares that he must die.

Alerted to the approach of Thanatos (Death), Sisyphus and his wife quickly try to devise a way to escape Death. When Thanatos arrives, Sisyphus is not intimidated by him and tries to argue his way out of dying. Thanatos grows more and more frustrated until he forcefully drags Sisyphus down into Tartarus. Hoping to intimidate Sisyphus, Thanatos shows him the eternal punishment of Tantalus, a king who must remain forever thirsty and hungry—standing with a pool of water at his feet and a branch of fruit hanging overhead, just out of reach. The king earned this punishment by sacrificing his son and serving him up as a stew to the gods. Tantalus' fate has little effect on Sisyphus.

Thanatos produces the Chains of Death in order to eternally bind Sisyphus to a rock. Sisyphus mocks Thanatos, telling him that the chains will never hold. Completely frustrated, Thanatos clamps the chains on his own wrists to demonstrate their strength—only to realize he has just chained himself. With Thanatos bound, Sisyphus escapes Hades, and his spirit returns to his body.

With Thanatos chained in the Underworld, no mortals can die. At last Ares, the God of War, confronts Zeus about the fact that no one is dying in his battles. Zeus sends him to Hades to investigate, and Ares frees Thanatos from his chains.

Thanatos immediately seeks out Sisyphus to have his revenge, but the wily king has prepared for this. Sisyphus instructs his wife to throw his dead body into the street once his spirit has left it. Thanatos arrives and kills Sisyphus once again.

In the Underworld Sisyphus asks to speak to Hades and Persephone and tells them of his wife throwing his body in the street. He asks for permission to go back and chastise her for this injustice. (Unburied bodies prohibited their spirits from entering the Underworld.) Hades and Persephone allow this on the condition that Sisyphus will return to the Underworld once he has spoken to his wife.

Sisyphus returns to earth but has no intention of returning to Hades. Finally, Zeus sends Hermes to drag Sisyphus back to the Underworld. Once there Thanatos appears and declares that Sisyphus must push a boulder up a hill for eternity. Each time he reaches the peak, he will lose his grip, and the boulder will roll to the base of the hill once again. In spite of this grim punishment, Sisyphus faces his eternal fate boldly. He still does not fear death.

ESSENTIAL QUESTIONS

- How should we face death?
- Should we ever give up?

ANTICIPATORY QUESTIONS

- Can you escape death?
- What does "Death" look like?
- Who is the Grim Reaper?
- If you had a way to escape death, would you?
- Would you fight a battle if you knew there was no hope of ever winning it?

CONNECT

The Myth of Tithonus According to this myth, Tithonus is the mortal lover of the dawn, Eos. Since Eos is desperately in love with Tithonus, she asks Zeus to give him eternal life. Unfortunately, she forgets to ask Zeus to give her love eternal *youth*. Tithonus lives many years, but his body grows older and older, eventually rotting away. Does this story have a similar theme to that of Sisyphus?

TEACHABLE TERMS

- **Allusion** On pg. 100 Thanatos' letter to Sisyphus contains an allusion to John Donne's "Meditation 17" when it says, "Ask not for whom the bell tolls. It tolls for thee."
- **Mood** Even though this myth deals with the death(s) of the main character, the mood of the story is not the gloomy one you would expect. What is the mood of the story?
- **Word Connection** A task that is considered pointless or endless is sometimes called *Sisyphean* after the eternal punishment of Sisyphus in Hades.
- **Understatement** On pg. 103 as Thanatos explains the eternal torments that souls suffer in Tartarus, Sisyphus' responses are restrained in an ironic contrast to the type of response that is expected. This is one way that understatement is used to create humor.

RECALL QUESTIONS

1. Why does Zeus declare that Sisyphus must die?
2. How does Sisyphus trap Thanatos in Tartarus?
3. What does Sisyphus' wife do to his dead body?
4. How does Sisyphus trick Hades and Persephone into letting him return to earth?
5. What is Sisyphus' eternal punishment?

THE LIFE (AND DEATHS) OF SISYPHUS

CAST

SISYPHUS	*Tricky King of Corinth*
WIFE	*Wife of Sisyphus*
RIVER GOD	*Father of Abducted Maiden*
THANATOS	*Death Himself*
ZEUS	*Lord of the Gods*
ARES	*God of War*
HADES	*Lord of the Underworld*
PERSEPHONE	*Queen of the Underworld*
CHARON	*Boatman of Hades*
HERMES	*Messenger God*

NARRATOR: Sisyphus was a clever man—some said the cleverest man who ever lived. He was always engaging people in confusing conversations, weaving verbal webs of trickery, and making fools out of everyone. One day Sisyphus was sitting near the river when he saw an enormous eagle flying overhead.

SISYPHUS: Hmmm.

NARRATOR: The eagle clutched a screaming maiden in its talons. *(screech of an eagle, scream of a maiden)*

SISYPHUS: That must be a god in disguise. It is too large to be a normal eagle. Plus there's the maiden. Hmmm. Must be Zeus—at it again.

NARRATOR: The eagle and its captive flew on and settled down on an island far out to sea. A nearby voice caused Sisyphus to turn.

RIVER GOD: Sir! Sir! Please! Have you seen my daughter pass this way?

NARRATOR: A river god had risen from the water nearby. He looked at Sisyphus desperately.

SISYPHUS: Does she have long, beautiful hair and a pretty face?

RIVER GOD: Yes!

SISYPHUS: Was she clutched in the talons of a giant eagle?

RIVER GOD: Yes!

SISYPHUS: Was she screaming and flailing her arms like this? Ahhhhh!

RIVER GOD: Yes!

SISYPHUS: Eh. I haven't seen her.

RIVER GOD: What do you mean you haven't seen her? You just described her to me exactly!

SISYPHUS: Well, yes, *technically* I saw her. But your daughter was obviously abducted by Zeus, so *officially* I saw nothing.

RIVER GOD: Please! Tell me where she has gone!

SISYPHUS: Sorry. No can-do. If I tell you where Zeus took your daughter, then he will come back and punish *me* for ratting him out. That's how it always works in these kinds of stories.

RIVER GOD: That's not fair. I need your help!

SISYPHUS: Life's not fair.

RIVER GOD: But you must help me! It's the right thing to do.

SISYPHUS: The right thing? Ha! Listen to this guy. The right thing *for me* to do is to keep my mouth shut.

RIVER GOD: Please! I'll give you anything!

SISYPHUS: Hmmm. Well, why didn't you say so? That's a different story. Let's see. From those gills you've got there, I assume you are a river god. My palace desperately needs a source of fresh water.

RIVER GOD: I'll give it to you—just tell me where my daughter is!

SISYPHUS: See that island in the distance there? That is where the eagle has landed. Just remember you didn't hear it from me! And I'll be expecting that fresh water soon.

NARRATOR: Unfortunately, for the river god, Zeus was not about to give up his latest girlfriend. As Sisyphus watched from a distance, the river god and Zeus battled. (*shazam!*) After a few well-placed thunderbolts, the river god left in defeat. But Zeus knew that someone had given away his whereabouts—and he suspected Sisyphus.

A week later Sisyphus was relaxing in his palace, now equipped with running water, when his wife came to him, bearing a piece of parchment.

WIFE: Sisyphus, this scroll has come to you by messenger.

SISYPHUS: What does it say?

WIFE: (*reading*) Dear miserable mortal (a.k.a. Sisyphus), this is a notice that you will soon be visited by Thanatos (a.k.a. "Death"). Prepare to die. Ask not for whom the bell tolls. It tolls for thee. (*scary noise*) Ooooooh!

SISYPHUS: It actually says, "Oooooh!"

WIFE: Yes! Right here.

SISYPHUS: I'll be darned.

WIFE: (*frightened*) Oh my! What do you think it means?

SISYPHUS: It means exactly what it says. It was a pretty straightforward death threat.

WIFE: Why is Death coming for you?

SISYPHUS: Zeus must have sent him in revenge.

NARRATOR: Just then there was a knock at the door. (*knocking on the door*)

WIFE: It's Death! He's come to kill you!

SISYPHUS: (*sarcastically*) You think? Just stay calm! It could be anybody! It might just be one of the neighbors—or a door-to-door chariot salesman.

NARRATOR: Sisyphus peeked out the window.

SISYPHUS: Nope. It's definitely Death. I'm a dead man!

WIFE: What are you going to do?

SISYPHUS: I don't know! Stall him? Outwit him?

WIFE: You can't outwit Death!

SISYPHUS: Thanks for your support! Just get out of here!

NARRATOR: As his wife scurried for cover, Sisyphus took a deep breath and opened the door. A tall, grim-faced god filled the doorway. Sisyphus kept his face calm.

THANATOS: *(evil-sounding voice)* Sisyphus?

SISYPHUS: *(calmly)* Yes? If this is about the local plague charity, we've already contributed.

THANATOS: I am Thanatos. I have come for your soul.

SISYPHUS: Is this a prank? I really don't have time for this tonight.

THANATOS: You have no more time at all. *(frighteningly)* I have come, and I am *Death*.

SISYPHUS: Death? I thought you said your name was Therma-toast?

THANATOS: *(hissing)* Thanatos! It means "Death" in Greek.

SISYPHUS: Then what language are we talking in? I guess it's all Greek to me.

THANATOS: *(angrily)* I am to take your soul to Tartarus—the fiery pit of Hades!

SISYPHUS: Wait a minute. I thought Hermes was supposed to come for mortal souls.

THANATOS: *(taken aback)* Well, technically he is, but I was sent on a special mission from Zeus. Consider this an express trip to eternal pain and suffering.

SISYPHUS: Nope. Sorry. You may be okay with breaking the rules, but I'm not. You go get Hermes. I'll wait here.

NARRATOR: Sisyphus tried to slam the door, but a bony foot barred the way. Thanatos pushed his way inside.

THANATOS: Nice try! No one escapes Death!

SISYPHUS: I don't know. I can run pretty fast.

THANATOS: You cannot run. You are already dead.

SISYPHUS: Impossible. I feel fine. I'm probably just dreaming this whole thing.

THANATOS: *(dramatically)* If this is a dream, then I am your worst nightmare!

SISYPHUS: You've been waiting a while to say that, haven't you?

THANATOS: Actually yes. Now come with me.

SISYPHUS: Right now? It's the middle of the night.

THANATOS: Death exists beyond time.

SISYPHUS: Oh good. So you wouldn't mind waiting until morning—or maybe next Thursday.

THANATOS: No! That's not what I meant. I meant...ummm...Death waits for no man. Yeah. That's what I meant.

SISYPHUS: I really could have used some advance warning.

THANATOS: Didn't you get my note?

SISYPHUS: I did. *(sarcastically)* Thanks for that whole five minutes. But I ran your note by my legal representatives, and they found some loopholes.

THANATOS: There are no loopholes in death! Now come with me.

SISYPHUS: You know what your problem is? You're not thinking "big picture" here. You've got to think outside the box—outside the coffin so to speak!

THANATOS: *(yelling)* Silence! Enough of your babbling!

SISYPHUS: Hey, you can't intimidate me!

THANATOS: I am Death! What is more intimidating than that?

SISYPHUS: Well, somebody's full of himself.

THANATOS: *(screeching)* Read my lips— You—are—dead!

SISYPHUS: I tried, but you don't really have any lips. You have this skeletal-face thing going on.

THANATOS: I am tired of these shenanigans. Come with me!

NARRATOR: Sisyphus folded his arms.

SISYPHUS: No.

THANATOS: What do you mean, "No"? You can't just say, "No!" to Death.

SISYPHUS: I just did.

THANATOS: Don't make me angry!

SISYPHUS: What are you going to do? Make me *more dead*?

THANATOS: *(hellish shriek)* Argh!

NARRATOR: Thanatos grabbed the wrist of Sisyphus, and they sank down through the ground. When they stopped sinking, they were standing in a dark cavern. Cries of pain flew out from the darkness. *(cries of pain)*

THANATOS: What do you think now? Do you doubt I am Death?

SISYPHUS: Eh. I'm still not buying it. I saw special effects like this when I was at a play in Athens. Only they were more believable.

THANATOS: Fine! Convince yourself that this is all some joke, but you are in the very belly of Tartarus.

SISYPHUS: Oooh. The belly of Tartarus, huh? I hear this is much nicer than the bowels of Tartarus—for obvious reasons.

THANATOS: Then consider this the bowels of Tartarus.

SISYPHUS: Which is it? The belly or the bowels? Or is this more like the entire digestive system of Tartarus?

THANATOS: Shut up! Here in Tartarus your eternity will be filled with pointless tasks and endless agony.

SISYPHUS: So it's kind of like life, huh?

THANATOS: Grueling toil and hideous torture will fill up your days!

SISYPHUS: Oh good. At least I won't get bored. I hate being bored.

THANATOS: Your ears will be filled with the endless cries of those around you.

SISYPHUS: And I won't be lonesome. This is sounding better and better.

NARRATOR: Thanatos leaned in and glared at Sisyphus.

THANATOS: I really hate you. (pause) Now behold! Look upon the tortures of Tantalus—another foolish king who laughed at death!

NARRATOR: A greenish light appeared, illuminating a pool of water. In its midst stood an emaciated man, his parched lips quivering in agony. A branch laden with fruit hung just out of his reach, and with the weakest of energy he stretched his arms toward it.

THANATOS: What do you think now? Gruesome, huh?

SISYPHUS: Eh. What's his punishment? Standing in water? So what if his feet get all pruney? Big deal!

THANATOS: He is eternally starving, yet he cannot reach the fruit that dangles above him. He is eternally thirsty, but he cannot bend down and drink from the water that surrounds him.

SISYPHUS: You could really use some counseling. (pause) What's he in for anyway?

THANATOS: He murdered his son and served him up as a stew to the gods.

SISYPHUS: Did the gods not like how the son tasted or something?

THANATOS: Oh no. Actually he was quite good. A little salty. (angrily) I mean, it was an abomination!

SISYPHUS: Let me get this straight. I'm here on the same level as some child murderer turned gourmet cook—and all I did was rat out Zeus? Wow. That's not very fair.

THANATOS: Life's not fair.

SISYPHUS: Apparently death isn't either.

THANATOS: Now! Behold! The Chains of Death!

NARRATOR: A pair of rusty chains appeared in Thanatos' bony grip.

SISYPHUS: If they're the Chains of Death, sounds like they belong to you. Maybe *you* should wear them.

THANATOS: Nice try. They will bind *you* forever!

SISYPHUS: These chains! Nah. I could wiggle out of them in ten minutes—tops.

THANATOS: No one has ever escaped these chains!

SISYPHUS: Then why are they empty?

THANATOS: What?

SISYPHUS: All right! Give me these things! I'll show you what I'm talking about. Look here. I'm trying to chain myself to this rock, and I just can't. See? They're broken or something. They're just not working.

THANATOS: That is because you're doing it all wrong. Here. Give them to me. You do it like this. See? *(click)* Whoops.

NARRATOR: Sisyphus grinned broadly.

SISYPHUS: Now what were you saying? No man escapes death?

THANATOS: *(yelling)* Sisyphus!

SISYPHUS: That's my name. Don't forget it.

NARRATOR: And so Sisyphus left Death trapped there in his own chains.

Back in the palace of Sisyphus, his weeping wife had laid out his dead body for burial. She had already placed the ceremonial coin in his mouth and was waiting for the professional mourners to arrive.

WIFE: *(weeping)* Oh, my dear! We had some good times, didn't we?

NARRATOR: All of a sudden, Sisyphus' eyes flew open.

WIFE: *(shriek)* Ahh-eeee!

SISYPHUS: *(frightened as well)* Ahhhhh! *(sudden hacking and choking)*

NARRATOR: Sisyphus, choking and turning a bit blue, spat the coin across the room.

SISYPHUS: Ptoo! *(gasping)* What are you trying to do, woman? Choke me to death!

WIFE: Sisyphus! I thought you were dead!

SISYPHUS: Well, I was! But you should have known that wouldn't stop someone like me.

WIFE: How did you escape?

SISYPHUS: Let's just say I had to tame a mean three-headed pooch and bargain with a boatman, but I made it. Thanks for the coin by the way. It came in handy.

WIFE: You beat Death! I mean, you really did it! No one has ever done that before! What will you do now?

SISYPHUS: *(yawn)* I might go lie down. Dying really took it out of me.

NARRATOR: Over the next few months things in the world took an odd turn. With Thanatos bound in Tartarus, no mortal being could perish. Just for a cheap thrill people started jumping off high cliffs, impaling themselves with spears, and drinking poison just to see what it tasted like. It was Ares, the God of War, who finally went to Zeus to complain about this problem.

ARES: Father! No one is dying! It's ridiculous!

ZEUS: Why is that?

ARES: My battles have become complete disasters! The warriors stab and stab at each other, but nobody dies! Now, they're finally deciding that war isn't worthwhile and they're—I can barely say it—making peace!

ZEUS: Isn't that a good thing?

ARES: You tell me. Picture a bunch of warriors hugging—singing songs—handing each other flowers. Yuck. It makes me want to vomit.

ZEUS: Well, don't do it in here. We just had the floors cleaned.

ARES: Think about it, Father! We're the gods! We're supposed to have the corner on this whole immortality thing. If the mortals are actually *immortal*, what makes us better than they are? Our stock will plummet!

ZEUS: Interesting point. You look into it! Figure out what has happened to Death.

NARRATOR: Ares departed and went directly to the Underworld. A large sign had been placed in the doorway of Hades' palace. Ares read it in disgust.

ARES: (reading) On vacation until further notice. Have a nice day! (in disgust) Has the whole world—and Underworld—gone insane?

NARRATOR: Ares pressed on and finally found Thanatos where he was still chained to a rock.

ARES: Thanatos! Has some powerful god or great warrior done this to you?

THANATOS: No, it was some pasty, little weakling from Corinth!

ARES: Did he possess some almighty weapon—a weapon that is powerful enough to subdue Death?

THANATOS: No. He basically just tricked me with confusing words.

ARES: Oh.

THANATOS: Now release me, so that I can drag him back down into Hades!

ARES: (dramatically) I shall release you! Let Death be unleashed on the mortal world once again! (loud laughter) Bwuhahaha! (pause) (rattling) Hmmm. These suckers are on here pretty tight.

THANATOS: Here! Give me your sword!

(snicker-snack, chains snapping)

THANATOS: (yelling) Sisyphus! Sisyphus!

NARRATOR: On earth Sisyphus sat up in bed. A terrible cold had seized his heart.

SISYPHUS: Death is coming for me!

WIFE: What? Again?

SISYPHUS: Yes! Only this time he's serious!

WIFE: What are you going to do?

SISYPHUS: Let me think! (pause) Ah-ha! When I die this time, throw my naked body out in the street!

WIFE: Naked? I can't do that! What will the neighbors say?

SISYPHUS: Who cares? Just do it! It's the only way I can escape Death—again!

WIFE: Fine! Fine! I'll do it. But at least let me throw it out back where it won't draw a lot of attention. I'm having friends over tomorrow.

NARRATOR: An enormous shadow rose at the end of Sisyphus' bed. In its shadowy face glowed two red eyes.

THANATOS: There will be no tricks this time—no chance to elude me! Death has returned for what is rightly his!

NARRATOR: There was a flash, and the body of Sisyphus fell back in the bed—his spirit gone.

WIFE: (*yawn*) See you soon, darling. Take care.

NARRATOR: Thanatos dragged Sisyphus down into the depths of Tartarus.

THANATOS: I am taking you directly to Lord Hades this time. No funny business!

NARRATOR: They tore past the snarling jowls of Cerberus, and at last the River Styx spread out in front of them.

THANATOS: First, we must cross the river. Oh good. There's not a line. Hmmm. You don't happen to have a coin on you? I can't carry a coin purse in this robe.

NARRATOR: Thanatos turned. Sisyphus had a smirk on his face.

THANATOS: You can't smirk at Death!

SISYPHUS: You cannot take me past the River Styx.

THANATOS: What?

SISYPHUS: My body is not properly buried. Even as we speak, my wife is throwing my lifeless body out in the road. According to the rules of the Underworld, now I must tarry on the banks of the Styx for one-hundred years.

THANATOS: Blast!

SISYPHUS: Hey, I'm a pro. This isn't my *first* death!

THANATOS: Fine! Rot here! See if I care! Here comes the boatman now.

NARRATOR: Charon, the old boatman of the Styx, was poling his ferryboat across the water.

THANATOS: Charon, this is one of the worst mortals you will ever meet. Keep an eye on him.

CHARON: What is his name?

THANATOS: Sisyphus.

CHARON: Sounds like some kind of disease.

THANATOS: He is! (*to Sisyphus*) Don't worry! This is not the last time we shall meet, Sisyphus. When your hundred years are up, I shall be here waiting to receive you. You have an appointment with Death, and I never miss an appointment.

NARRATOR: Thanatos disappeared.

SISYPHUS: He must have a lot of spare time or something. How does he come up with that stuff?

NARRATOR: Charon shrugged.

SISYPHUS: Look, my good man, this is all a big misunderstanding. I must talk to the Queen of the Underworld. I must speak with Persephone!

CHARON: I don't think so.

SISYPHUS: Aren't I entitled to one call? Isn't that one of my rights?

CHARON: You're dead. You have no rights.

SISYPHUS: Listen, Sharon.

CHARON: It's *Charon*. The *ch* makes the "k" sound.

SISYPHUS: Hey, I don't care if you have a girl's name.

CHARON: It's not a girl's name! I am the dreaded Ferryman of the Styx!

SISYPHUS: Oh yes. Fairies are sooo scary.

CHARON: Hush up! You're in Hades now! You're dead, so get used to it! You're going to be dead for a long time.

SISYPHUS: *(sudden sadness)* Oh, you're right! *(crying)* I just can't believe that I'm really dead!

CHARON: Stop crying.

SISYPHUS: I—just—can't—help—it! *(loud crying)* Wah! Wah!

CHARON: Grrrrr.

SISYPHUS: *(sniffly)* I'm just glad I'll have you here for the next one-hundred years. I really need a shoulder to cry on. You're the best, Sharon.

CHARON: That's it! You want to talk to Queen Persephone, huh? I'll get her for you.

SISYPHUS: Okay. Thanks. Try to hurry. I'm getting a leg cramp.

NARRATOR: Soon the King and Queen of Hades stood on the bank of the River Styx beside Sisyphus. Hades was wearing a floppy traveling hat, and Persephone carried a sack of Athenian knick-knacks.

HADES: What's the meaning of this, Charon? We were in the middle of our vacation! Why are all these souls piled up here?

NARRATOR: A line of souls had amassed on the banks.

CHARON: It's Thanatos, Your Deadliness. He was chained for so long, and now he's making up for lost time.

HADES: *(sigh)* I hate Mondays. Who is this miserable sad-sack?

CHARON: His name is Sisyphus.

HADES: Sounds like some kind of disease.

SISYPHUS: Oh, Lord and Lady of Death! Please hear my cry! I have been wronged most grievously.

PERSEPHONE: What is the matter?

SISYPHUS: It's my wife—the foul shrew! She has thrown my body out into the road and just left it there! Now the crows will pick my bones—and the dogs will lick my wounds—and the rats will make little holes in my—

PERSEPHONE: *(disgusted)* We get the idea!

HADES: *(enjoying it)* No please! Go on!

PERSEPHONE: Many of these souls waiting here on the banks of the Styx have been dishonored by their relatives. What makes you any different?

SISYPHUS: I am a king! It's bad for my image. All I ask is for a chance to go back and tell her the correct way to dispose of my body. Then I will gladly return.

CHARON: Be careful, majesties. Thanatos said this one is a mighty trickster.

PERSEPHONE: A trickster, huh? Then you shall stay here with Charon for the next one-hundred years!

CHARON: But on the other hand, I say, give the lad a chance.

PERSEPHONE: Oh very well. But you must promise to return. We can't have people rising from the dead all over the place. It would cause havoc.

SISYPHUS: That would be terrible, Your Highness.

PERSEPHONE: Now go!

NARRATOR: Sisyphus' wife had given up on her husband's return. His body had lain in the road for days. Then one night as she sat alone in their darkened chambers, his corpse came barging in through the door.

WIFE: Ahh-eeee!

SISYPHUS: Quiet! It's me! It's me!

WIFE: Oh, I know, my dear! But you look so gruesome. I guess the buzzards got to you a bit.

SISYPHUS: Oh well! The important thing is I'm back—for good this time!

WIFE: Thank goodness! The neighbors were really starting to complain about the smell.

NARRATOR: But Sisyphus' triumph was short-lived. One day as he sat by the river, a man wearing winged sandals and bearing a strange staff appeared out of thin air right in front of him.

SISYPHUS: (*sadly*) Hello, Hermes. You've come to take me back to Hades, haven't you?

HERMES: Yes. And just let me say, if anyone is a match for your wits, it is I. So don't try any of your tricks.

SISYPHUS: (*sigh*) Very well.

HERMES: It's nothing personal, Sisyphus. I admire your spunk. After all, you tricked Death—twice. You looked that old sourpuss straight in the eye and defied him. If it was up to me, I'd let you live. But Zeus says that you must die.

SISYPHUS: Well, third time's the charm.

HERMES: If it makes you feel any better, someday people will hear the name Sisyphus and think of your cleverness—instead of just thinking it's some kind of disease.

SISYPHUS: I guess that won't be so bad. (*pause*) Just let me get one last look at this world. (*thoughtfully*) It's an absurd life, isn't it?

NARRATOR: Hermes carried Sisyphus down into the Underworld. Sisyphus had sent word to his wife to bury his body. There would be no tricks this time. She could not risk the wrath of Zeus.

In the lower intestine of Tartarus, beside a high hill, Sisyphus came face to face with Thanatos once again.

THANATOS: (*evilly*) See? I told you we'd meet again.

SISYPHUS: (*happily*) Therma-toast! My, my. It's a small Underworld after all.

THANATOS: I've asked special permission to create an especially horrible torture for you.

SISYPHUS: Awww. You shouldn't have.

THANATOS: Behold! The instrument of your torture!

NARRATOR: Thanatos laid his thin hand on a huge boulder beside him.

SISYPHUS: A rock. How creative. How long did it take you to think of that one?

THANATOS: *(defensively)* Actually quite a while! This is no normal boulder. Once you touch it, you will be bound to it forever. It will become your eternal task to roll this boulder up the high hill you see before you.

SISYPHUS: All the way up—or just halfway? Straight up, or sort of to the side? Here. Show me how you want me to do it.

THANATOS: It's perfectly simple! You just roll it like this! *(catching himself)* Oh! I see! No, you will not trick me again! This will be your eternal fate—and yours only.

NARRATOR: Thanatos grinned cruelly.

THANATOS: Ha! You see it now, don't you? There is truly no escape. Eternity stares you in the face.

NARRATOR: For the first time the full magnitude of this broke in upon Sisyphus—he was trapped in Hades, and there was no way for him to escape.

THANATOS: It will take the whole effort of your body to roll this stone. Then when you have pushed it all the way to the peak, it will elude your grip and roll back to the base. Then your toil begins anew. What do you have to say about that?

NARRATOR: Sisyphus glanced up to the heights of the hill.

SISYPHUS: Let it begin.

NARRATOR: Sisyphus shook his finger in the face of Death.

SISYPHUS: Just as I loved life, I hate death. I have nothing but scorn for these gods that punish men on a whim. Now you want me to despair. But I will not be overcome by my fate. I will conquer it. I will be stronger than this rock.

NARRATOR: Something like a look of fear came into the eyes of Thanatos. He had never heard such words.

SISYPHUS: Chew on that!

NARRATOR: Sisyphus reached out, braced himself against his boulder, and began to push.

DISCUSSION QUESTIONS

- Do you feel sorry for Sisyphus? Explain.
- Was Sisyphus right to help the river god find his daughter? Explain.
- How should people react when they are faced with death?
- How is Sisyphus' eternal punishment symbolic of his efforts to escape death?
- Who has it worse—Sisyphus or Tantalus, the other tortured king? Explain.
- It has been said that the best way to deal with death is to laugh at it. How does this myth laugh at death?
- In the end does Sisyphus win? Explain.
- Is Sisyphus a hero? Explain.
- Is it noble when people fight battles they cannot win? What are some examples?

HERACLES: THE TRUE STORY
TEACHER GUIDE

BACKGROUND

Heracles (or *Hercules* to the Romans) is Greece's greatest hero, and his exploits are almost too many to name. In his career he defeats a long list of monsters and villains and somewhere along the way founds the Olympic Games and creates the Milky Way. It is no wonder that at the end of his life, Heracles was taken up to Olympus to become one of the gods.

In spite of all his strength and all his success, Heracles lived a life of suffering. To the Greeks suffering was part of being a hero. Heroes didn't live charmed lives. They had real problems and struggles that they had to overcome. Pushing through these obstacles, this suffering, was the essence of being a hero.

SUMMARY

Clio the Muse of History (and No-Nonsense Journalism) is doing a feature story on the great Greek hero Heracles, only she feels like there is some hidden dirt to uncover in his life—something that disqualifies him from being a true hero. She travels throughout Greece, interviewing those who interacted with him during his adventures. Through these interviews Clio pieces together the major events of the life of Heracles.

Zeus fathers Heracles by visiting the princess Alcmene in the form of her husband. When it comes time for Heracles to be born, Hera tries to prevent his birth by prolonging his birth for seven days, but one of Alcmene's servants tricks the Goddess of Childbirth into allowing the baby to be born. Next Hera sends a pair of vipers into the baby's crib to end his life, but Heracles strangles them both. Alcmene names the baby Heracles ("Glory of Hera") in an effort to mollify the angry goddess. Fearing for her own life, Alcmene leaves her baby in the wilderness to die. Athena takes pity on the baby and leads Hera to where it lies and tricks her into breastfeeding the baby herself. Heracles is so hungry that he bites down on Hera and causes milk to spray across the sky, resulting in the formation of the Milky Way. Hera puts a hold on her revenge until Heracles is grown and has a family of his own. Then she sends a madness upon him that causes him to kill his wife and children. Heracles is going to end his life, but the hero Theseus begs him to reconsider. The Oracle of Delphi tells Heracles that he can be forgiven if he performs twelve labors for an evil king, Eurystheus.

King Eurystheus, a complete coward, sends Heracles on the twelve worst labors he can think of. Subduing a giant lion, bull, boar, and stag make up four of the labors. Then comes the challenge of defeating the Hydra—a three-headed monster that sprouts new heads when one is severed. Heracles' nephew, Iolaus, helps him defeat this monster by searing the neck stumps once they are severed—preventing them from sprouting new heads. The boy also accompanies the hero on four other labors—defeating a flock of dangerous birds, feeding an evil king to his team of man-eating mares, and stealing the girdle of the Amazon queen, Hippolyta. The next labor, cleaning the manure-piled stables of Augeas in one day, presents Heracles with a unique challenge. To accomplish this task, the hero diverts the course of two rivers to wash the stables clean.

The final three labors take Heracles to the edge of the world. He defeats a three-headed monster named Geryon and steals his cattle. Then he collects the golden apples of the

Hesperides by making a deal with the titan Atlas. Heracles offers to hold up the sky for Atlas, while the titan fetches the apples for him. Atlas agrees, but when he returns, he decides not to take the sky back. Heracles cleverly asks Atlas to hold the sky, just for a second, while he adjusts his grip. But once the titan has taken the sky, Heracles leaves him to his punishment. Along the way Heracles frees the titan Prometheus from his punishment. For his final labor the hero captures Cerberus and drags him back to Eurystheus, who hides in a giant pot at the sight of the hell-hound. The twelve labors are completed.

Later in life Heracles is tricked by the woman he loves, who gives him a poisoned, flaming robe. As his mortal body dies, Zeus takes Heracles' spirit to Olympus and makes him a god. There is wed to Hebe, the Cupbearer of the Gods.

As Clio collects the events of Heracles' life, she comes to respect and admire the hero.

ESSENTIAL QUESTIONS

- What makes a person heroic?
- Why is point-of-view important?

CONNECT

Myth-Information Write a skit where a character from Greek mythology is being interviewed (in a way similar to this story). Make sure the character's viewpoint creates a new angle on the original myth.

ANTICIPATORY QUESTIONS

- Who are the muses?
- What do you know about Heracles?
- What were some of his deeds?
- Can learning about someone's life cause you to gain or lose respect for him or her?

TEACHABLE TERMS

- **Bias** Clio demonstrates bias (prejudice in favor of or against one thing, person, or group compared with another) in her attitude toward Heracles.
- **Point-of-view** Why is each character's point-of-view important in this version of the Heracles myth? Can point-of-view sometimes be unreliable or slanted?
- **Jargon** This script uses journalistic jargon associated with the news media. For example, "exposé" pg. 113, "scoop" pg. 114, "feature" pg. 116, "blow the whistle" pg. 120, "put a spin on" pg. 120, "news flash" pg. 121, "off the record" pg. 121, "angle" pg. 123, "exclusive" pg. 124, and "that's a wrap," "sign off" pg. 125. What does this terminology add to the story?
- **Alliteration** Clio frequently employs alliteration in the titles of her articles. "Living Life Liverless" (pg. 122) and "Father Learns Strongman Son Is Actually Heavenly Hand-Me Down" (pg. 115) are examples.
- **Dynamic Character** Clio is an example of a dynamic character as she experiences a change of heart toward the hero Heracles.
- **Onomatopoeia** On pg. 119 Iolaus uses examples of onomatopoeia such as *shoom*, *raar*, and *bam* when he describes Heracles' battle against the Hydra.

RECALL QUESTIONS

1. What does Heracles' name mean?
2. What horrible crime does Heracles commit?
3. Who is Heracles' greatest enemy?
4. What are three of Heracles' labors?
5. What happens to Heracles at the end of the story?

HERACLES: THE TRUE STORY

CAST

CLIO	*Muse of History*
BOY	*Random Boy*
ZEUS	*Lord of the Gods*
ALCMENE	*Mother of Heracles*
HERA	*Queen of the Gods*
EURYSTHEUS	*King of Tiryns*
IOLAUS	*Heracles' Nephew*
PROMETHEUS	*Kindly Titan*
ATLAS	*Punished Titan*
HERACLES	*Hero*

CLIO: Hello, all you news-hungry folks out there. This is Clio, the Muse of History and No-Nonsense Journalism. As you know, Greece is gaga over its "greatest hero," Heracles—*but* my gut tells me that he is a bit too good to be true. And as you know, my gut never lies. Every hero has a weakness—a juicy secret just waiting to be discovered. You might remember my last hard-hitting exposé,

"Achilles: Hero or Heel?" Well, tonight I present "Heracles: The True Story."

Let's begin by finding out what the average Greek-on-the-street knows about this man of steel. *(to boy)* You, boy! Yes, you! What can you tell me about this alleged hero Heracles?

BOY: *(confused)* Uh…who?

CLIO: *(to audience)(sigh)* How sad. Look how our schools are failing this child. He is completely ignorant.

BOY: I can hear you…

CLIO: *(to boy)* What about *Hercules*? Have you heard of him? That's Heracles' Roman name.

BOY: Oh, Hercules! Yeah! He is the greatest hero of all time!

CLIO: Yeah. Yeah. Whatever. But what *dirt* do you know on him?

BOY: Nothing! He is a model Greek. A noble warrior and a real family man!

CLIO: A family man? He murdered his wife and children in cold blood!

BOY: Eh. Accidents happen. *(pause)* But he is really good at killing monsters!

CLIO: *(to audience)* See? This is what is wrong with Greece! Our children are glorifying murderers! I blame heavy metal lyre music.

BOY: Can I leave now?

CLIO: Whatever. *(to audience)* As I was saying, at the bottom of every crystal-clear pool there's some muck to rake! Today, using my muse-powers, I will travel throughout

Greece, appearing to both mortals and immortals and conducting personal, in-depth interviews to find out: Just who was this Heracles fellow? And what's all the fuss about? *(tinkle-tinkle music)*

To get to the bottom of something, sometimes you have to go right to the top—of Olympus, that is. You might remember Zeus, Lord of the Gods, from my ongoing series *All Zeus' Children*. Ah, there he is! *(to Zeus)* Zeus! Zeus! Clio here! The muse with the news!

ZEUS: *(a little too friendly)* Well, hello there. A muse, huh? How *amusing*!

CLIO: Okay. Easy, buddy. Don't get me mixed up with one of your nymphy girlfriends.

ZEUS: *(playfully)* And why not?

CLIO: I'll have to double-check the family tree, but I think I might actually be your daughter. Soooo…unless you'd like to make a new Greek tragedy, back off!

ZEUS: Err…sorry about that. How have you been…dear?

CLIO: Emotionally confused. But I have some questions about your son.

ZEUS: Which one? I have 120—and counting…

CLIO: My question is about the "hero" Heracles. How exactly did you father him?

ZEUS: Erm. Didn't your mother have that talk with you?

CLIO: I don't mean that! You're into this weird animal-transformation type of romance. So what form did you choose when you visited Heracles' mother? A swan? A bull? Some kind of ant-eater?

ZEUS: Oh, I see. Yes, I'd fallen terribly in love with a beautiful mortal princess named…what was her name again?

CLIO: Alcmene.

ZEUS: That's it! You've got a good memory!

CLIO: My mother is Mnemosyne—Memory herself!

ZEUS: Oh, I remember her! We had a thing once.

CLIO: Who *didn't* you have a thing with? Continue with your story.

ZEUS: Anyway, I intended to romance princess what's-her-name, and I had exhausted almost every option for an animal disguise. I was thinking of taking the form of tortoise—but that one was even too creepy for me. So I tricked her by taking the form of her husband instead.

CLIO: And that *wasn't* creepy? Thanks for the juicy scoop, Zeus. You're always good for a lurid love story.

ZEUS: Thanks—I think.

CLIO: Rest assured, there is much more to this story. Now let's speak to the mother, Alcmene. I bet we will find her in her home in Thebes. The last time I was in Thebes I was doing a special on Oedipus called "Getting the Heebie-Geebies in Theebies." *(tinkle-tinkle music)*

ALCMENE: *(frightened)* Ah! Where did you come from?

CLIO: I'll ask the questions, missy! Are you Alcmene, the mother of Heracles?

ALCMENE: Yes! Are you from his fan club? I get requests for autographs all the time.

CLIO: Hardly. Tell me what Heracles was like as a child!

ALCMENE: Obviously, Heracles was incredibly strong. Sometimes he was so strong that he frightened his father and me.

CLIO: By his father, do you mean Zeus?

ALCMENE: No. I mean his earthly father.

CLIO: How did your husband feel about Zeus taking you for a harlot?

ALCMENE: I beg your pardon?

CLIO: You should be begging your husband's. Just answer the question.

ALCMENE: Well, I never told him.

CLIO: Are you telling me that your husband, Amphitryon, thinks that Heracles is his real son?

ALCMENE: Umm. Well, yes. How do you break news like that?

CLIO: I'll show you! Let's just find your husband and reveal this heartbreaking news to him—in front of a live studio audience, of course. I can see the caption now: Father Learns Strongman Son Is Actually Heavenly Hand-Me-Down!

ALCMENE: No!

CLIO: You're no fun. Fine. Just tell me more about Heracles' childhood.

ALCMENE: Oh, our baby had such great strength, and as he grew up, he also developed a horrible temper.

CLIO: Hmmm. I've heard of his temper. Apparently, once he tried to kill the sun because it was shining too brightly.

ALCMENE: Yes, he is a bit emotional.

CLIO: Emotional. Stupid.

ALCMENE: We hired our little Heracles the best music teacher money could buy—a lyre teacher named Linus. But Heracles wasn't a musician, and he hated his lessons. One day he hit his teacher upside the head with his lyre so hard that it broke.

CLIO: What broke? The lyre?

ALCMENE: No. His teacher.

CLIO: *(to audience)* Interesting. Sounds like the great Greek idol is actually a brutish killer!

ALCMENE: Well, he didn't mean to. And we grounded him a whole week for it!

CLIO: *(sarcastically)* I bet that showed him. Now, tell me this: Why is Heracles named after his greatest enemy, Hera? I mean, I appreciate irony as much as the next muse, but what's up with that?

ALCMENE: I'm responsible for that actually. The goddess Hera had it out for him from the beginning. She was not happy about Zeus' and my affair.

CLIO: Were you expecting her to be?

ALCMENE: Well, no. But she didn't have to be so rude about it. When it came time for

Heracles to be born, Hera commanded the Goddess of Childbirth to prolong my labor for seven days.

CLIO: Yikes. How did that make you feel?

ALCMENE: How do you *think* that made me feel? My handmaiden finally tricked the Goddess of Childbirth, and Heracles entered the world. Have you ever seen a twenty-pound baby?

CLIO: Holy Harpies!

ALCMENE: I named him Heracles—"Glory to Hera." I thought that might keep her off my back, but it didn't work. I could see that she meant business, and I panicked. I'm so ashamed to admit it, but I did something terrible.

CLIO: Finally something juicy! Spit it out!

ALCMENE: I left my darling baby out in the woods to die.

CLIO: Hmm. Pretty dark. I can use that. But obviously your "darling" did not die.

ALCMENE: No! The goddess Athena took pity on my baby and tricked Hera into breastfeeding him. She had no idea she was feeding her hated enemy! But Baby Heracles was a bit of a biter and so hungry that he caused a nursing accident by—well, uh—use your imagination. Milk sprayed all over the sky, and that's why we have the Milky Way.

CLIO: That's disgusting!

ALCMENE: I know! I feel such shame for leaving him out in the woods that way!

CLIO: No. I mean the whole Milky Way thing. I'm going to have that image in my head for a week! Yuck.

ALCMENE: I can tell you more.

CLIO: Uh. No thanks. It looks like I need to speak to Hera, the world's worst stepmother! She may have her own side to the story. *(tinkle-tinkle music)* You might remember Hera from my recent feature, "Zeus and Hera: Heavenly Bliss or Nuptial Nightmare." There she is! Hera!

HERA: Oh, good Gaea, it's that snoopy reporter muse. *(to Clio)* You know we have a saying around here—no muse is good news. What do you want? Whatever it is, I'm busy.

CLIO: I'm here to smear the name of Heracles.

HERA: *(happily)* Well, why didn't you say so? By the way, thank you for that article you did on all Zeus' offspring. I found it most helpful—in dealing out my punishments.

CLIO: Speaking of offing Zeus' offspring, what about Heracles?

HERA: Oooh. I hate him completely!

CLIO: Don't you hate everyone?

HERA: Well, yes and no. There are different levels to my hatred. Heracles occupies the highest level of that hatred.

CLIO: So Heracles is hated by one of the mightiest goddess of Olympus—

HERA: Excuse me?

CLIO: I mean, *the* mightiest goddess of Olympus. But if that is so, then why is he still alive today?

HERA: Because the little booger would not die—no matter what I did! First, when he was just a baby, I sent deadly vipers into the crib where he slept.

CLIO: Wow. Killing a baby. That's low.

HERA: You have no idea how low I can go. It didn't work though. The brat strangled the snakes in his chubby, little hands!

CLIO: Kids do the darnedest things.

HERA: I finally got him though! It took me years, but I finally had my revenge. Yes! It was perfect!

CLIO: Tell me more.

HERA: Heracles grew up—won himself a wife—had some kids—did all the typical mortal stuff. But I waited. And then when he least expected it, I sent a madness upon him, and in a demonic rage he murdered his wife and his children.

CLIO: I stand corrected. You *can* go lower.

HERA: Heracles wanted to kill himself, and that's what I was hoping for! I wanted to be right there when he jabbed that dagger into his heart!

CLIO: You really need to get out more.

HERA: But that blasted hero do-gooder, Theseus, talked Heracles out of killing himself. Oh well, I thought. Because he has murdered his family, at least the Furies will drive him to madness. But the Oracle of Delphi—that meddling wench—told Heracles

that the gods would forgive him if he performed twelve labors. Can you believe it?

CLIO: Of course. Forgiveness sells.

HERA: The Oracle sent him to serve a king called Eurystheus and do whatever twelve labors he commanded him. But luckily I was there to inspire that weak-minded king with the most challenging labors ever concocted.

CLIO: Hmmm. The Twelve Labors of Heracles. It has a ring to it. Tell me more.

HERA: *(psychotic anger)* Grrrr. When I think about those twelve labors, I become so angry that I just have to strangle something!

CLIO: Err...well, in that case. Moving along. Can you tell me more about how the Milky Way came into existence?

HERA: *(in a rage)* No comment! This interview is over!

CLIO: Apparently the Milky Way is a painful subject for the Queen of Heaven. It's time to move on to Eurystheus, the cowardly king whom Heracles was forced to serve. Eurystheus has recently been ridiculed in Greece for his tendency to hide in large pots during times of danger. This all came out when a daring news muse published a report titled "King Cowers in Crock." *(tinkle-tinkle music)* There he is! *(to Eurystheus)* King Eurystheus! King Eurystheus!

EURYSTHEUS: *(screaming in fright)* Aieeee!

CLIO: Good grief! Get out of that pot. I'm not going to hurt you!

EURYSTHEUS: *(covering)* Uh...I wasn't scared. I crawl in this pot sometimes for—for—relaxation.

CLIO: Yeah right. You've got chicken written all over you. Anyway, tell me about Heracles. Why did you assign such trying tasks to our so-called strongman?

EURYSTHEUS: Because I was jealous of his strength and his popularity. I knew I could not kill him directly, so I sent him on missions that would kill him for me.

CLIO: *(sarcastically)* How brave of you.

EURYSTHEUS: First I sent him to slay the Nemean lion.

CLIO: A big cat? You sent the mightiest hero of Greece against a giant cat? *(sarcastically)* Good one.

EURYSTHEUS: It's not a giant cat! *(pause)* Well, it is—but it's a man-eater! Its skin cannot be pierced by any blade! I saw it once, and I about soiled myself.

CLIO: Yes, but you about soiled yourself when you saw me, too. So how did Heracles do against your overgrown pussycat?

EURYSTHEUS: He defeated it easily!

CLIO: How? Did he dangle some yarn in front of it?

EURYSTHEUS: No! Since the beast's hide couldn't be pierced, Heracles strangled it. Then he dragged it back here.

CLIO: And you jumped into your pot, didn't you?

EURYSTHEUS: *(defensively)* I just happened to slip and fall into the pot.

CLIO: Speaking of pots, on most Greek vases Heracles is shown wearing that lion's skin. If its skin is so tough, how did he remove it?

EURYSTHEUS: Heracles used one of the lion's own claws to skin it. And he kept the pelt and wore it as a shield against weapons! My plan to end Heracles' life completely backfired! He became even stronger!

CLIO: Haven't you heard? What doesn't kill you makes you stronger.

EURYSTHEUS: Yes, but not everyone makes it into that second category.

CLIO: Okay. Surprise, surprise, the big cat didn't defeat Heracles. What other beasts did you send him against?

EURYSTHEUS: I sent him to capture a giant gold-horned stag, a man-eating boar, and a massive bull. Unfortunately, he was able to capture them all—and bring them back here.

CLIO: Let me guess. You fell into your pot again.

EURYSTHEUS: They were terrifying!

CLIO: A pig, a deer, and a side of beef. Frightening.

EURYSTHEUS: Yes! But they were enormous! And they had really bad attitudes!

CLIO: Ooooh.

EURYSTHEUS: Then I sent him against the most deadly beast I could think of—the dreaded nine-headed Hydra. When one of its heads is cut off, two more grow in its place.

CLIO: Now that's more like it! How did he fare against the Hydra?

EURYSTHEUS: He beat it, too. But he would have failed if it hadn't been for that pesky nephew of his—some brat named Iolaus.

CLIO: Nephew? Thanks for the tip, Eurystheus. You can get back in your pot now. Sounds like I need to talk to this Iolaus guy and get the real skinny on the Hydra. (tinkle-tinkle music) If my facts are correct—and they always are—I can find Iolaus at the official Heracles fan club headquarters.

IOLAUS: Hello. Are you here to sign up for the Heracles fan club?

CLIO: Fat chance. I am Clio the muse. Are you Iolaus, the nephew of Heracles?

IOLAUS: I am.

CLIO: My sources tell me that you helped your uncle defeat the Hydra.

IOLAUS: You bet I did!

CLIO: Just the facts, man.

IOLAUS: Heracles came up against the Hydra. He was all like, "Ahhhh!" And the Hydra was all like, "Raar!" Heads were going in all direction. Shoom! Shoom! Shoom!

CLIO: Very descriptive. Just get to the point. How did Heracles beat the Hydra?

IOLAUS: Well, he wasn't getting anywhere. Heads kept sprouting in all directions. Bam! Bam! Bam!

CLIO: Okay. Sound effects. I get it.

IOLAUS: That's when I came up with the idea of burning the neck wounds once we'd cut a head off. Kind of like, "Shhhh! Aaah!" That way they couldn't grow back. Then

Heracles dropped a big rock on the final head. Ka-chow!

CLIO: It sounds like *you* beat the Hydra, and Heracles stole the credit for it.

IOLAUS: Gee. I don't know.

CLIO: Work with me here, kid.

IOLAUS: He really did most of it.

CLIO: Face it, sonny. You're the victim. Heracles stole your moment in the spotlight.

IOLAUS: Well, to be honest, I didn't like my uncle Heracles much at first. Our personalities clashed—and he *did* kill my cousins and my aunt.

CLIO: I'll quote you on that. Now continue your story. What happened after the Hydra was dead?

IOLAUS: Heracles dipped his arrows in the Hydra's poisonous blood. That way all his arrows were poisoned...you know, from the blood...that was poison.

CLIO: I get it.

IOLAUS: Then that sourpuss king sent Heracles on another labor—the grossest one yet—to clean the stables of Augeas in just one day. Talk about a smelly job! Those stables were piled with more manure than you've ever seen.

CLIO: I don't know. I've seen a lot of manure in my day.

IOLAUS: There was so much manure it would have taken Heracles a lifetime to shovel it all. But using boulders he changed the course of two streams—running them through the stables, which removed all the dung from the stables. So see? He wasn't just a dumb muscle-head.

CLIO: That's debatable. Did you go with Heracles on any other labors?

IOLAUS: Eurystheus sent him to clear a swamp of these dangerous birds. Their dung was poison.

CLIO: More dung? Does this guy have dung on the brain or something?

IOLAUS: They could shoot their feathers out like arrows, and their beaks were like spears. Heracles had me beat some cymbals, which flushed them out of their trees, and then he picked them off with his bow and poisoned arrows.

CLIO: I guess no one told him that those birds were a protected species. I can't wait to blow the whistle on that one!

IOLAUS: Then he had to battle the Amazons—fierce female warriors—and steal the girdle of Hippolyta, their queen. Heracles did not think it would be much of a challenge, but it was.

CLIO: Ha! He underestimated us women, didn't he? The Amazon queen was more than he bargained for.

IOLAUS: No, he killed her pretty easily. It was getting that girdle off her. That was the real beast.

CLIO: Killing innocent females and robbing them of their garments. How heroic.

IOLAUS: I wouldn't exactly call the Amazons defenseless. They're so into war that they cut off one of their…errr…y'know,

woman parts—so that they can fire a bow and arrow easier.

CLIO: Before you say more, let's move on. What was Heracles' next labor?

IOLAUS: He had to defeat an evil king called Diomedes, whose horses dined on human flesh. When Heracles was done with him, he was food for his own horses.

CLIO: Didn't all this carnage bother Heracles?

IOLAUS: Not really. Heracles is a monster-killer. But he is more than that, too. I can't explain it. He is just—well, a hero.

CLIO: *(disappointed)* It sounds like you developed respect for Heracles along the way.

IOLAUS: I realized that he was truly sorry for what he had done to his family. At night I would hear him crying out for his lost wife and children.

CLIO: *(quietly)* Yes. That's hard to put a spin on—even for me.

IOLAUS: Then I learned those murders were all Hera's fault, and I forgave him.

CLIO: Did he resent his twelve labors?

IOLAUS: Once I asked him if he resented his fate. With tears in his eyes, he told me that he deserved every bit of his punishment. Suffering is part of being a hero, he said. Then I figured out that these twelve labors weren't just to get Heracles out of trouble. They were his way of forgiving himself for the death of his family. In the process he became the hero of Greece. And he became my hero, too.

CLIO: Well, enough of this sob story. I'm not here to make a sappy tribute to the guy. What else do you know?

IOLAUS: That's it. For his final three tasks he went beyond the known world, and he had to leave me behind.

CLIO: Hmmm. Then I know just who to talk to about the last labors. Thank you, Iolaus.

IOLAUS: So would you like to join the Heracles fan club or what?

CLIO: Ha! *(tinkle-tinkle music)* Next we will go to the big guy—Atlas—the titan who holds up the heavens—also known as the sky's biggest supporter. Luckily for me, I know just where to find him. He doesn't get out much. Atlas! Clio the news muse here!

ATLAS: *(angrily)* You've got a lot of nerve showing your face here!

CLIO: What *are* you talking about?

ATLAS: I'm talking about that interview I did with you. You completely misquoted me! Plus, you told all of Greece that I had body odor.

CLIO: Trust me. That wasn't much of a news flash.

ATLAS: You try holding up the sky for a couple thousand years, and we'll see if you don't sweat a bit!

CLIO: Whole rivers are birthed from your armpits. And excuse me, *you're* offended? *I* had to sit here and smell you through that whole interview. But if it means anything, I'm sorry, and I'll never do it again.

ATLAS: *(sniffing)* It was just hurtful, you know.

CLIO: Now I have some questions for you.

ATLAS: I don't think so!

CLIO: I'm trying to bring down Greece's number one hero, Heracles.

ATLAS: Oooh! I hate that little twerp! He caused a lot of trouble in this part of the world.

CLIO: Is this on or off the record?

ATLAS: On! I want all of Greece to know how dishonest that pipsqueak is. He is a murderer and a thief!

CLIO: Tell me more! What damage did he cause around here? I've already heard about his first nine rampages.

ATLAS: For this tenth labor he stole the cattle of Geryon.

CLIO: *(gasp)* Not the cattle of Geryon! *(pause)* Okay. I give up. What are the cattle of Geryon?

ATLAS: Geryon is a monster who has three heads. Or wait—does he have one head and three bodies? I never can remember.

CLIO: Is he the one who's part lion, part goat, and part Chihuahua?

ATLAS: No! No! It doesn't matter now anyway. He's dead. Heracles shot him with one of his poisoned arrows.

CLIO: Alas! Poor Gerlon! He will be missed!

ATLAS: Geryon.

CLIO: Whatever.

ATLAS: Then Heracles came sniffing around here for his eleventh labor. He said he needed some golden apples from the garden of my daughters, the Hesperides. He thought maybe I could help him.

CLIO: Didn't you tell him that you kind of have your hands full?

ATLAS: I did, but the rude little beggar persisted. He looked like a beefy guy, so I told him to hold the sky for me while I nipped out for a bit. I had to do something I've needed to do for a long time.

CLIO: Take a bath?

ATLAS: Grrrr. Actually to visit my daughters. And while I was there, I agreed to pick up some apples for him.

CLIO: So Heracles holds up your end of the bargain while you pick up his groceries.

ATLAS: Yeah, but, you see, once I got the sky off my shoulders, I felt like such a weight had been lifted. I kind of liked the feeling. My back has been killing me for the last thousand years or so. So I went and picked him a few apples, but on the way back I decided, I was through! If Heracles was stupid enough to take the sky from me, he could hold it up for a while.

CLIO: The old switcheroo. Sounds fair to me.

ATLAS: He was straining pretty hard when I returned. I told him to lift with his legs. It was kind of funny actually. The puny mortal had bitten off more than he could chew. I told him that I'd decided not to take the sky back! But listen to how selfish and deceitful Heracles is!

CLIO: Do tell!

ATLAS: He pretended to be fine with holding the sky for me. He only asked for me to take it off his hands—just for a second—while he got a better grip.

CLIO: The old hang-onto-the-sky-for-a-second-while-I-get-my-grip-back trick, huh? And you fell for that?

ATLAS: Hey, I'm a kind and trusting person! Once I had the sky back in my hands, he skipped away—snatching up the apples and laughing as he went.

CLIO: After all you had done for him? Tsk. Tsk.

ATLAS: Exactly!

CLIO: What happened to him after that?

ATLAS: I don't know, and I don't care! You might ask my brother, Prometheus. He's chained to the mountains at the end of the world. I think Heracles went that direction.

CLIO: Thanks for the tip. Keep up the good work, Atlas. (*tinkle-tinkle music*) You've probably heard of Prometheus. He is the eternally-chained titan whose liver is ripped out each day. This is broadcasted daily on the Tragedy Channel—all tragedy, all the time. I once had the pleasure to interview Prometheus for a blurb entitled "Living Life Liverless." Now here I am on the peak of Mount Caucasus to ask him if—what? (*gasp*) He's gone! Stop the presses! Prometheus has escaped! Prometheus is gone!

PROMETHEUS: No. I am here.

CLIO: Where are your chains? And look! There's your liver! Completely intact!

PROMETHEUS: Heracles freed me of my chains and slew the eagle that persecuted me.

CLIO: Prometheus, I do not doubt your noble word, but are you sure? I can't believe Zeus allowed that to happen. What's his angle?

PROMETHEUS: I bartered with Zeus over some very sensitive information. I told him to steer clear of a nymph named Thetis.

CLIO: What could possibly make Zeus swear off nymphs?

PROMETHEUS: I saw the future. Thetis is destined to give birth to a son greater than his father.

CLIO: That would do it. Power is everything to these gods.

PROMETHEUS: I owe my freedom to Heracles. It was he who took my bargain to Zeus and arranged for my freedom. Of course, I had seen in a vision that he would help free me.

CLIO: Is there anything you *don't* see in a vision? Speaking of that, tell me more about next year's Olympics. I might want to lay some bets.

PROMETHEUS: Heracles founded the Olympics. Did you know that? And after Heracles freed me, he completed his twelfth and greatest labor. He descended into the Underworld and captured Cerberus, the three-headed hound of Hades.

CLIO: (*surprised*) Wow! He basically conquered death. Is there anything that guy can't do? (*catching herself*) I mean…psh-sha. Cerberus. No big deal.

PROMETHEUS: Why should you look down on his deeds?

CLIO: Hey, it's nothing personal. I just need a good story, and hero worship doesn't sell.

PROMETHEUS: Doesn't sell? Where is your journalistic integrity?

CLIO: Never heard of it!

PROMETHEUS: Clio! I can tell that deep down you admire Heracles!

CLIO: Lies.

PROMETHEUS: Is that a Heracles fan club button you're wearing there?

CLIO: (*defensively*) No! (*fake shock*) What? Where did that come from?

PROMETHEUS: Shame on you, Clio! You have been trying to slander the good name of Heracles and make light of his mighty labors, just so you can stir up controversy! I know that you think that there was some trick—some deception—in Heracles, but in your heart you know that he was truly a great hero.

CLIO: *Was*? What do you mean?

PROMETHEUS: Heracles is dead.

CLIO: (*in shock*) Dead? How?

PROMETHEUS: Well, it's complicated. A situation arose involving a love triangle with two princesses, an evil centaur, and a poisoned robe. In the end the hero was consumed by the flames of the poisoned robe and begged to die. Zeus took pity on him and allowed him to depart the mortal world.

CLIO: *(slowly)* I began this investigation thinking I knew all the answers. But, you know, I was wrong. Heracles was truly an amazing hero, and Greece will never be the same without him. *(sniff)* That's right. Clio is shedding a tear for the death of Heracles.

PROMETHEUS: Yes. Heracles is gone from us forever. Never again shall we see his noble face—

CLIO: *(in shock)* Look! There in the sky! It's Heracles! It's really him!

PROMETHEUS: You are right!

CLIO: *(to audience)* This just in—the golden form of Heracles has appeared on the peak of Caucasus. It's time for this muse to get her first *post-mortem* interview with the hero. Heracles! Heracles!

HERACLES: *(booming)* Clio, Muse of History, I've got a bone to pick with you!

CLIO: *(innocently)* Whatever you've heard, I'm completely innocent!

HERACLES: You've been looking for the real story of Heracles, right? Well, now you can get it straight from the hero's mouth. I've got a secret to tell—a real exclusive.

CLIO: *(frantically)* Wait! Wait! Let me make sure I'm getting all this!

HERACLES: Heracles the mortal hero has passed way, but he has become Heracles the god!

CLIO: That's fantastic! God of what?

HERACLES: We're still working out the details. But as I died, Zeus took my spirit to Olympus. I have proved myself worthy to be among the gods.

CLIO: Well, I'm completely speechless!

HERACLES: That's a first.

CLIO: So, Heracles, now that you are a god, what are you going to do next?

HERACLES: I shall be married to Hebe, the beautiful Cupbearer of the Gods.

CLIO: Oooh! A new celebrity couple! The public will flip! Give me all the details. What first attracted you to Hebe? Her fabulous cup-bearing skills?

HERACLES: That—and her goddess-level good looks.

CLIO: Yes, we are all cursed with that burden.

HERACLES: Erm. Some more than others.

CLIO: Any other plans?

HERACLES: I plan to inspire heroes for generations to come. I plan to show them the Heracles method for solving the problems that are placed before them.

CLIO: When you face an obstacle in life, hit it really hard with your club? And if that doesn't work, use your brain!

HERACLES: Exactly! And I'm choosing you to share my story with all of Greece.

CLIO: Me? Are you sure? I have been known to get *creative* with the facts.

HERACLES: My story is so inspirational that not even *you* can mess it up! So spread the news! Make sure I go down in history as the greatest hero of all! If I don't, I will sue you for slander!

CLIO: Ermm...

HERACLES: Only kidding. Farewell!

CLIO: Heracles is quickly ascending back into the heavens as I speak. What an investigation this has been! I did end up getting the *true* story of Heracles—it just wasn't the story I was expecting. Well, that's a wrap, folks. It's time for me to sign off. This is Clio the Muse saying, "I'm history—literally."

DISCUSSION QUESTIONS

- After listening to Clio the Muse's report, do you think Heracles is a hero? Explain.
- Heracles tells Iolaus that suffering is part of being a hero. Do you think this is true? Explain.
- What un-heroic acts are included in Heracles' past? Explain.
- Heracles' life story is interpreted through Clio the Muse's point-of-view. How does this put a slant on the events of his life? Why is point-of-view important?
- Clio uses many examples of journalistic jargon (terms and phrases associated with the news media). What are some examples? What do they add to the story?
- Can news stories be slanted or biased in their delivery? What about accounts of history? What does the saying "History is always written by the winners" mean?
- Have you ever begun something with firm convictions only to find out along the way that your convictions were wrong? What changed them? Explain.

ATALANTA'S RACE
TEACHER GUIDE

BACKGROUND

Atalanta, Greece's foremost female hero, lived a life full of adventure. As a baby, she was abandoned by her kingly father in the wilderness. Her life was saved by a passing she-bear, and she was raised by a band of nomadic hunters. She became a famous and ferocious warrior. Among her accomplishments were slaying a pair of murderous centaurs, tracking and wounding the giant Calydonian Boar, and assisting the hero Jason on his fantastic voyage in search of the Golden Fleece. As beautiful as she was brave, Atalanta was desired by many men, but none of them ever swayed her heart, and much like the goddess Artemis, she preferred the single life of maidenhood.

During the hunt for the Calydonian Boar, a young prince named Meleager fell in love with Atalanta. This prince had a strange backstory. When he was born, the Three Fates appeared to his mother and prophesied that he would die when the log burning on the fire expired. To protect her son, Meleager's mother removed the log from the fire and kept it in a safe location for the entirety of his life. But Meleager's infatuation with Atalanta caused him to betray his family, and in anger his mother burned the fateful log—bringing about Meleager's death.

SUMMARY

Hippomenes is a young man who first sees Atalanta competing at a series of funeral games in the city of Iolcus. The Argonauts have just returned from their journey to the ends of the earth. Atalanta defeats a warrior named Peleus at wrestling, and Hippomenes is impressed by her abilities. Someone else is impressed, too—an old man who reveals himself to be Atalanta's long-lost father, King Iasus. He apologizes for abandoning her in the wilderness many years ago, invites her to return to his kingdom, and suggests she find a husband to rule the kingdom with her. Initially, Atalanta refuses as she does not wish to become a dainty princess and especially does not wish to marry. She declares that she will not marry a man unless he is her equal. This gives her father an idea. He tells Atalanta that she can propose any kind of physical contest to compete with the men who wish to win her hand. If they manage to beat her, they will win the right to marry her and inherit the kingdom. Atalanta is intrigued by the idea and suggests a footrace, but she wants to add a deadly twist—if the suitors lose, they must die. She returns with her father to his kingdom, and their bizarre contest begins.

Although many men desire Atalanta's hand and her father's kingdom, few of them want to pay with their lives. Atalanta is so swift that is impossible to beat her, and the few suitors who do try the contest lose and are executed.

Hippomenes, who fell in love with Atalanta at the funeral games and wishes to be her husband, receives the help of Aphrodite. The love goddess dislikes Atalanta because the maiden has always shunned the power of love. Aphrodite offers Hippomenes three golden apples that no woman can resist. He must use these to win the race.

Hippomenes travels to Atalanta's kingdom and vows to race her. Atalanta is impressed by his bravery but warns him that he is bound to lose. The race begins, and Hippomenes uses his magical golden apples to divert Atalanta from the race course three times. Atalanta does not understand why she is drawn to the golden apples, but she cannot resist them. Hippomenes wins the race. Afterward Aphrodite appears to the boy and orders that he become a demanding husband and break Atalanta's spirit. Hippomenes refuses, and Aphrodite vows to have her revenge.

Hippomenes and Atalanta are deliriously happy together. One day they go for a walk, and a rain drives them into a temple of Zeus. As they embrace and express their love for one another, Aphrodite reports this to Zeus, who frowns on mortals using his temples as romantic getaways. In punishment Zeus transforms Hippomenes and Atalanta into a pair of lions. (The Greeks believed that lions could not mate with their own species but mated with leopards instead.) Yet the two lions break the rules of their kind and spend the rest of their lives together.

ESSENTIAL QUESTIONS

- Is romantic love for every person?
- Is love worth risking everything for?

CONNECT

Women in Ancient Greece Research the conditions under which women in ancient Greece lived. What rights did they have? Who determined whom they would marry? What were their lives like? Compare and contrast their situation with the events presented in Atalanta's myth.

ANTICIPATORY QUESTIONS

- Who is Atalanta?
- Do you know anyone who has sworn off love?
- Can a person fall in love even when they're trying not to?

- What is a type of contest you think you could win every time?
- Would you risk your life to win the person you love?

TEACHABLE TERMS

- **Motif** Magical golden apples show up frequently in Greek mythology (making them a motif). In this myth Aphrodite offers Hippomenes golden apples on pg. 133. Think of other myths, legends, or fairy tales where apples are important.
- **Ethics** Discuss whether or not it is ethical for Hippomenes to use the magical apples to win Atalanta's race. Discuss Atalanta's ethics as well: Was her race fair to begin with? Do two wrongs make a right?
- **Simile** On pg. 136 Atalanta says that "freedom can still feel like a cage," which is a simile contrasting *freedom* and *cage*. Think about what she means by this statement.
- **Idiom** On pg. 133 Aphrodite advises Hippomenes to take Atalanta "down a peg or two," which is an idiom for reducing her self-esteem.
- **Stereotypes** On pg. 133 Aphrodite makes the comment that "no man wants a woman who claims to be better than he is." What stereotypes, for both men and women, is she promoting here? How do Hippomenes and Atalanta both break stereotypes?

RECALL QUESTIONS

1. Atalanta beats Peleus at what sport?
2. What type of contest must Atalanta's suitors participate in?
3. What happens when they lose?
4. How does Hippomenes win the contest?
5. Hippomenes and Atalanta are both transformed into what type of animal?

ATALANTA'S RACE

CAST

ATALANTA	*Famous Female Warrior*
HIPPOMENES	*Young Man*
PELEUS	*Famous Warrior*
MAN	*Man in the Crowd*
IASUS	*Old King*
APHRODITE	*Goddess of Love*
ZEUS	*Lord of Olympus*

NARRATOR: A young man named Hippomenes entered the teeming Greek city of Iolcus. A celebration was underway—the funeral games of Pelias, the corrupt king of that city-state. Jason and his famous Argonauts had just returned from their legendary journey.

Hippomenes drew near to a tight knot of people amassed in the street. A wrestling match was in progress. One of the wrestlers pinned the other and yelled in triumph. *(cheering from the crowd)*

PELEUS: I win! I win! All right! Who's next?

NARRATOR: Hippomenes turned to a man beside him.

HIPPOMENES: Who is that wrestler?

MAN: He is Peleus the Argonaut. His strength is legendary.

HIPPOMENES: Has he defeated everyone who has challenged him?

MAN: Naturally. They say he *can't* be beaten.

NARRATOR: The wrestler continued his taunting.

PELEUS: Come on! Are all of you afraid? Won't any of you *ladies* wrestle me?

ATALANTA: I will!

NARRATOR: A tall, beautiful girl had stepped forward from the crowd. *(murmuring from the crowd)* Peleus grinned in amusement.

PELEUS: You?

ATALANTA: Yes. And wipe that stupid smirk off your face.

PELEUS: This is a *men only* contest.

ATALANTA: Maybe I'll show you men what a lady can do!

PELEUS: *(laughing)* Trust me. I know what a lady is good for—tending the children, cooking the meals, and scrubbing the floors.

ATALANTA: Ha! I'll scrub the floors with you.

NARRATOR: Watching this argument from the sidelines, Hippomenes was entranced by the maiden's loveliness.

HIPPOMENES: Who is *that*? She's gorgeous!

MAN: That is Atalanta. She, too, went on the quest of the Golden Fleece.

HIPPOMENES: Who is her husband?

MAN: No one. She is fiercely independent. They say she had a suitor once—but he died under mysterious circumstances. Since then, everyone else keeps their distance.

NARRATOR: Peleus and Atalanta were continuing their disagreement.

ATALANTA: So are we going to wrestle or not?

PELEUS: Atalanta, knock it off! Be serious!

ATALANTA: I am!

MAN: *(shouting)* Do it, Peleus! Maybe if you win, she'll give you a kiss.

ATALANTA: Oh, I'll give you a kiss all right—with my fist.

PELEUS: Fine! We can wrestle. But if you end up getting hurt, it's your own fault. And for that matter—

NARRATOR: Atalanta pummeled into him—cutting him off in mid-sentence.

PELEUS: *(sound of pain)* Oof! Wait! Wait!

NARRATOR: The two furiously struggled.

MAN: Get her, Peleus!

NARRATOR: The match ended sooner than anyone expected. Showing her speed and strength, Atalanta hurled Peleus into the crowd of spectators.

PELEUS: Ah! *(cry of surprise)*

(shouts of surprise from the spectators)

NARRATOR: Atalanta wiped the dust from her hands.

ATALANTA: Who's smirking now?

PELEUS: Ugh! I can't believe it! I am defeated by a woman!

ATALANTA: I don't see what's so surprising about that.

PELEUS: *(angrily)* It wasn't a fair contest. I wasn't ready.

ATALANTA: Care to go again?

PELEUS: Um. No. I'm good. Please don't tell any of the other Argonauts about this.

ATALANTA: Tell them what? That you were foolish enough to challenge me?

NARRATOR: Atalanta turned to the crowd.

ATALANTA: Who else wants a piece of me?

NARRATOR: Hippomenes was staring intently at Atalanta. He had already fallen deeply in love with the fiery maiden.

ATALANTA: What are you looking at, farm boy?

HIPPOMENES: Nothing! Nothing!

ATALANTA: Are any of you powerful enough to defeat Atalanta?

MAN: No way! I'm out of here!

(muttering of the crowd)

NARRATOR: The crowd dispersed—except for Hippomenes. He stepped forward to speak to Atalanta, but an old man in a traveling cloak beat him to it.

IASUS: *(old man voice)* Miss.

ATALANTA: Sorry, gramps. I don't wrestle the elderly.

IASUS: I have information that might interest you.

ATALANTA: I doubt that.

IASUS: Are you interested to know that...I am your father?

NARRATOR: Atalanta stared at the man intently and then turned away.

ATALANTA: No.

IASUS: Wait! At least speak to me!

ATALANTA: I have nothing to say to you. You left me to die in the wilderness.

IASUS: But you did not die!

ATALANTA: Thanks to a bear. A beast showed me the kindness that you could not.

IASUS: You're right. I was cruel. I foolishly threw you away. But I see how powerful you've become. I want to invite you to come home with me and live in my palace.

ATALANTA: I'm not that kind of girl. Walls just make me antsy. I have sailed with Jason and seen the ends of the earth. I can never live in a cage.

IASUS: Please. I'm an old man, and I need an heir. You may rule my kingdom after I am gone.

ATALANTA: *(surprised)* You would make a woman the ruler of your kingdom?

IASUS: *(in shock)* Of course, not! You will have to marry.

ATALANTA: I thought as much. Nevermind. No deal.

IASUS: But you *can* rule by your husband's side!

ATALANTA: Let me explain this to you. I have sworn never to marry simply because I have never met a man who is my match. Therefore, I will stay a virgin like the goddess Artemis.

IASUS: What if you found a man who *was* your match?

ATALANTA: Impossible.

IASUS: Do you want to make a wager on that?

ATALANTA: What do you mean?

IASUS: You propose a contest—wrestling, footracing, javelin-throwing, whatever you wish. And if any man is able to beat you, he will be your husband.

ATALANTA: No man will ever win against me.

IASUS: Then there can be no danger in agreeing to the contest!

ATALANTA: Hmmm. It would be a nice way to prove a point. And, luckily, you have caught me between adventures. A contest might be a nice diversion.

IASUS: Excellent! Then what sport do you choose?

ATALANTA: It must be a footrace. But let's make this contest more interesting. What happens to the men who lose?

IASUS: You decide.

ATALANTA: Death.

IASUS: Death? That's a little harsh, don't you think?

ATALANTA: No. It's death or nothing.

IASUS: It will be as you say. *(excitedly)* Oh, the men will be lining up to accept this challenge!

ATALANTA: Then they race to meet their doom.

NARRATOR: Hippomenes, who had been eavesdropping on this conversation, watched the maiden and her father depart.

HIPPOMENES: I must find a way to win her hand! I was trained by Chiron the centaur to be a great warrior, and I am very swift, but something tells me I could not beat Atalanta. There must be another way!

NARRATOR: Atalanta returned home with her long-lost father to his kingdom. The word was sent out that King Iasus desired suitors— men to vie for the hand of the princess, Atalanta. Many suitors answered the king's invitation, but most of them withdrew when they heard the steep penalty for failure.

ATALANTA: Did you have to describe me as the *princess* Atalanta? Princess is so demeaning. It makes me sound like some helpless airhead. So where are all my suitors?

IASUS: Well, many of them are terribly fond of you, but they're also fond of living.

ATALANTA: That's what I thought.

IASUS: For some men love cannot overpower their fear of death.

ATALANTA: Love? These greedy pigs don't love me. They only want your kingdom.

IASUS: Don't underestimate your beauty, my dear.

NARRATOR: In spite of the risk, some men still took Atalanta's challenge. She beat them easily, and they paid with their lives.

ATALANTA: Men are so stupid. Is it their pride that they die for?

IASUS: Maybe it's love.

ATALANTA: Even stupider.

NARRATOR: Meanwhile, Hippomenes had spent months trying to devise a way to conquer the woman he adored. One night Aphrodite, Goddess of Love, appeared to him in his dreams.

APHRODITE: Hippomenes! It is I— Aphrodite! I have heard your prayers!

HIPPOMENES: What? There must be some mistake, goddess. I haven't prayed to you!

APHRODITE: Oh please! You're a lovesick young man. Your achy, breaky heart has been sending up signals to me like crazy.

HIPPOMENES: It is true! I am in love with Atalanta!

APHRODITE: (sigh) I really don't know what you see in her, but I'm here to help you all the same. Atalanta has always shunned the power of love, and I want to teach her a lesson! I will help you win against her in a footrace—if you will promise to marry her.

HIPPOMENES: Of course!

APHRODITE: Perfect! I can't stand all these unmarried women running around. It's unnatural!

HIPPOMENES: How shall I beat her?

APHRODITE: Oh! That's the best part. I picked these for you.

NARRATOR: The goddess drew three golden apples from her robe.

HIPPOMENES: Golden apples? How will these help me?

APHRODITE: You are handsome, but you're not very smart, are you? These are magical apples that no woman can resist. During your race, use them to your advantage. Wherever you throw them, Atalanta will follow.

HIPPOMENES: Isn't that kind of strange—to win someone's love through a trick?

APHRODITE: You don't know much about love, do you?

HIPPOMENES: I will do it!

APHRODITE: Now be careful. Even with these golden apples, there is a chance you might lose. Atalanta is fleet of foot.

HIPPOMENES: Don't worry. Something tells me I will win myself a wife!

APHRODITE: After you are married, just remember to take that girl down a peg or two. No man likes a woman who claims to be better than he is!

NARRATOR: Hippomenes accepted the apples offered by the goddess, and upon the morning, he journeyed to King Iasus' kingdom. There he appeared before the king and his daughter.

HIPPOMENES: I want to race for the right to marry Atalanta.

IASUS: (excitedly) Oooh. It's been a few weeks since our last execution—I mean, event.

ATALANTA: What is your name, boy?

HIPPOMENES: Hippomenes.

ATALANTA: What does that mean? Horse-keeper or something? Sounds like you come from a long line of servants. What makes you think you can beat me and become a king?

HIPPOMENES: I have the speed of a horse. And I was trained by Chiron the centaur.

ATALANTA: Trained by him? Or were you the stable boy who cleaned up his dung?

IASUS: Atalanta! There is no need to be rude!

ATALANTA: (sigh) These executions are getting so tedious! Look, buddy, you seem like a nice guy. Why not just quit while you're ahead?

HIPPOMENES: *(earnestly)* I can't. From the first time I saw you, I knew I had to have you.

ATALANTA: As a possession?

HIPPOMENES: *(passionately)* As an object of admiration. Something to give my life for.

ATALANTA: Don't make me throw up. Everyone knows that this race isn't about me. It's about my kingdom.

HIPPOMENES: Not for me. I race only for you. If I win, this kingdom will just be a perk. We'll rule it together.

ATALANTA: Rule whatever you like, but you'll never rule me. It's a moot point anyway. There is no way you can win.

HIPPOMENES: Then I will die for love.

ATALANTA: Then you die in vain. *(sadly)* A pity. You seem very brave. We shall race tomorrow.

NARRATOR: In spite of herself Atalanta was impressed with the young man's bravery.

IASUS: I have a good feeling about this one. He's a handsome lad! Perhaps you might want to lose on purpose.

ATALANTA: Never!

IASUS: *(grumbling)* I would like to have some grandchildren before I die.

NARRATOR: The next day the race was held in the valley below the king's fortress, and the whole city-state turned out to see it.

IASUS: Let the contestants take their marks!

NARRATOR: Atalanta walked boldly to her mark, and Hippomenes, grinning at the princess, did the same.

ATALANTA: Okay, horse-boy. Prepare to know the true meaning of speed.

HIPPOMENES: I think I will be the winner today.

NARRATOR: He patted the golden apples, which he had secured beneath his tunic.

ATALANTA: Ha!

IASUS: *(yelling)* Race!

NARRATOR: Atalanta dashed forward in a burst of speed. Hippomenes, too, darted forth.

ATALANTA: *(shouting)* Not a good start, horse-boy!

NARRATOR: Although Hippomenes was swift, Atalanta was easily winning. *(cheering of the crowd)* When the course had been almost halfway run, Hippomenes freed the first of the golden apples from their hiding place.

HIPPOMENES: Here goes nothing!

NARRATOR: Hippomenes hurled the apple to a spot by the side of the path where it would catch Atalanta's eye. But much to his surprise, the girl dashed on past—ignoring the apple.

HIPPOMENES: *(in shock)* What? Impossible!

NARRATOR: Just then Atalanta's head whipped to the side—summoned by the sheen of the golden apple. To everyone's shock, she ran from the course and stooped to pick up the apple.

ATALANTA: *(dreamlike)* What a gorgeous apple!

NARRATOR: Hippomenes sped on by, and the crowd cheered. *(cheering of the crowd)* The noise jarred Atalanta loose from her daydream.

ATALANTA: *(in shock)* What? How did he get ahead? Grrrr.

NARRATOR: She stuffed the apple into her tunic and returned to the race. Hippomenes ran for all that he was worth, but Atalanta was soon by his side.

ATALANTA: *(between breaths)* Nice trick! I won't be fooled by that one again!

HIPPOMENES: We'll see.

NARRATOR: Hippomenes dropped the second apple from his pouch, and Atalanta screeched to a halt—bending down to retrieve it.

ATALANTA: What am I doing? Why can't I resist these…*(suddenly dreamlike)* beautiful apples? *(snapping out of it)* No! No! I must win! I must!

NARRATOR: Hippomenes saw the finish line ahead, and he pushed himself to run even faster.

HIPPOMENES: I'm going to win!

NARRATOR: Just then Atalanta shot past him—her long legs extended like those of a deer.

ATALANTA: Feast on this, horse-boy! I'm going to win, and you're going to—*(dreamlike)* Oooh! Shiny!

NARRATOR: Hippomenes had hurled the final apple—far into the grass at the side of the course. Atalanta sidetracked, and Hippomenes crossed the finish line. *(cheering of the crowd)*

HIPPOMENES: Yes!

IASUS: At last! At last! I have a husband for my daughter! My kingdom has an heir!

NARRATOR: Hippomenes, exuberant and breathless, turned. Atalanta was staring him down—holding the last golden apple in her hand.

ATALANTA: I am *not* happy about this! I ought to cram these apples down your throat! You cheated!

HIPPOMENES: Not necessarily. You never said anything about magical items being against the rules.

ATALANTA: *(angrily)* The rules don't say anything about me clobbering you either!

HIPPOMENES: Wait! *(pause)* You said that you wanted a husband who was your equal, right? Well, I knew I couldn't beat you in an honest race, so I decided to—

ATALANTA: Cheat.

HIPPOMENES: Use my resources. That *should* make you happy. It was the only way anyone could beat you.

ATALANTA: Hmmm. I guess you're right. *(sigh)* Fine. I will be your wife—even though I find the whole thing demeaning.

HIPPOMENES: How about a kiss for the winner?

ATALANTA: Don't push it.

NARRATOR: Not long after the race Atalanta and Hippomenes were married.

HIPPOMENES: I love you, Atalanta!

ATALANTA: Good! Don't forget it either.

NARRATOR: In spite of her resistance, Atalanta had fallen in love as well. Once again Aphrodite appeared in Hippomenes' dreams.

APHRODITE: The apples worked perfectly! Now that you are her husband, it's time to make her suffer for all that haughtiness she showed you before. Show her who's boss!

HIPPOMENES: No. Atalanta is my partner in life.

APHRODITE: What? Partner? Don't you know how marriage is supposed to work? You're supposed to crush her spirit!

HIPPOMENES: Never! Her spirit is what I love most about her.

APHRODITE: You owe me that much!

HIPPOMENES: Sorry.

APHRODITE: (*to herself*) Oooooh. No one double-crosses me!

NARRATOR: Aphrodite determined right then and there to ruin the happiness of Hippomenes and Atalanta.

One day the happy couple went for a stroll in the countryside. A sudden rain caught them by surprise, and they were driven inside a temple to take shelter. In the darkness of the temple, they embraced.

HIPPOMENES: I love you! The greatest day of my life was when I won you for my wife!

ATALANTA: Hmmm. As much as I try to resist it...I guess I love you as well.

HIPPOMENES: Are you truly happy?

ATALANTA: (*thoughtfully*) My whole life I've tried to live wild and free. But, you know, sometimes wildness is lonely, and freedom can still feel like a cage. So, yes, I am happy.

NARRATOR: Meanwhile, up on Mount Olympus Aphrodite was consulting Zeus, Lord of the Gods.

APHRODITE: Zeus! I want you to punish a pair of young lovers for me.

ZEUS: Sounds like an ironic request from the Goddess of *Love*.

APHRODITE: Oh, they've earned my hate! Trust me!

ZEUS: And why should I punish them?

APHRODITE: Well...uh. They're incredibly happy...

ZEUS: And?

APHRODITE: And they're rubbing it in everybody's face.

ZEUS: (*sarcastically*) My goodness! We must put a stop to this!

APHRODITE: Really?

ZEUS: No. Now, if they had done something horrible—like desecrating one of my temples or something—that would be a different story.

APHRODITE: Actually, they're in one of your temples right now. On a completely unrelated topic, how exactly *would* a mortal desecrate your temple? I'm just asking.

ZEUS: Well, I certainly don't allow loud talking there—or murder. And definitely no embracing or romantic situations—if you know what I mean.

APHRODITE: Zeus doesn't allow romantic affairs to happen in his own temple? Who's being ironic now?

ZEUS: Just come back when you have an actual reason to punish these mortals.

APHRODITE: Well, don't look now, but those two mortals have decided to use your temple for a little romantic getaway!

NARRATOR: Aphrodite pointed down to where Hippomenes and Atalanta embraced.

ZEUS: What? Didn't they read the signs posted there? They shall pay dearly for this!

NARRATOR: Without another thought, Zeus struck. *(shazam!)*

A lion and a lioness emerged from Zeus' temple into the evening gloom. The great Lord of the Sky had transformed Hippomenes and Atalanta into these animal forms to separate them forever. For, as every Greek knows, lions do not marry.

Yet somehow these lions seemed different from the rest of their kind. At first they looked at one another with confused expressions. Then they drew near, nuzzled, and licked the other's cheek. Swishing their tails behind them, they sauntered off into the wilderness—side by side.

DISCUSSION QUESTIONS

- What do you think about Iasus, Atalanta's father? Is he a good father? Explain.
- Is it fair that Atalanta was tricked into marriage? Explain.
- Is Hippomenes a cheater? Does this make him an unlikeable character? Explain.
- Should Atalanta be angry at Hippomenes for cheating? Explain.
- Do you think this last portion of Atalanta's story complements or contradicts the other parts of her story? Explain.
- Would you risk *your* life to gain someone whom you loved? What about someone you love *and* a kingdom? Explain.
- Does Aphrodite have a good cause for wanting to punish Atalanta or Hippomenes? Explain.
- Does Zeus have a good cause for wanting to punish them? Explain.
- In the original ending of this myth the fact that Atalanta and Hippomenes are turned into lions separates them from one another forever. The ancient Greeks believed that lions could not mate with their own species but mated with leopards instead. This modified version of the myth alters that conclusion slightly to give the lovers a happier ending by implying that they stay together. Which ending do you prefer? Explain.
- Is it fitting that Atalanta ends her life as a wild animal? Explain.

THESEUS: THE ROAD TO ATHENS
TEACHER GUIDE

BACKGROUND

Heracles was by far the greatest Greek hero simply because no other hero came close to accomplishing as many amazing feats as he did. But his hometown was the city-state of Thebes, which held bragging rights over all the other city-states of Greece. "Heracles is from *our* town, not yours!" This tended to get under the skin of the other city-states.

Athens had their own hometown hero, Theseus, which wasn't too shabby. Theseus did defeat the Minotaur. But as Athens grew in power, the Athenians started to suffer from hero-envy. Sure, Theseus was great, but Heracles had the better résumé. The ultimate city-state deserved the ultimate hero. So the story of Theseus was "spruced up" to put the Athenian hero on the same level as the Theban Heracles.

Since Heracles was the son of Zeus, Poseidon was revealed to be Theseus' second father—in addition to his mortal father—a biological impossibility. They also added several episodes to Theseus' quest (before and after the Minotaur) such as battling supernatural thieves, capturing man-eating beasts, and descending into the Underworld. Many of these events mimicked the Twelve Labors of Heracles. Since Athens became committed to democracy, they also added the idea that it was Theseus who united the local city-states under the banner of Athens and then gave up his crown to make the city-state a democracy! For all of their trouble, Heracles still remained first in the eyes of the Greeks— or at least the non-Athenian Greeks. And Theseus? He placed a strong second.

SUMMARY

Sixteen-year-old Theseus has grown up in Troezen with no knowledge of his father's identity. One day his mother tells him that his father is Aegeus, the king of Athens, and before he left to accept his kingship, Aegeus buried his sword and sandals below a boulder. When Theseus is strong enough to lift the boulder, he may journey to Athens to be reunited with his father. Theseus lifts the boulder and retrieves the artifacts. His mother recommends that he go to Athens by ship. Instead Theseus decides to take the dangerous, sea-side road that is plagued by supernatural bandits.

On his way Theseus encounters Procrustes, a bandit who lays his victims upon his iron bed and hacks off whatever body parts hang over the edges. Theseus defeats him and then fits him to his own bed. Theseus also encounters Sinis the Pinebender, who ties his victims between two bent pine trees. Then he releases the trees, tearing his victims in half. Theseus defeats this bandit and subjects him to his own method of killing. The third bandit is Sciron, an old man who tricks travelers into helping him remove a thorn from his foot. When they are bent down, he kicks them off a cliff into the awaiting mouth of his pet sea turtle. Theseus falls for the bandit's trick, plummets into the sea, and uses his sword to wound the giant sea turtle. While he is underwater, he hears the voice of Poseidon, who declares that he is Theseus' second father (in addition to King Aegeus). Both of them visited the mother of Theseus on the same name—imbuing Theseus with attributes from both fathers. After hearing this information, Theseus returns to defeat Sciron and feeds him to his own turtle.

Theseus arrives in Athens and declares that he has cleared the sea-side road of all bandits. This entitles him to an audience with the king. King Aegeus is now married to Medea, the witch from the myth of Jason and the Argonauts. She has borne Aegeus a young son, whom she hopes to place on the throne. When Theseus arrives to feast with the king, Medea convinces Aegeus to poison the cup of Theseus, whom he has not recognized. Theseus rises to present a toast, and Aegeus recognizes his own sword slung at Theseus' side, realizes his son's true identity, and cries out for him not to drink. In anger Aegeus turns on Medea. Her plans thwarted, Medea flees Athens with her son.

The reunion between Theseus and his father is short-lived. Theseus has heard of the human sacrifices that Athens sends to King Minos, the King of Crete, every nine years. These captives are fed to the Minotaur, a half-human, half-bull creature Minos keeps in an enormous maze called the Labyrinth. Theseus declares that he will go as one of the sacrifices and defeat the monster. Aegeus reluctantly agrees and gives his son specific instructions to change the color of his ship's sails from black to white when he returns, so that Aegeus will know if he is successful.

ESSENTIAL QUESTIONS

- How important is strength?
- What are the different types of strength?

CONNECT

The Hunger Games **by Suzanne Collins** In this popular novel teenagers are selected by lottery to compete in a televised battle to the death. According to the author, the sacrificial youths in Theseus' myth and their fate in the Labyrinth inspired the plot of her novel.

ANTICIPATORY QUESTIONS

- What is the Minotaur?

- What is the Labyrinth?
- What are the different ways to define strength?
- How much impact do fathers have on their children's lives?

TEACHABLE TERMS

- **Pun** Theseus uses expressions such as "You've made your bed. Now lie in it!" (pg. 144), "Why don't you split?" (pg. 146), and "I hate it when people fall apart like that" (pg. 146) in a way that indicates two different meanings of the phrases.
- **Dialect** The street urchin on pg. 149 uses a dialect with phrases such as *ain't, don't know nothing,* and *nobody knows nothing.*
- **Xenia** On pg. 151 Theseus references the concept of Greek *xenia* (or "guest-friendship"), a code of conduct that required all guests to be treated with respect. Guests were not even required to identify themselves or state their business until after they were given hospitality.
- **Backstory** Medea is a character with a lengthy backstory, which is referenced through the dialogue on pg. 151. She was once the lover of the hero Jason. She bore him two sons and then later murdered those sons when Jason left her for another.
- **Foreshadowing** On pg. 153 Medea makes a prediction that Aegeus will die at the hands of his own son. How might this come about?

RECALL QUESTIONS

1. What task must Theseus perform to prove he is the son of Aegeus?
2. How does Sinis kill his victims?
3. Who is Theseus' "second father"?
4. To whom is King Aegeus married?
5. Theseus volunteers to do what in order to save the young people of Athens?

THESEUS: THE ROAD TO ATHENS

CAST

THESEUS	*Young Hero*
AETHRA	*Mother of Theseus*
PITTHEUS	*Grandfather of Theseus*
PROCRUSTES	*Otherworldly Bandit*
SINIS	*Otherworldly Bandit*
PERIGUNE	*Daughter of Sinis*
MAN/SCIRON	*Otherworldly Bandit*
POSEIDON	*God of the Seas*
SOLDIER	*Watchman of Athens*
AEGEUS	*King of Athens*
MEDEA	*Barbarian Witch*
OLD MAN	*Brokenhearted Father*
URCHIN	*Street Boy*

NARRATOR: Prince Theseus grew up in Troezen, a small, seaside city-state. His life was filled with many advantages—wealth, privilege, a loving mother and grandfather. Yet it had always lacked one thing—a father. As to the true identity of this mystery man, his mother spoke little. All she would say was…

AETHRA: Work hard, grow strong, and when you are strong enough, I will tell you of your father.

NARRATOR: It was not the answer Theseus wanted, but his mother was a stubborn woman. So he took her at her word and did just what she suggested. He became strong. He spent his days training—strengthening his body and his will.

THESEUS: One day the truth about my father will take me far away from this place. I can feel it.

NARRATOR: Theseus' old grandfather, the king of Troezen, laughed at his grandson's constant training.

PITTHEUS: All this is for nothing. *I* know who your father is. Your father is Poseidon—God of the Sea. Your mother went for a swim one day, and after that she was with child.

THESEUS: I think there's more to it. I think my father is a great hero, and someday I will go and meet him—wherever he is.

PITTHEUS: Nonsense! You'll stay here in Troezen and become the king after me. Here you'll be happy.

NARRATOR: When Theseus turned sixteen, he was a head taller than the other boys and much stouter. His mother saw that he was ready, and one morning she came to him with news in her eyes.

THESEUS: It's time, isn't it?

AETHRA: All these years I have kept your father's identity a secret from you. That is what he commanded me to do—before he went away.

THESEUS: Who is he? Grandfather says my father is the God of the Sea.

AETHRA: No, he is as mortal as you and me. He visited Troezen once—just for a short time—and left before you were born. He would have stayed longer, but he learned that his cousin had died—and he was the next in line to become the king of Athens.

THESEUS: *(in awe)* My father is Aegeus, the king of Athens?

AETHRA: Yes. Before he departed, he dug a hole on the high hill, and inside he placed his sandals and his sword. Then he used his great strength to push a boulder over that spot and seal it. He said that if you were truly his son, you would one day grow strong enough to move that boulder and discover your destiny. Your father is a man who values strength.

THESEUS: Apparently. What if I had been a weakling? Would he not want me for a son?

AETHRA: Since you are his son, he knew you could not be weak.

THESEUS: Perhaps I do not want to meet a father who puts such a condition on his love.

AETHRA: It is your choice. You may stay here in Troezen and inherit your grandfather's throne. It will be a boring life—but a safe one.

NARRATOR: Theseus looked up to the high hill.

THESEUS: Show me this boulder.

NARRATOR: It was a boulder that Theseus had passed many times during his boyhood—never guessing that the truth of his identity was hidden beneath it.

AETHRA: Today is the day that I have feared for many years. Either you will fail, and my heart will break for you—or you will succeed, and my heart will break for me.

THESEUS: *(determined)* I will not fail!

NARRATOR: Theseus seized the rock and strained against it with all his might. His muscles shuddered, and his bones ached, but at last the boulder began to budge. *(rumbling of a boulder)*

THESEUS: *(grunting)* Ergh!

NARRATOR: Then the rock shifted from the spot it had occupied for sixteen years. Panting from the exertion Theseus beheld what lay beneath—a hollow and within, a dust-covered sword and a pair of sandals.

THESEUS: *(cry of triumph)* I did it!

AETHRA: Behold! Your birthright!

NARRATOR: Theseus knelt and brushed the dust from the magnificent sword. The sandals were well-crafted and still supple after so many years.

AETHRA: You must go to your father now. He will recognize you as his son by this sword and these sandals. Athens lies across the gulf. You must sail there. That is the safest way.

THESEUS: I'll go by the coastline road.

AETHRA: Theseus, no! There are terrible killers along that path—butchers!

THESEUS: If I am to one day be the king of Athens, I will need to be a great hero. I will defeat these bandits and earn my reputation.

AETHRA: They are more than just bandits. They are demented, murderous men! Some even say that they are not even men at all—but dark creatures that have crept out of the Underworld to prey upon the living.

THESEUS: Mother, it cannot be as bad as all that.

AETHRA: You have not heard the stories that I have! One of the savages is Procrustes the Stretcher. He offers travelers a place to sleep—on his iron bed. But in the night, he makes his victims *fit* the bed. If you are too big, he chops off whatever hangs over the edge. If you are too short, he puts you on the rack and stretches you until you fit the bed perfectly.

THESEUS: Ha! A bed of death? *(sarcastically)* How frightening.

AETHRA: You should be frightened. Another bandit is called Sinis the Pinebender. He ambushes travelers and ties them between two trees he has bent to the ground. Then he releases the trees, and his victims are ripped in half.

THESEUS: Not to worry. A fool and his saplings do not intimidate me. If he challenges me, *he* shall be ripped in half.

AETHRA: *(sniffling)* I don't know what I will do. First, your father left and now you.

THESEUS: Mother, all will be fine. When I am a king and a great hero, I will send for you. We will see each other again. I'm sure of it.

NARRATOR: After a tearful goodbye Theseus departed. He struck out upon the coastline road. The first leg of his journey was uneventful. As twilight set in, the path grew rougher and led between looming rock walls. Dank caves opened out of the rock like black mouths, and out of them rose wisps of smoke and a foul smell.

THESEUS: Ugh. What is that smell?

PROCRUSTES: Death.

NARRATOR: The huge form of a man had appeared on the path before Theseus. His face was seamed with scars, and in his hand he carried a metal club.

THESEUS: I just want to pass peacefully.

PROCRUSTES: I only demand one thing from you.

THESEUS: What is that?

PROCRUSTES: Die! *(battlecry)*

NARRATOR: The bandit swung his club with incredible speed. Theseus ducked, and the strike missed his skull—barely—connecting instead with the rock wall behind him. *(shattering of rock)* Rubble flew in all directions.

PROCRUSTES: Argh! Curses!

NARRATOR: The bandit swung again—striking Theseus' sword and sending it flying out of his hand. *(clang)* Then the bandit palmed Theseus' head and bashed it roughly against the rock wall.

THESEUS: Ughn.

NARRATOR: The scar-faced thief seized up the stunned boy and began to drag him toward one of the larger caves.

PROCRUSTES: Heh heh! Care for a sleepover? I'm sure my bed will suit you. It is one-size-fits-all.

NARRATOR: Inside, the cave was littered with bones. The brute slammed Theseus down onto a blood-crusted, iron bed. *(metallic clang)*

PROCRUSTES: I may have to take a bit off the top, but you'll fit just fine.

NARRATOR: To his horror Theseus saw that his head and feet extended past the limits of the bed. Procrustes had noticed this too, and smiling a rotten smile, he seized up an enormous axe.

PROCRUSTES: Oh, I love having guests. I admit, I like the stretching more, but the hacking is fun, too. Nighty-night.

NARRATOR: Procrustes raised the axe above his head. As the axe-strike fell, Theseus darted from the bed, grabbed up a rock, and bashed the bandit brutally across the face. *(thwack)* Procrustes blinked but otherwise did not react. Then he roared with laughter.

PROCRUSTES: Ha! Ha! *(loud laughter)* You thought you would defeat Procrustes with a rock? *(laughter)*

THESEUS: Actually, that was just to distract you.

PROCRUSTES: Huh?

NARRATOR: With all his strength Theseus barreled into the bandit—knocking him backward—tripping him over the end of the iron bed.

PROCRUSTES: What? Huh? Argh!

(crashing sound)

NARRATOR: As Procrustes landed upon his own bed, Theseus seized up the villain's fallen axe.

THESEUS: You've made your bed. Now lie in it!

(snicker-snack)

NARRATOR: As it turned out Procrustes was a bit too big for his own bed—and he lost his head.

Some would have found it hard to sleep in the den of a mass murderer. But Theseus' day had exhausted him. He settled down in the cave of Procrustes and slept peacefully—even with the bandit's dismembered body dripping nearby.

The next morning Theseus journeyed on—not before retrieving his sword from the spot it had fallen the day before.

THESEUS: I must be more wary. These thieves are more than I bargained for.

NARRATOR: Soon enough the road moved more inland, leading Theseus into a dark grove of pine trees.

THESEUS: Mother spoke of one called the Pinebender. Any creature who can bend mighty pine trees to the ground must be a worthy adversary.

NARRATOR: The dark firs seemed to blot out the sun. Theseus drew his sword. *(shing)* He had not taken many more steps into the grove when the hairs upon the back of his neck suddenly stood up. Someone or something was behind him.

THESEUS: Here we go again.

NARRATOR: He spun around.

THESEUS: (*battlecry*) Argh!

PERIGUNE: (*cry of fright*) Ah!

NARRATOR: His sword was pointed right in the face of a frightened girl.

THESEUS: (*angrily*) It's not wise to sneak up on an armed warrior! Who are you? You could have been killed!

PERIGUNE: I am Perigune. I was trying to warn you—about my father!

THESEUS: Your father?

PERIGUNE: Sinis, the Pinebender! He does such horrible things to anyone who passes this way! Run while you still—

THESEUS: Still what?

NARRATOR: The girl's features were frozen in fright—her eyes fixed on something behind Theseus.

THESEUS: There's something horrible behind me, isn't there?

SINIS: (*creepy voice*) Yes.

NARRATOR: The boy spun around again. Towering over him was a shadowy man that seemed nearly as tall as the surrounding pines. Two red eyes burned where a face should be.

THESEUS: Okay. That's more like it.

SINIS: (*hiss*) Trespasser!

NARRATOR: As the girl darted for the underbrush, Sinis went for Theseus—clawing at him with his bony hands. Theseus dodged to the side and brought his sword down swiftly upon one of the large wrists, cutting it deeply.

SINIS: (*howl of pain*) Rargh! Now you have made me angry.

NARRATOR: Sinis seized Theseus by the throat and lifted him into the air.

SINIS: I'm going to enjoy watching you die.

THESEUS: You first! (*battlecry*)

NARRATOR: Theseus thrust his sword into the chest of his dark attacker.

SINIS: (*cry of pain*) Argh!

NARRATOR: But Sinis' grip did not loosen.

SINIS: Stab me all you want. You will not kill me that easily. I am born of Hades, and that is where I will send you now.

NARRATOR: Sinis seized Theseus' sword and flung it aside. (*clang*)

SINIS: Your death has been prepared.

NARRATOR: Sinis carried the struggling boy to the edge of the clearing, where a huge pine tree was bent over and staked down. Sinis dropped Theseus to the ground, where the boy wheezed for life.

THESEUS: (*gasping for breath*) Ughn. (*coughing*)

SINIS: Can you imagine feeling yourself torn in two different directions? If not, you might get used to the idea.

NARRATOR: Sinis picked up a rope that was attached to the top of a nearby pine. He wrapped the other end of the rope tightly around his arm.

SINIS: Now, behold my strength!

NARRATOR: With phenomenal strength, he began to inch the tree-top down toward the ground, looping the excess rope about his arm. *(creaking of the tree)*

SINIS: *(grunting)* Grrrr.

PERIGUNE: Father! No!

NARRATOR: The girl had appeared again.

SINIS: Hush up, girl! Tie this fool's arm to the bent pine. Hurry! I am bending down this one.

NARRATOR: She picked up the looped end of a rope that ran from the staked-down pine. She paused.

PERIGUNE: No! This is an evil thing you do! I won't help you any longer!

NARRATOR: Sinis trembled, the length of rope still curled around his arm, all his strength straining against the pine he had forced down almost to the ground.

SINIS: Do it now! This pine is ready. Put the loop about his arm.

NARRATOR: The girl threw down the rope and ran into the trees.

SINIS: Argh! Nothing is worse than teenagers! I'll deal with her later! Just as soon as I deal with you. *(shocked)* What? Where did he go?

NARRATOR: Theseus appeared at Sinis' side, furiously securing the end of the bent-pine rope around the thief's free arm.

SINIS: *(in shock)* What?

THESEUS: Why don't you split?

SINIS: Noo!

NARRATOR: With both of Sinis' arms now secured to either pine tree, Theseus kicked loose the stake that held the bent pine to the ground. *(sproing!)* Both pine trees shot upward. *(tearing sound)*

SINIS: *(hideous cry of pain)*

NARRATOR: Sinis was split into half, and the bits of him flew high into the air.

THESEUS: I just hate it when people fall apart like that.

NARRATOR: Theseus once again reclaimed his sword from where it had fallen.

THESEUS: I may need to tie this to my hand.

NARRATOR: A sniffling from the underbrush drew his attention. Perigune had hidden herself within the thicket. Theseus stooped and extended a friendly hand.

THESEUS: Come out. Do not be afraid.

NARRATOR: After much coaxing Perigune came forth from the bushes. She tearfully warned Theseus about the final bandit who lived along the road to Athens.

PERIGUNE: His name is Sciron. They say he feeds his victims to an enormous sea turtle that he keeps for a pet.

THESEUS: What is he like? Is he a clubber or a butcher or a pinebender?

PERIGUNE: No one knows. The turtle they have seen—glutting itself on the flesh of Sciron's victims—but no one has ever seen Sciron himself and lived to tell about it.

NARRATOR: Theseus spent that night in the pine grove—with pieces of Sinis still hanging from the treetops. The next morning he took his leave.

The road now climbed high and ran along the top of the sea cliffs. Theseus paused on the edge for a moment. The waves crashing below reminded him of his home. *(sounds of waves crashing)*

MAN: Be careful!

NARRATOR: Theseus jumped at the sudden voice. A plump, old man was sitting on a nearby rock.

MAN: I didn't mean to startle you. I'm just a traveler from Athens. But I wouldn't get too close to these cliffs. That's quite a drop!

THESEUS: What are you doing out here? Don't you know there's a murderous thief on this road?

MAN: *(in shock)* Oh dear! Are you serious? I better turn around then. I just had to stop here because I got a thorn in my foot! I hate thorns!

NARRATOR: The old man strained to reach down to his sandal, but his large belly prevented him.

MAN: *(grunting)* Errr. *(sigh)* It's no use. I'm a big eater—as you can see.

NARRATOR: Theseus looked hastily up and down the pathway. This bumbling old man was making him vulnerable to attack.

THESEUS: Here let me help you.

MAN: Oh, would you? What a nice young man!

NARRATOR: Theseus knelt before traveler and removed his sandal. The old man's toenails were strangely yellow and gnarled.

THESEUS: *(confused)* Sir? You are mistaken. There is no thorn in your foot.

NARRATOR: Theseus looked up. There was a peculiar light in the old man's eyes.

MAN: See you later, turtle-bait!

NARRATOR: The old man's leg shot out and kicked Theseus with the force of a bull. The kick sent the boy sprawling backward out over the edge of the cliff.

THESEUS: *(cry of fright)* Ahhhh!

NARRATOR: Theseus caught spinning glimpses of landscape as he fell—sky, sea, sky—and finally the sea again. *(loud splashing)* The foam surrounded him, and he sank down into darkness.

A sudden warmth revived him. He was still in the water, and his sword was floating before him. He reached out and grasped it.

Through the dimness of the sea, he saw a shadowy leviathan approaching. It swam with incredible speed, and opened its enormous mouth—the scaly, razor-sharp beak of a turtle—to claim the morsel it craved. Theseus stabbed upward, into the soft roof of the sea turtle's mouth, and its blood filled the water. *(underwater roar of pain)* The beast veered away into the depths.

Theseus started to swim toward the surface, but through the swirling blood, a sudden light appeared. His lungs were aching for air, but the light was warm, and it begged him to stay. Then Theseus found that somehow he could breath, and a voice spoke to his mind—a voice like crashing waters.

POSEIDON: I am Poseidon. Theseus, you are my son.

THESEUS: Son? Aegeus of Athens is my father.

POSEIDON: I am your father, too. We both visited your mother on the same night. My strength is in you, and it will allow you to do great things. It will send you across the sea— to Crete, a kingdom I have cursed. You will exact my revenge on the evil king there.

THESEUS: But I was sent to be reunited with my father—

POSEIDON: Go. Face your enemy who waits on the cliffs above and defeat him.

NARRATOR: Sciron the bandit had been scanning the seas ever since he sent his victim tumbling to his death. Much to his disappointment his pet sea turtle had not emerged with the mangled body of Theseus in her mouth.

SCIRON: *(grumbling)* Where's my girl? I wanted to see her pull him apart.

NARRATOR: Something exploded up from the waves in a geyser of water. *(sound of whooshing waters)* Sciron barely had time to scramble backwards before Theseus was

standing before him—brandishing his sword. He seized the villain by his collar.

SCIRON: Impossible! No son of a mortal could have defeated my darling pet!

NARRATOR: Theseus dragged the thief toward the cliff's edge.

THESEUS: That's because I'm not just the son of a mortal. I'm also the son of a god.

NARRATOR: Theseus brought his fingers to his lips and whistled. *(whistle)* Below the monster sea turtle had risen from the waves. It clicked its beak in hunger. *(hungry clicking of a turtle's beak)*

SCIRON: No! Bad girl! No! You will not eat Daddy!

THESEUS: Looks like you two have a dinner date.

NARRATOR: Theseus hurled the thief out over the cliff's edge.

SCIRON: *(cry)* Ahhhh! *(dying sounds)*

NARRATOR: Theseus continued along the coastline road. Soon Athens appeared on the horizon—its temples and palaces perched high on the Acropolis.

THESEUS: There it is! The kingdom of my father! Or the kingdom of one of my fathers anyway!

NARRATOR: Near the city there was a roadside guard station where a pair of bored soldiers stood watch. When the soldiers saw Theseus coming down the road, they jumped in shock.

SOLDIER: Boy! Where did you come from?

THESEUS: *(confused)* Down the road.

SOLDIER: What do you mean? You came down the coastline road?

THESEUS: Yes.

SOLDIER: And you weren't killed?

THESEUS: Not to my knowledge. No.

SOLDIER: No one travels that way anymore. There are bloodthirsty thieves along that road that ambush travelers.

THESEUS: Not anymore. They have been dealt with. I, Theseus of Troezen, have dispatched them.

SOLDIER: *(laugh)* You? You're barely old enough to shave.

THESEUS: Go see for yourself. You will find Procrustes fitted exactly to his bed—the halves of Sinis swaying silently from the treetops—and Sciron becoming a seafood snack.

NARRATOR: The soldiers looked at him in confusion.

THESEUS: Go ahead. Don't worry. It's perfectly safe now. When you see that I am correct, just remember my name—Theseus of Troezen.

NARRATOR: The soldiers, their mouths hanging open in wonder, watched the boy continue toward the city.

When Theseus arrived at Athens, he made his way toward the Acropolis. There a large crowd of mourners was gathered around a platform on which stood seven youths and seven maidens. *(wailing of the crowd)* An old man near Theseus was wailing and beating his head feebly with his fists.

THESEUS: What is the matter?

OLD MAN: *(crying)* My daughter is up there.

NARRATOR: He pointed to those standing on the platform.

THESEUS: Is she being sold as a slave?

OLD MAN: I wish she was a slave! That would be a kinder fate. Instead she will be meat for a monster.

NARRATOR: On Theseus' other side stood a young boy, a street urchin.

THESEUS: Boy, what does he mean? What is the meaning of all this sadness?

URCHIN: Athens is a sad place, mister. I ain't never seen it before, but every nine years there is a lottery, and if your number is drawn, you go to be killed.

THESEUS: Killed? By whom?

OLD MAN: *(ranting)* A demon! An abomination! A curse from the gods!

URCHIN: Don't you know nothing, mister? They send you to the island of Crete on a black-sailed ship and feed you to King Minos' monster.

THESEUS: What kind of monster?

URCHIN: Nobody knows nothing about it— except its name—the Minotaur.

THESEUS: That name means "the bull of Minos." But a bull would not eat human flesh. Hmmm. Your king, King Aegeus, allows this sacrifice to happen?

URCHIN: He ain't got no choice!

THESEUS: There is always a choice.

OLD MAN: (*numbly*) You do not know the power of King Minos. He is a son of Zeus. He controls the seas. He is a dangerous warlord.

THESEUS: I cannot believe that the king gives up these lives without a fight.

OLD MAN: What does it matter to him? It is not his sons or daughters going to their deaths. But my poor daughter is no great loss. (*weeping*)

NARRATOR: Theseus placed his hand on the weeping man's shoulder.

THESEUS: I do not know what I can do, but I will try to save the life of your daughter.

OLD MAN: All is lost. I must mourn now, but in time I will forget her.

NARRATOR: Theseus turned to the street urchin.

THESEUS: Boy, can you show me where I might spend the night? I will need a place to stay until I receive an invitation from the king.

URCHIN: Holy Hermes! The king? I know all about the king. My mom is one of the servants at the royal palace.

THESEUS: What is he like?

URCHIN: She says he's quiet mostly. His wife does most of the talking.

THESEUS: His wife? I did not know he was married!

URCHIN: You're really not from around here, are you? My mom calls her a *consort* but I guess that means "wife." Her name's Medea, and the rumor is she's a witch. They say she flew to Athens in a chariot pulled by dragons. Anyway, she has the king under a spell.

THESEUS: What kind of a spell?

URCHIN: They say the king used to be a big guy—like you—but since his witchy wife showed up, he's gotten all old and weak. They have a son together even.

THESEUS: A son! Hmmm.

URCHIN: Anyway, that's all I know. If you're meaning to head for the palace, just watch your step.

THESEUS: Thank you.

URCHIN: C'mon. I live over this way. It ain't much, but I'm willing to share.

NARRATOR: The urchin led Theseus to his humble home—nothing more than rough shelter on the back streets.

THESEUS: Thank you. I won't forget this. Maybe someday I can repay you. Maybe someday things will be different in Athens.

URCHIN: My mom has a saying—"Kings come and go, but nothing never changes."

THESEUS: Hmmm.

NARRATOR: A few days later as Theseus made his way through the city, he was stopped by a soldier—the one whom he had met outside Athens.

SOLDIER: Theseus, right? We have verified your story. There are no signs of the robbers along the coastline road. If you have killed those butchers, you are a hero!

THESEUS: I told you so.

SOLDIER: The king would like to meet you.

THESEUS: Then I accept his invitation.

NARRATOR: A few hours later Theseus was ushered into the dark banquet hall of the king. At the long table were seated many elderly, finely-dressed men—the nobles of Athens. At one end sat Aegeus, the old, shrunken king—Theseus' father. At the other end sat a regal woman adorned with exotic jewelry—obviously Medea, the king's consort. The king and his nobles continued to sip their soup while Medea addressed Theseus.

MEDEA: Welcome to the royal banquet hall, hero. We have heard so much about you. There is a special seat prepared just for you.

NARRATOR: Theseus was seated near his father. The old king did not greet him. Instead he eyed him with distrustful glances. Medea snapped her fingers at a sickly, young boy who sat by her side.

MEDEA: Sit up, Medus! Sit up!

NARRATOR: Theseus realized this must be the child of Medea and Aegeus that the urchin had spoken of.

MEDEA: There is a report that you have cleared the coastline road of the murderous bandits.

THESEUS: That is true.

MEDEA: It sounds like you must be quite a murderer yourself.

THESEUS: Is it murder to bring criminals to justice?

MEDEA: I'll ask the questions here. So why have you come to Athens? What do you want from us? Glory? Power? The throne?

NARRATOR: The king was glaring at Theseus with unconcealed hatred now.

THESEUS: I can tell you are not a Greek, Lady Medea. In our country it is rude to ask a guest his business before he has been treated with hospitality.

MEDEA: Fine. Keep your secrets. *(to her son)* Sit up! This is my son, Medus. He must learn his manners. One day he will be king here.

THESEUS: Is he your first child?

MEDEA: *(coldly)* No.

THESEUS: Are you not the same Medea who was brought back from Colchis by the famous hero, Jason?

NARRATOR: At the mention of Jason, Medea's eyes grew fiery.

THESEUS: I heard you *murdered* your two young sons.

MEDEA: *(slowly)* All kinds of lies are told about us foreigners. I suppose you've also heard that I am a witch.

(muttering from all the nobles)

MEDEA: *(yelling)* Silence!

NARRATOR: The hall once again grew silent. Then, for the first time, the king spoke.

AEGEUS: *(strangely)* Medea, my dear. We must treat this boy in the correct fashion. He is our guest.

MEDEA: Of course. Where *are* my manners? Perhaps Theseus would like a drink. He looks incredibly thirsty.

AEGEUS: *(strangely)* Yes, a drink!

NARRATOR: The old king motioned to the goblet before Theseus. Something bizarre was in their invitation, and Theseus did not trust it. Yet refusing a king's invitation was inhospitable—the sign of a criminal. Theseus took the cup into his hand—but instead of drinking, he stood.

THESEUS: I must thank you King Aegeus and Lady Medea for hosting me at this lovely banquet. I drink to your health.

NARRATOR: Theseus tipped his glass to the old king, but Aegeus was not meeting his glance. Instead he was staring wide-eyed at the sword hanging from Theseus' belt. Theseus lifted the cup to drink.

AEGEUS: *(yelling)* Stop!

MEDEA: Aegeus! You fool!

AEGEUS: Do not drink! The cup is poisoned.

(murmuring from the nobles)

MEDEA: Dear? What *are* you talking about? He's getting a little senile in his old age.

AEGEUS: *(to Theseus)* That sword! Where did you get that sword?

THESEUS: It was left for me—by my father.

NARRATOR: Aegeus' face lit up.

AEGEUS: *(breathlessly)* My son?

NARRATOR: Aegeus stood, tall and straight, and pointed his finger toward Medea.

AEGEUS: *(angrily)* You tried to make me murder my own son in cold blood! You did not tell me who he was! Yet you knew the whole time, didn't you?

MEDEA: Medus is your son! You wanted me to give you an heir—and I did!

AEGEUS: Medus? That weakling is a disgrace! Who even knows where he came from?

NARRATOR: Theseus stared in pity at the sickly boy. He remembered what it was like to be an unwanted son.

AEGEUS: I'm through with your lies! Theseus is my true son! He is my true strength!

MEDEA: Maybe he is your son, but I say he has come to kill you and take your throne! Be a man! Have the strength to put the knife to your own child—like I did!

AEGEUS: You are a murderous witch!

MEDEA: Watch your tone, Aegeus!

AEGEUS: Your hold over me has been broken! Guards! Arrest this woman and her child! Banish them from my kingdom!

NARRATOR: The guards, who had been accustomed to following Medea's orders instead of the king's, paused in confusion.

MEDEA: A curse on all of Athens! Aegeus, you will die for this. I say you will die at the hands of your own son!

AEGEUS: Seize them!

MEDEA: Don't bother! I'll show myself out!

NARRATOR: There was a flash of fire. (*shazam!*) Everyone within the hall recoiled from the blast. When the smoke cleared, Medea and Medus had vanished from Athens forever.

AEGEUS: Guards! Search the palace! Make sure that witch is truly gone.

NARRATOR: After the guards had reported that Medea had in fact vacated the palace, Aegeus turned to Theseus and clapped him on the shoulders.

AEGEUS: Thank you, my boy! The sight of you was enough to free me from that sorceress' spell. Now let's look at you! Ha! I can see much of myself in you. I knew you would be able to lift that boulder. You possess your father's strength—that's why.

THESEUS: King, there is something troubling me—

AEGEUS: You must call me *Father*. And don't worry. I will announce you as my heir as soon as possible. You will be king of Athens after me.

THESEUS: That is not what I'm worried about. Our people, the Athenians, are in pain. They are mourning the sacrifices to Crete.

AEGEUS: Oh. Has it been nine years already? Well, it can't be helped.

THESEUS: Can't be helped? Why not?

AEGEUS: Many years ago the son of King Minos came to Athens to compete in the annual games, but there was an accident, and he was killed while competing. Minos vowed to destroy Athens. All I could do was beg for mercy. Minos agreed to spare our city if I sent him these sacrifices.

THESEUS: Why did you not challenge him?

AEGEUS: No one goes against King Minos! No one! He is the Bull-King! A son of Zeus! He rules the seas with his mighty navy. To challenge him would be suicide.

THESEUS: Father, you just praised me for my strength—*your* strength. Why are we too weak to defend our own people?

AEGEUS: We are defending our own people by giving him these sacrifices.

THESEUS: Innocent lives?

AEGEUS: It's only every nine years.

THESEUS: I must go.

AEGEUS: What? You're leaving already? You just got here!

THESEUS: No. I must go to Crete. Make me one of the sacrifices.

AEGEUS: Out of the question! You are the son of the king. You are exempt from the lottery!

THESEUS: My people suffer, so I must suffer as well.

AEGEUS: No one knows what kind of horror the Minotaur is! All we know is that it gorges itself on human flesh! Not only that, but it lives in the Labyrinth—an enormous maze of passageways beneath Minos' palace. It makes a game toying with its victims before it picks them off one by one! I will not send you to such a fate!

THESEUS: I am sending myself! I will slay this beast or man or whatever it is—and bring Minos' reign of terror to an end.

AEGEUS: Please, my son. I admire your bravery, but reconsider! This quest will only end in death.

THESEUS: Then I shall join a long line of martyrs.

NARRATOR: Aegeus tried to dissuade his son, but Theseus was adamant. In the Athenian harbor the sacrificial ship was prepared—displaying the black sail of mourning. One of the sacrificial youths was released, for Theseus would take his place.

AEGEUS: That boy is lucky. You have saved him from certain death.

THESEUS: I will save them all from death before it is over.

NARRATOR: Aegeus smiled at his son.

AEGEUS: You are so sure of yourself. You are so sure of your strength. I was that way once.

NARRATOR: Aegeus grasped his chest.

AEGEUS: My old heart can barely take your leaving. I will pray that you are successful. I have told the captain of the ship to wait in Crete. Then if somehow you survive, you will have a way back to me. I will watch the seas every day for your return. I have included a white sail on the ship. If you indeed kill the Minotaur, change the sails of your ship from black to white. That way I will know from afar whether or not you have survived.

THESEUS: I'll come back to you, Father, and I won't forget.

NARRATOR: Theseus took his place among the sacrifices. The youths and maidens all had hollow eyes, filled with visions of their own doom. As the black-sailed ship navigated away from Athens, Theseus saw a figure standing upon the high cliffs. It was the king watching his departure.

DISCUSSION QUESTIONS

- The theme of strength and weakness runs through this story. How important is strength? Are there different types of strength presented in the story? Which characters are strong and which are weak? Explain.
- Is Aegeus a good father? Explain.
- Ancient Greeks believed that a person could have two fathers—such Theseus being both the son of Poseidon *and* Aegeus. How does Theseus have a mixture of immortal and mortal qualities?
- Which enemy presents the biggest challenge for Theseus? Explain.
- At the beginning of the story Theseus believes that discovering the identity of his father will be the key to his destiny? Is he right? Explain.
- What is noble about Theseus trying to save his people from King Minos?
- What do you think will happen in the second part of Theseus' story?

LOST IN THE LABYRINTH
TEACHER GUIDE

BACKGROUND

When archeologist Sir Arthur Evans discovered the remains of the palace of the historical King Minos on the island of Crete, his discovery shed new light on the myth of Theseus. The many rooms of the palace are connected by tight passageways with maze-like turns that often lead to unexpected or even secret rooms. It is believed that this disorienting architectural design is probably the inspiration for the mythic Labyrinth. Frescoes decorate the walls of the palace. These paintings show a society devoted to the divinity of the bull. One shows youths (sacrifices or maybe performers) leaping over the horns of a bull. Another is a portrait of a man wearing a bull mask—a possible inspiration for the half-bull, half-human Minotaur.

During the time that the myth was formed, Crete was a major military power in the Mediterranean, thanks to its superior navy. The Greeks, jealous of Crete's success, used their stories to paint the Cretans as blood-thirsty barbarians, who mated with animals and performed human sacrifices. At some point Crete lost its power and was subdued by mainland Greece. This defeat is reflected in the myth by Theseus' triumph over Minos.

SUMMARY

Ariadne is the daughter of Minos, the king of Crete. From her tutor, Daedalus, she learns how her father was cursed by Poseidon. The sea god presented the king with a bull, but Minos refused to sacrifice it back to him. Poseidon caused Minos' queen, Pasiphae, to mate with the bull. This union produced a half-human, half-bull child, the Minotaur. The creature is trapped in the Labyrinth, the maze beneath the palace.

When Ariadne is older, Minos makes her the Priestess of the Labyrinth, and Daedalus teaches her all of its secrets. Feeling sympathy for the Minotaur, Ariadne sneaks into the Labyrinth and tries to befriend it. She even teaches the beast its human name: Asterion.

Soon after this Ariadne's human brother is murdered by the Athenians, and Minos declares that a group of fourteen sacrifices must be sent from Athens to Crete every nine years. When the first sacrifices arrive, Minos commands Ariadne to feed them to the Minotaur. Ariadne tries to prevent the Minotaur from killing them—appealing to his human side, which she still believes to exist. After Ariadne fails and the monster even tries to attack her, she resigns herself to the fact that the Minotaur is truly a mindless beast.

Nine years pass, and once again sacrifices arrive in Crete. Among the sacrifices is a bold Athenian named Theseus, who claims to be a son of Poseidon. To test this claim Minos throws a ring into the sea and commands Theseus to fetch it. Theseus completes this task, and Ariadne is impressed by his bravery.

The night before Theseus will be let into the Labyrinth, Ariadne comes to him and proposes a bargain. If Theseus will take her away from Crete and make her his wife, she will give him the tools to defeat the Minotaur. Theseus agrees. Ariadne provides him with a crown of light and a spool of golden thread that, by her holding the other end, will lead him back to the entrance of the Labyrinth. She offers him a sword as well, but Theseus vows to face the monster weaponless.

Theseus makes his way into the Labyrinth, battles the Minotaur, and kills it with one of its own horns after it is severed from the monster's head. As the Minotaur lies dying, Ariadne arrives, and the beast bellows its own name and Ariadne's as well. Ariadne notices that in his lair the Minotaur has kept a bit of the blanket it had a child. Convinced that she was wrong to bring about the Minotaur's death, Ariadne begins to suffer a nervous breakdown. Theseus leads her away and frees the other captives. They drill holes in the Cretan ships and sail away in the black-sailed ship that brought them to Crete.

As they sail for Athens, Ariadne's actions grow stranger, and Theseus begins to doubt his decision to marry her. When the crew stops on the island of Naxos, Ariadne lies down to sleep, and Theseus leaves her behind. Stranded on Naxos, Ariadne is discovered by the god Dionysus, who makes her his wife.

With the cliffs of Athens in sight, Theseus sees his father standing upon the heights, waiting for his son's return. But Theseus has forgotten to change the color of his sails from black to white, and, believing Theseus to be dead by this signal, his father jumps to his death. Theseus becomes king of Athens. After many years of ruling, Theseus hands over control of Athens to the people and goes adventuring once again.

ESSENTIAL QUESTIONS

- What is it that makes us human?
- Is every person a beast deep down?

CONNECT

The King Must Die by **Mary Renault** This novel re-tells the myth of Theseus using historical explanations for the story's fantastic elements. Theseus travels to Crete, where he is forced to perform in the ring with live bulls and must face off against King Minos' dreaded general, the Minotaur.

ANTICIPATORY QUESTIONS

- Where is the island of Crete?
- Who is Daedalus?
- What request did King Aegeus ask of his son Theseus before they parted?
- What is the difference between a beast and a human?

TEACHABLE TERMS

- **Protagonist** On pg. 162, halfway through this story, the protagonist of the story switches from Ariadne to Theseus. What effect does this have on the story?
- **Theme** On pg. 159 Daedalus tells Ariadne, "Deep inside, men are no better than beasts." The theme of bestiality vs. humanity runs through this story. Examine which characters are beast-like and which are human. Is every person a beast deep down?
- **Character Motivation** On pg. 165 Ariadne asks Theseus to take her back to Athens with him. Examine her motivation: Is this because she loves him? Or is it because she wants to escape her life on Crete?
- **Theme** The theme of mazes and being trapped runs through this story. Examine which characters feel helpless and trapped.

RECALL QUESTIONS

1. What causes Ariadne to lose her sympathy for the Minotaur?
2. How does Theseus prove he is Poseidon's son?
3. What two items does Ariadne give to Theseus?
4. What happens to Ariadne?
5. What happens to King Aegeus?

LOST IN THE LABYRINTH

CAST

ARIADNE	*Princess of Crete*
MINOS	*King of Crete*
DAEDALUS	*Athenian Inventor*
MINOTAUR	*Half-Man, Half-Bull Monster*
THESEUS	*Athenian Hero*
GUARD	*Cretan Guard*
CAPTIVE	*Young Athenian*
CAPTAIN	*Captain of the Ship*

NARRATOR: Princess Ariadne grew up in the palace of Knossos, the capital city-state of Crete. The fearsome warlord, Minos the Bull-King, was her father, and her mother was the mad queen, Pasiphae. Ever since Ariadne could remember, her mother had been shut away from the rest of the royal family in a far wing of the palace. Her father was absent, too—in a different way—busy with plans of expanding his empire with his mighty navy.

As a girl, Ariadne would spend hours wandering the maze-like corridors of the palace, gazing at the vibrantly painted frescoes. Her favorite one depicted a woman riding on the back of a white bull in the middle of the blue sea. One day while she gazed upon it, her father put in a rare appearance.

MINOS: This picture is a favorite of mine as well. Did you know our family is descended from the gods?

ARIADNE: You are the son of Zeus, and my mother is the daughter of Helios. But who is the woman in the picture?

MINOS: That is my mother, Europa. She once lived among the barbarian Greeks. The bull is Zeus. He pretended to be a tame bull and tricked Europa into climbing onto his back. Then he dived into the sea and swam all the way here to our island. Here, on Crete, he made her his wife. That is why we hold the bull to be sacred above all beasts.

NARRATOR: Ariadne could not remember a time when her father had spoken so much to her. She plucked up the courage to ask him another question that had always puzzled her.

ARIADNE: At night I hear a noise. It sounds like something moving beneath the palace floor.

MINOS: Rats. All palaces have them.

ARIADNE: No, it's something else— something big. Sometimes it bellows and shakes the foundations of the palace, and sometimes it just moans.

MINOS: It is nothing.

ARIADNE: Mother says it is a monster.

MINOS: (*suddenly angry*) Your mother is mad. You know that! I forbid you to speak to her any more on this subject!

ARIADNE: But, Father! I—

MINOS: (*harshly*) I have spoken! (*calming*) Don't worry. You will find out the truth soon enough.

NARRATOR: The next day, Ariadne sat in a lesson with her tutor, Daedalus. He had once been an inventor in Athens before he came to Crete.

ARIADNE: Tell me about the monster that lives under the palace.

NARRATOR: Daedalus was tinkering with some invention as he always did.

DAEDALUS: Hmmm. What?

ARIADNE: The sound under the floors. Surely you've heard it! My mother says it's a monster.

DAEDALUS: (*dry chuckle*) Heh. She would know.

ARIADNE: My father hired you to teach me, right? I'm asking you a question! He will be angry with you if you refuse to tell me.

DAEDALUS: Trust me. He wants me to keep this secret from you. And, boy, is it ever a juicy secret!

ARIADNE: Hmph!

DAEDALUS: (*sigh*) Look. When you are old enough, you will become the priestess, and you will know everything you need to know.

ARIADNE: Priestess?

DAEDALUS: Why else would your father waste education on a girl? *You* will be the keeper of your father's greatest secret. You will be the Priestess of the Labyrinth.

ARIADNE: The Labyrinth?

DAEDALUS: I've said too much. Just be patient. Soon you will know all the secrets, and then you'll be like me—and wish you didn't know.

NARRATOR: This conversation only deepened Ariadne's curiosity. At night she would place her ear against the floor and listen. The strange sound would begin with a shuffling and then progress to a clacking of hooves and a snorting cry—half roar, half moan. To her it sounded sad.

Years passed in this manner, and finally it was announced that Ariadne was old enough to become the Priestess of the Labyrinth.

DAEDALUS: It is my unfortunate duty to fill you in on all of the royal family's dirty secrets. Below this palace is the Labyrinth, a complicated maze of passageways filled with all kinds of traps that mean instant death for the uninitiated.

ARIADNE: Amazing!

DAEDALUS: Yes, actually it is. It is my greatest work. Unfortunately, it is also what has trapped me here. Since I know its secrets, I can never go free.

ARIADNE: I am sorry.

DAEDALUS: Don't be. Once I teach you all I know, you will be just as trapped as I am. Neither of us shall ever leave Crete.

ARIADNE: Why would I ever want to leave Crete?

DAEDALUS: (dry chuckle) Heh. I have not told you what lives in the Labyrinth.

ARIADNE: The monster!

DAEDALUS: Yes, a monster—a creature with the body of a man and the head of a bull. The Minotaur he is called—"the bull of Minos."

ARIADNE: How did he come to be there?

DAEDALUS: Years ago, a white bull walked right out of the sea. It was a present to your father from the sea god, Poseidon.

ARIADNE: Like the one who took Europa!

DAEDALUS: Exactly. Only Poseidon commanded your father to sacrifice this bull back to him. Instead your father kept the bull among his herds. This enraged Poseidon, so he polluted the mind of your mother.

ARIADNE: That is why she is mad!

DAEDALUS: No, that came later. Poseidon infected her with an unnatural passion. It led her into the fields—to the white bull. It is not proper for me to tell you more. Needless to say, the Minotaur is your half-brother. Your mother went mad after the birth of the beast. At times she could not bear to look at her bull-baby. Other times she would hold it lovingly upon her lap and call it Asterion, her "shining one." It was all very bizarre.

ARIADNE: And now he is trapped down there?

DAEDALUS: As he should be. He is a beast.

ARIADNE: You said that he was half-man!

DAEDALUS: What good is that? Deep inside, men are no better than beasts. I am ashamed of the part I played in all this. I was seduced by your father's riches. When he found out about the Minotaur, he commissioned me to build a maze—one from which the beast could never escape.

ARIADNE: And I must be a part of this, too?

DAEDALUS: See? You want to leave now, don't you? Of course, you will be part of it. You are the Priestess of the Labyrinth. Your duty is to guard its mysteries and make sure the Minotaur is forever trapped.

NARRATOR: Daedalus held up the latest invention he had been toying with. It was a crown that glowed with a green light.

DAEDALUS: Here you are. If you ever dare to venture into the Labyrinth, wear this.

ARIADNE: I must go into that terrible place? Is there some kind of map?

DAEDALUS: The map exists only here.

NARRATOR: Daedalus tapped his head.

DAEDALUS: Not even Minos knows the way. Nor does he want to know. Although he would love to destroy the Minotaur, the symbol of his shame, he is terrified of it. He, like the rest of us, is trapped.

NARRATOR: From Daedalus Ariadne learned her priestess duties and the secrets of the Labyrinth—its twistings and turnings—its branching hallways, dead-ends, and pitfalls. Then soon after that Daedalus simply disappeared, and no one at the palace ever mentioned his name again. As for the Minotaur, instead of hatred or fear, Ariadne felt pity for it.

ARIADNE: *(to herself)* Daedalus said that deep inside every man is a beast. But what if deep inside this beast, there is man? I must know!

NARRATOR: One night, Ariadne stole a plate of food from the palace kitchen and snuck down to the secret passageway that led into the Labyrinth. She touched a spiral wall-etching, and the design began to spin and sink inward. *(sliding of a door)* A small hatch, designed barely large enough for a human to enter, opened at her feet. A musty smell came from within.

ARIADNE: If I die, at least the secrets of the Labyrinth will die with me.

NARRATOR: Ariadne crawled into the stuffy passageway, and the hatch closed behind her. She was in the Labyrinth. Her glowing crown lit the few feet of passageway before her.

ARIADNE: Hello?

NARRATOR: At first all that could be heard was the skittering of rats. Then Ariadne heard the sound of heavy hooves upon stone. *(bellow of the Minotaur)* A pair of glowing eyes appeared from the gloom—followed by a looming figure whose horns nearly scraped the tunnel-roof.

ARIADNE: *(to herself)* It's not a beast. It's my brother. *(to the Minotaur)* I am Ariadne—your sister. I am a friend.

NARRATOR: Keeping her eyes upon the beast, Ariadne placed the platter of food carefully upon the floor. Her free hand she rested on the door-trigger.

ARIADNE: Here! I brought you this food.

NARRATOR: Just then the beast bellowed and lunged toward her. *(bellow of the Minotaur)* Ariadne screamed, fumbling for the wall-switch and opening the hatch.

Seconds later, safely back on the other side of the wall, Ariadne heard the beast ravenously devouring the food she had left behind. *(slurping and smacking sounds)* She calmed her shaky nerves.

ARIADNE: He has been treated like a beast his entire life. He does not know any better. I will try again.

NARRATOR: Each time Ariadne visited the Minotaur, she brought food and attempted to speak to it, but its beastliness would always cause her to flee. Then one night instead of diving after the food, the beast hunched down and met her gaze. For a moment its eyes looked almost human.

ARIADNE: I am Ariadne. I am your sister. You are Asterion. You have been treated cruelly, but I am your friend.

(curious moan of the Minotaur)

NARRATOR: The princess slid the platter of food across the tunnel floor. The Minotaur lowered its head to eat—all the while keeping its eyes on Ariadne.

ARIADNE: I have come here to teach you that you are a not a beast. You are a man.

NARRATOR: She laid her hand on her chest.

ARIADNE: *(slowly)* Ariadne.

NARRATOR: Then she motioned to the beast.

ARIADNE: *(slowly)* Asterion.

NARRATOR: Each time she visited the Minotaur, Ariadne tried to teach it these two simple things. It took many months, but finally one day the beast spoke its name—after a fashion.

MINOTAUR: *(beastlike)* Assssteeeeriiiion.

ARIADNE: Very good! I knew you were not just a beast! I don't know how, but I will show my father! And he will free you!

NARRATOR: But that would never be. It happened that Ariadne's brother, Androgeos, journeyed across the sea to the annual games in Athens. While there, he was ambushed and killed by the Athenians. Minos, fueled into a fiery rage, sailed to Athens to burn it to the ground. Yet when he returned, Athens still stood—and in his ship he carried seven boys and seven girls, captives from Athens.

ARIADNE: Father, have you avenged my brother's death? Have you destroyed Athens?

MINOS: I have done something better. I have broken its spirit.

ARIADNE: Who are these captives?

MINOS: They are sacrifices. I have found a use for my monster and its maze. You shall feed them to the beast. Every nine years the young of Athens will be meat for the monster.

ARIADNE: Father, no! That is cannibalism!

MINOS: It is not cannibalism for a beast to eat a man!

ARIADNE: Asterion is not a beast!

MINOS: *(yelling)* That name will never be spoken again!

ARIADNE: *(weeping)* Please, Father! Do not make me do this thing!

MINOS: You will do as you are commanded!

NARRATOR: There was nothing Ariadne could do to defy her father.

MINOS: Guards, take these Athenian captives to the Labyrinth immediately! The priestess will open the Labyrinth, and the monster will feed.

NARRATOR: As the captives were led to the entrance of the Labyrinth, Ariadne's mind was racing. Somehow she must accompany the captives into the maze and reach Asterion first—to explain this to him. If the captives remained unharmed, her father would see that Asterion was not a beast.

Ariadne did her duty and opened the passage into the Labyrinth, and the guards shoved the captives into the darkness. But Ariadne followed quickly behind them.

GUARD: Princess! It is not safe!

ARIADNE: Leave me alone!

(hungry bellow of the Minotaur)

CAPTIVE: *(frightened)* What is that?

NARRATOR: Ariadne turned to the frightened boys and girls.

ARIADNE: You have nothing to fear if you do what I say. Stay here! Do not move from this spot!

NARRATOR: Ariadne raced through the passageways—searching for her brother.

ARIADNE: Asterion! Asterion!

NARRATOR: She reached the central hub of the Labyrinth. The Minotaur was not there. Then a horrible sound reached her ears. *(Minotaur roar, dying cries from the captives)* The Minotaur had found the captives.

ARIADNE: *(yelling)* No!

NARRATOR: When Ariadne finally made her way back the entrance, she witnessed a grisly mess of gored bodies. The Minotaur was already feasting on some of the captives.

ARIADNE: *(weeping)* No! Asterion! No!

NARRATOR: The Minotaur looked up—its jowls dripping with blood. The human look in its eyes had faded. A look of blood-lust was there instead. It charged toward her. *(Minotaur roar)*

ARIADNE: Nooo!

NARRATOR: Ariadne bolted—the Minotaur in pursuit. She barely found the wall switch in time to escape.

Safely outside the Labyrinth, Ariadne sank to the floor and wept. The beast pounded against the door. *(booming and growling)* Ariadne sat and listened as the beast hunted down the remaining captives throughout the maze.

CAPTIVE: *(faraway dying sounds)* Ahh!

NARRATOR: Then all sound ceased completely. Ariadne wanted to flee—leave her home forever. Then it broke in upon her—she was trapped—just like the Minotaur.

MINOS: Are they all dead?

ARIADNE: Yes.

MINOS: Do you still call it cannibalism?

ARIADNE: That *thing* down there is a beast—and I was foolish to think otherwise.

MINOS: Yes, you were. But now you have learned your lesson. There are beasts, and there are men in the world.

NARRATOR: Something of Ariadne's soul was lost in the Labyrinth that night. From then on she did her duty heartlessly, sacrificing Minos' enemies to his monster.

Nine years passed. The black-sailed ship once again arrived from Athens. Unbeknownst to the Cretan royal family, one of the sacrifices was an Athenian prince, Theseus.

Theseus had experienced many adventures and proved himself to be a great hero. Now he had come to Crete to slay the creature called the Minotaur and save his people from the oppression of Minos. He had no idea how he was going to accomplish this, but he did not doubt that he could do it.

Theseus and the other captives sat with blank faces as the black-sailed ship pulled into port. Cretan guards bearing the symbol of the Bull-King came aboard and bound the sacrifices before escorting them from the boat.

GUARD: Come on, you Greek scum!

NARRATOR: A crowd of Cretans had gathered at the port to see the arrival of the captives. Sitting upon a platform was a large man wearing a horned crown. The captives were led before him.

THESEUS: *(to himself)* This must be the mighty King Minos!

GUARD: Silence!

NARRATOR: The guard struck Theseus across the mouth.

MINOS: Miserable Greeks, your king has offered up your meaningless lives as a tribute to Crete! You shall be meat for my monster—the Minotaur.

NARRATOR: Several of the captives began to weep in fright. *(weeping sounds)*

MINOS: Rest in the knowledge that your sacrifice will spare your cowardly city for another nine years. Where is the Priestess of the Labyrinth?

NARRATOR: A girl about Theseus' age stepped forward wearing ceremonial robes. It was Ariadne. She raised her arms in a grand gesture.

ARIADNE: Tomorrow you shall enter the Labyrinth, and it shall claim you. Bring the captives forward for inspection!

NARRATOR: One of the captives, a stunning Greek girl, caught Minos' eye.

MINOS: My, my. What a beauty! She should not have to spend the night in the dungeon. Perhaps she would like to stay in the king's chambers.

NARRATOR: Minos touched his hand to the young girl's face, and she shied away.

THESEUS: Leave her alone!

MINOS: Who said that?

NARRATOR: Theseus faced the Bull-King boldly.

THESEUS: I did. This girl may be your prisoner, but she is not your harlot! Leave her alone!

MINOS: How dare you speak to me in such a way! I am the son of Zeus!

THESEUS: And *I* am the son of Poseidon.

(murmuring of the crowd)

NARRATOR: A sudden fear came into Minos' eyes. More than any other god he feared Poseidon.

MINOS: *(laugh)* A son of Poseidon? What proof do you have?

THESEUS: I could ask you the same question. You claim that your mother was visited by Zeus in the form of a bull. Perhaps that is a lie. Maybe she just got a little too friendly with the livestock!

MINOS: Why you—! *(calming)* Very well. *(shouting)* Almighty Zeus! Father! Show this upstart that I am your son!

NARRATOR: Although the sky was perfectly clear, a thunderbolt sliced across the heavens. *(shazam!)* Minos turned to Theseus with a satisfied smile.

MINOS: What further proof could you need? Now, it is your turn. Prove that you are the son of Poseidon.

NARRATOR: Minos removed his royal ring from his finger and handed it to his guard.

MINOS: *(to the guard)* Fling this into the deepest part of the harbor.

NARRATOR: The guard hurried to carry out his king's command.

MINOS: Now, if you are the son of Poseidon, you can surely retrieve that ring from the bottom of the sea for me. *(chuckling)*

THESEUS: I can. Loose my bonds.

NARRATOR: As the guards freed him, Theseus noticed that Ariadne was staring at him. Her face was emotionless, but her eyes were dancing.

THESEUS: I will return with your ring.

NARRATOR: Theseus ran to the edge of the Cretan dock and dived into the sea. Everyone waited for many minutes, but the boy did not resurface.

ARIADNE: Father! You should not have let him go! He's escaped.

MINOS: Don't worry. He is dead. No mortal could survive so long underwater.

ARIADNE: Perhaps he *is* the son of Poseidon.

MINOS: Ha!

NARRATOR: A sudden spray of water drew their attention. *(splashing of water)* Theseus stood upon the end of the dock—his clothes perfectly dry. *(murmuring of the crowd)* Theseus approached Minos and flung the ring up into his face.

THESEUS: Here is your ring! And I bring a message from my father—do not challenge him again! Your reign of terror is over!

MINOS: Grrrr! Take them away!

NARRATOR: The guards ushered the captives away. Ariadne's eyes followed Theseus. A corner had turned in her mind. She saw something in Theseus—a way out of Crete, a way out of the labyrinth of life that she had come to loathe.

MINOS: That boy made a fool of me! I want him dead! I want the Minotaur to mutilate his body, and I will send it back to Athens in pieces! No one mocks me!

ARIADNE: The boy is very brave. He could have swum away, but he did not.

MINOS: Do not defend him!

ARIADNE: I wasn't.

MINOS: Tomorrow he will die.

ARIADNE: *(to herself)* Not if I can help it.

NARRATOR: That night Ariadne visited Theseus in the dungeon of Knossos.

ARIADNE: Psst. Boy, are you awake?

THESEUS: Of course. What are you doing here? Aren't you the witch of the Labyrinth?

ARIADNE: I am the *Priestess* of the Labyrinth. But I have a name. I am Ariadne. I can help you escape.

THESEUS: I do not wish to escape. I came here to slay the Minotaur—whatever it is.

ARIADNE: It is a half-bull, half-man creature—the offspring of my mother and a bull.

THESEUS: Talk about a dirty family secret. So this thing is your brother?

ARIADNE: It is no brother of mine! It is a murderous beast! If you are determined to fight it, I will help you defeat it!

THESEUS: So why would *you* help *me*?

ARIADNE: I have my reasons. But you must do something for me in return.

THESEUS: What could I do for you?

NARRATOR: The girl's deathly cold hand reached through the bars and grasped his.

ARIADNE: You can give me a life—a life away from this madhouse. I cannot explain it, but from the moment I saw you, I loved you. I'll free you from your cell and tell you how to reach the Labyrinth's center. That's the monster's lair. But you must swear to take me with you—back to Athens—and make me your wife.

NARRATOR: Theseus knew there was no other way for him to navigate the perilous maze, and the girl *was* beautiful.

THESEUS: I swear.

NARRATOR: That was all Ariadne needed to hear. She summoned the guards and had them release Theseus. Then she led him through the winding halls of the palace.

ARIADNE: The entrance to the Labyrinth is here. I have some items that will help you slay the beast.

NARRATOR: From her cloak she drew forth a crown that emitted an odd green glow.

ARIADNE: Here is a treasure given to me by Daedalus the craftsman. It will light your way.

NARRATOR: She placed the crown on Theseus' noble head.

ARIADNE: And, secondly, a sword. It's nothing fancy. I stole it from the armory.

THESEUS: No. The Minotaur does not fight with a weapon. So neither will I.

ARIADNE: Then you will die. I have seen this beast. He will rip you apart.

THESEUS: When Minos sees that I have beaten his Minotaur with only my bare hands, he will truly fear me and my homeland.

ARIADNE: You are right. (pause) Most of all, you will need this.

NARRATOR: Ariadne held up a spool of glittering thread.

THESEUS: Thread?

ARIADNE: Because of the Labyrinth's design, all paths lead to its center, but it is nearly impossible to find your way back. This string will lead you back—to me.

NARRATOR: She placed the thread tenderly into his hand.

ARIADNE: I will hold one end, and you will hold the other.

THESEUS: Thank you. You are giving me so much, but I have nothing to give you.

ARIADNE: If you take me from this place, you will give me everything.

NARRATOR: Ariadne touched the wall-trigger, the hatch opened, and the stagnant air of the Labyrinth filled their noses. Ariadne leaned forward and kissed Theseus.

ARIADNE: Don't fail me.

NARRATOR: Without hesitation Theseus crawled into the Labyrinth. He tied his end of

Ariadne's thread about his wrist, adjusted his crown of light, and walked warily into the darkness.

The passageways seemed to run straight ahead, but as he walked, Theseus sensed a curve in their path. The Labyrinth formed an enormous spiraling web of passageways. Some paths led to dead-ends. Some led to deep drop-offs—pits of no return. Some curved back on themselves.

THESEUS: *(to himself)* I have to watch my step.

NARRATOR: It might have been some trick of the echo, but as Theseus journeyed through the darkness, he thought he heard soft footsteps behind him. When he would stop, the footsteps would stop as well.

THESEUS: *(to himself)* It must be my imagination.

NARRATOR: Theseus entered a large circular chamber where passageways entered from all directions. He knew it was the heart of the Labyrinth—the creature's lair. A large pile of bones and rags occupied the center of the room. On the top was a ragged bit of silk. It looked like the blanket of a child. *(Minotaur roar)*

The bellow of the Minotaur shook the walls. Theseus spun in the midst of the room, scanning the blank doorways, sensing an attack, but unsure from which direction it would come.

There was a sudden snorting, rushing sound, and Theseus turned just in time to see the Minotaur bearing down on him—its horns lowered for an attack. A horn gored Theseus in the thigh, and he was thrown across the room by a fling of the monster's muscular neck.

THESEUS: *(cry of pain)* Ah!

NARRATOR: Theseus painfully rose, facing his monstrous opponent. The Minotaur pawed the ground, snorting and throwing its head from side to side. Its horn dripped with Theseus' blood. With incredible speed it lowered its head and charged again. *(Minotaur roar)*

Theseus waited for the perfect moment—the moment when the creature would be unable to reverse its momentum—and then he sprang to the side. The beast rammed directly into the wall behind him—burying its horns into the stonework. *(tremendous crash)*

MINOTAUR: *(roaring)* Argh.

NARRATOR: The monster grunted, thrashing about trying to wrench itself loose from the wall. Theseus grasped one of the thick horns and brought his elbow down hard upon it. *(cracking of bone)* Now in his hand Theseus held the severed horn of the Minotaur.

Stonework flew through the air as the Minotaur tore itself loose. Blood was oozing from its horn-stump. Theseus held up the missing horn.

THESEUS: Looking for this? Come and get it.

NARRATOR: The Minotaur lowered its remaining horn and charged again. *(snorting and charging sound)* Theseus bent his knees and braced himself. He remembered the long hours he had spent wrestling back in Athens. He knew how to throw an opponent many times his size. As the Minotaur charged toward him, Theseus ducked under its head, caught ahold of the monstrous chest, and pushed upward with all his might.

MINOTAUR: *(confused roar)*

NARRATOR: The monster flipped over Theseus and landed in a heap behind him. He sprang upon the beast and forced its enormous head to the side. Then he plunged the severed horn into the monster's neck. *(frightful bellow)*

THESEUS: Athens is avenged!

NARRATOR: Theseus sprang away. The wound gushed, and the Minotaur tried to rise—but fell back to the floor. *(dying sounds from the Minotaur)* Its blood pooled around it. Although the Minotaur could not rise, it dragged itself across the floor to its nest and placed its head upon the tiny, silken blanket.

ARIADNE: You have done it.

NARRATOR: Theseus turned in shock. Ariadne was standing in one of the chamber doorways.

THESEUS: Ariadne, what are you doing here? You could have been killed.

ARIADNE: *(strangely)* I came to see him die. He chose to live like a beast, so I came to see him die like one.

NARRATOR: The Minotaur's head lifted a bit, and its dimming eyes locked onto its sister.

MINOTAUR: *(slowly)* Arrriaaadneee.

NARRATOR: With a feeble gesture from its final ounce of strength, the beast pointed toward itself.

MINOTAUR: Asssteeerion.

NARRATOR: Then the light went out of its eyes. Ariadne burst into tears.

ARIADNE: *(weeping)* What have I done? I thought he would die like a beast!

THESEUS: What are you talking about?

NARRATOR: Ariadne knelt and lifted the bloodstained bit of silk.

ARIADNE: He knew! This is the blanket he had as a child. I have done wrong! I have helped you murder an innocent being! My brother!

THESEUS: Innocent being? He was a killer. And you said you wanted the beast dead!

ARIADNE: Beast? He's not the beast! *I'm* the beast! All I wanted was to leave this place. But I killed him to free myself.

THESEUS: *(annoyed)* There is no time for this. Your father will find you here and kill you! He'll know you've betrayed him.

NARRATOR: Ariadne did not respond. All she could do was stare at the fallen form of the Minotaur.

THESEUS: *(forcefully)* You must pull yourself together! What's done is done!

NARRATOR: Ariadne nodded. They followed the golden thread back through the curves of the Labyrinth to the entrance where Ariadne had tied it off.

Theseus freed the other Athenian captives, and they made their way to the port of Crete. The black-sailed ship was still moored there.

CAPTAIN: I cannot believe you survived! We must hurry! Minos' fleet will soon follow after us!

THESEUS: No, it will not. We drilled holes in the hulls of his ships. The power of Minos is broken. Never again will he plague the city-states of Greece.

NARRATOR: Theseus displayed the severed horn of the Minotaur to his comrades.

THESEUS: I have slain the beast!

ARIADNE: *(strangely)* No. The beast still lives—within us.

NARRATOR: The captain of the ship nodded toward Ariadne.

CAPTAIN: Who is this? A prisoner?

THESEUS: A guest.

NARRATOR: The ship pulled out to sea. As the sun rose, Ariadne stood at the railing watching her island home fade into the distance.

THESEUS: I appreciate what you have sacrificed for me. You will be welcomed in Athens.

ARIADNE: *(numbly)* Will I? Or will Athens just be another prison for me?

THESEUS: It will be what you make of it.

ARIADNE: I cannot see anything but him dying before me.

THESEUS: You must put these memories out of your mind.

ARIADNE: I cannot.

NARRATOR: On the journey back to Athens, the ship pulled in close to the island of Naxos for the passengers to take a rest from the unforgiving sun. Ariadne lay down under the shade of a bush and slept. Theseus sat watch nearby.

ARIADNE: *(in her sleep)* Asterion! No!

NARRATOR: Theseus tried to imagine this tormented girl as his bride. She was the daughter of Athens' greatest enemy—the sister of a monster. What would the people say? He imagined her wandering the royal hallways, haunted by the ghosts of her past, trapped in a labyrinth all her own. The ship's captain interrupted his thoughts.

CAPTAIN: Theseus, the tide is with us. It's time to sail on.

NARRATOR: Theseus looked at Ariadne. She had calmed. She seemed finally at peace. He stood and walked away. The ship pulled out to sea again without the princess. No one questioned this.

THESEUS: I pray that some god will take pity on her and give her what I cannot.

NARRATOR: Some said that when Ariadne awoke to find herself abandoned on that island, she wept out her life. Other said that the god Dionysus found her there, dried her tears, and spirited her away to make her his wife.

The rest of the voyage, Theseus could think of nothing but Ariadne. He knew she could not find happiness in Athens. But had he done the right thing?

CAPTAIN: There are the cliffs! We are home!

NARRATOR: The cliffs of Greece had come into view—the same cliffs where Theseus' father, King Aegeus, had promised he would stand watch.

CAPTAIN: There is your father!

NARRATOR: This drew Theseus from his contemplation.

THESEUS: You are right.

NARRATOR: A figure, dressed in royal purple, stood upon the cliffs. Theseus raised his hand to hail him. But as he did, the figure pitched forward, plummeting down into the sea.

THESEUS: *(crying out)* Father! No!

NARRATOR: It was only then that Theseus remembered his promise. He had vowed to change his sails from black to white as a signal of his survival. Thinking his son and heir had perished, King Aegeus had jumped to his death.

While Athens mourned the death of their king, they also rejoiced that Theseus had returned the captives safely and broken the power of Minos. Theseus at last became the king of Athens.

Years passed, and Theseus learned that he did not enjoy kingship. He saw the evils within it. He saw how power can turn men into beasts. He remembered the cruel tyranny of King Minos. He remembered the humble street urchin who had once shared what little he had.

So Theseus gave up his power and bestowed it upon the people. In his mind they were the ones who had the true right to rule anyway. Then he did what he enjoyed doing best—he went adventuring.

DISCUSSION QUESTIONS

- What do you think of the legend of Theseus bringing democracy to Athens? Does Theseus seem like the type of person who would give up his own power for the betterment of his people? Explain.
- The theme of humanity versus bestiality runs through this story. Which characters are beastlike and which are human?
- Is every person a beast deep down? Explain.
- The theme of prisons and feeling trapped runs through the story. Which characters are trapped by their circumstances?
- A *clew* is a term for a spool of thread. A *clue* is something that helps you solve a mystery. What is the connection between the two words, and how was it inspired by this story?
- Was it right for Ariadne to assist in the death of her half-brother, the Minotaur? Should she feel guilty? Explain.
- Who plays the most crucial role in this story—Ariadne or Theseus? Explain.
- Do you feel any sympathy for the Minotaur? Explain.
- Why didn't Ariadne or Theseus attempt to assassinate King Minos?
- Is Theseus cruel to leave Ariadne behind on the island of Naxos? Does it make him less of a hero? Explain.
- Why do you think Theseus decided to leave Ariadne behind?
- Did Theseus use Ariadne? Did she use him? Explain.
- The witch Medea predicted that King Aegeus would die at the hands of Theseus. Did her prophecy come true? Explain.
- Some have said that Theseus did not change his sails on purpose, so that he would become king sooner. What do you think about this theory?

THE CREATION OF THE UNIVERSE

Zeus and the other gods were not the first group of immortal beings to rule the heavens and the earth. Read about the first immortals and the creation of the universe according to the Greeks.

Chaos was the state of the universe when it first existed. From this chaos came cosmos, the ordered universe. Which god made the universe orderly was a mystery, but in the newly formed world there existed two immortal beings, Gaea (Mother Earth) and Uranus (Father Heaven). Coming together, these two forces produced their first batch of children. Yet, much to Uranus' displeasure, these children were hideously deformed: Some were Cyclopes (one-eyed giants), and the others had one hundred gangly arms and fifty heads each. Disgusted by their deformities, Uranus banished them to the deepest and darkest part of the Underworld, a pit called Tartarus. Gaea grieved for her lost children, yet her mourning was cut short. Uranus compelled her to produce a second batch of offspring. These children were the titans, giants who possessed mighty powers. Some had the strength to lift mountains, some were as strong as rushing waters, and some blazed like the sun. Since they were perfectly formed, Uranus allowed them to roam the earth freely, and there was peace for a time.

The craftiest of the titans, Cronus, envied his father's power, and his mind began to scheme. He heard the weeping of his mother, Gaea, who mourned for her deformed first-offspring, now locked beneath the earth. Using this to his advantage, Cronus convinced his mother that the only way to free her long-lost children was to murder Uranus. The grief-stricken Gaea agreed to Cronus' plan and gave him a scythe to help him accomplish his dirty deed. That night when Uranus materialized from the heavens to meet with his wife, Cronus leapt from his hiding place and, slashing with his weapon, emasculated his father.

Deeply wounded and his power gone, Uranus dissipated back into the sky, and there he lost substance. The blood of immortal beings had magical properties, and as the drops of Uranus' blood rained from the heavens, it gave birth to new creatures wherever it mingled with the dust of the earth. The three Furies, demonic spirits that torture criminals, arose with their eyes dripping blood. Also, giants were born from the fallen blood. Finally, a single drop of the magical blood landed on an ocean wave as it crested. Combining with the splendor of the sea foam, the blood produced Aphrodite, the Goddess of Love and Beauty.

With his father displaced, Cronus set himself up as the new master of the universe and, ignoring his promise to his mother, left his deformed brothers chained beneath the earth. As his new kingship began, Cronus decided to make sure his reign would last forever.

Every king must have a consort, so Cronus took his sister Rhea to be his queen. When the union produced its first child, Cronus knew there was a chance that this child might try to overthrow him—just as he had done to his father. It was not a risk he was willing to take. When the baby—the first of the gods—was at last delivered, Cronus swallowed it whole. Rhea was horrified at this, but it was just the first of many crimes. A grisly cycle of birthing and devouring began. Time and time again, Rhea delivered a perfectly formed infant god only to have it gobbled up by Cronus. The newborn Poseidon, Hera, Hades, Demeter, and Hestia were all devoured in this way. As Cronus' stomach swelled with the bodies of his own children, it seemed his appetite for power would never be satisfied.

At last Rhea reached her limit. In secret she delivered her next child, a sturdy baby boy, and sent him to be raised by the nymphs of Mount Ida on Crete. When Cronus demanded to see his latest son, crafty Rhea wrapped a stone in blankets and presented it to her husband. He greedily gobbled up the stone without a second thought, and Rhea smiled to herself. She knew her youngest son, Zeus, would grow to adulthood in exile and return to avenge his brothers and sisters.

DISCUSSION QUESTIONS

- In Greek mythology the question of which god brought the universe from chaos to cosmos is never addressed. Why do you think this question was never answered?

- Cosmos, meaning "in good order," was created from chaos. *Chaos* is a confusing term because it has progressed through several different meanings. Now it means "complete disorganization," but once it meant "wide gap." The Roman poet Ovid, who retells the creation story most poetically, imagined chaos as a primordial substance, a haphazard mess of elements—water, fire, earth, and air, all competing against one another—until an unnamed creator came along, tamed them, smoothed them into their appropriate places, and formed the cosmos. Why is this an interesting way for the universe to begin?

- Because the other gods have yet to be born when Aphrodite springs from the sea foam, she is actually the oldest of the gods. Why would a myth-maker choose Aphrodite (the personification of love) to be older than the other gods and the forces they personify (power, ingenuity, war, wisdom, etc.)?

- The physical appearance of the titans is never clearly described, even though they sound like giants. How do you picture them?

- The element Titanium, the adjective *titanic* meaning "enormous," Titan the largest moon of the planet Saturn, and a professional football team (the Tennessee Titans) are all named for the titans of mythology. Can you think of anything else that might be inspired by the titans?

- Cronus eventually became confused with Chronos, the Greek god of time. When artists depicted Cronus, they showed him holding an hour glass, to symbolize time, and a scythe, the weapon he used to dethrone his father. How did this image of Cronus (mistaken for the god of time) inspired the modern image of Father Time?

WAR OF THE TITANS

Cronus the titan ruled the universe with a tight fist. When his children were born, he swallowed them whole to keep them from ever challenging his rule. His wife, Rhea, finally rebelled by feeding Cronus a swaddled rock and secreting her newborn son away to be raised elsewhere. She hoped this son, Zeus, would return and free his brothers and sisters—still trapped inside of Cronus' belly.

Many years passed, and Zeus did return, grown handsome and strong. In secret he reunited with Rhea, his mother, and together they formulated a plan. Posing as Cronus' cupbearer, Zeus poisoned his father's drink. Poison could not kill an immortal, yet it would weaken Cronus long enough for Zeus to attack.

The plan worked perfectly. Cronus unknowingly drank the poisoned draught and, feeling the liquid burning, clasped his throat to halt its progress, but it was too late. As the titan's stomach began to churn and bubble, Zeus threw off his disguise. Cronus realized his worst fears had been confirmed: Somehow one of his children had survived. At that moment the titan's stomach convulsed, throwing him to the floor where he heaved and retched. One by one, Cronus vomited up his devoured children and, last of all, a cloth-swaddled rock. Hades, Poseidon, Hera, Demeter, and Hestia—fully grown gods, seething in anger—stood over the prostrate form of their father. But Cronus was not defeated yet. He called out hoarsely for his titan brothers and sisters to come to his aid. The palace began to shake as the great titans drew near.

What happened next was an all-out war, one that shook the heavens and the earth. Zeus and the gods battled against Cronus and the titans. The war lasted for ten years, and gradually the titans—being an older and stronger race—pressed an advantage. It became clear that the gods would lose if someone did not intervene. It was then that Gaea, the earth herself, called out to her godly grandchildren, reminding them of the malformed monsters whom Uranus had locked in Tartarus long ago—the same ones that Cronus had failed to free. Seizing upon this opportunity for aid, Zeus descended to the Underworld to free the chained creatures, the Cyclopes and the one-hundred-handed, fifty-headed monsters. They had never forgotten how the titans had abandoned them to prison for so many years. Now was their chance for revenge! Roaring in freedom, the one-hundred-handed monsters burrowed up through the earth to face their titan brothers and sisters. The Cyclopes paused only long enough to bestow a new weapon on Zeus—an all-powerful thunderbolt—before they flew into the battle as well.

Listen as the poet Hesiod describes the war as it reaches its climax: "A hundred hands stuck out of their shoulders, grotesque, and fifty heads grew on each stumpy neck. They stood against the titans on the line of battle holding chunks of cliff in their rugged hands. Opposite them, the titans tightened their ranks, expectantly. Then both sides' hands flashed with power, and the unfathomable sea shrieked eerily, the earth crashed and rumbled, the vast sky groaned and quavered, and massive Olympus shook from its roots under the immortals' onslaught...And now Zeus no longer held back his strength. His lungs seethed with anger, and he revealed all his power. He charged from the sky, hurtling down from Olympus in a flurry of lightning, hurling thunderbolts one after another, right on target, from his massive hand, a whirlwind of holy flame. And the earth that bears life roared as it burned, and the endless forests crackled in fire, the continents melted and the ocean streams boiled...The blast of heat enveloped the chthonian titans...and the incandescent rays of the thunderbolts and lightning flashes blinded their eyes, mighty as they were, heat so terrible it engulfed deep Chaos. The sight of it all...was just as if broad heaven had fallen on earth...And the battle turned" (Hesiod, translated in Brunet, Smith, & Trzaskoma, 2004, pgs. 150-151).

When the dusts of battle cleared, the gods were victorious. Terrified and defeated, Cronus fled to the far regions of the earth. The remaining titans were seized by many strong arms. For their crimes against the gods, they would be eternally punished—some chained in Tartarus (as their deformed brothers had been), while others would suffer earthly punishments similar to that of Atlas, who was forced to bear the awful weight of the sky on his shoulders.

Zeus now ruled on high, but he did not hoard power as his father had done. He gave his brother Poseidon dominion over the seas and his brother Hades dominion over the dead beneath the earth. Zeus declared his palace on Mount Olympus to be home to any god who desired peace. The Cyclopes, in thanks for their rescue, made mighty gifts for the gods. To Zeus they had already given the thunderbolt, but to Poseidon they gave a trident and to Hades a helmet of invisibility. The rule of the gods had begun.

DISCUSSION QUESTIONS

- Will Zeus be a better ruler than his father was?
- Sons overthrowing fathers is a common theme in mythology. Why do you think this is so?
- Hesiod imaginatively envisions this cosmic battle and uses descriptive language to emphasize its magnitude. What are some of the best details he uses? Explain.
- A shrine in the ancient city-state of Delphi boasted that it had found the stone that was substituted for Zeus and vomited up by Cronus. It became an ancient Greece tourist destination. Priests oiled the rock daily and on holidays decorated it. Does this seem like a strange item to visit? How does it compare to tourist attractions in our own time?
- The titans were probably deities worshiped before the gods arrived on the scene. As one religion replaced another, myths were created to explain why. This story was created during the time of the god-worship because it shows Cronus to be a monstrously cruel tyrant, begging to be overthrown. Some have even theorized that Cronus eating his children reflects a tradition of child-sacrifice that perhaps accompanied the older religion. Because such barbaric customs horrified the later Greek myth-makers, they created a story of how the "good-guy" gods overthrew the titans. What do you think of this theory? Why is the idea of one group of gods supplanting another interesting?

DEUCALION AND THE GREAT FLOOD

After reading "Prometheus the Firebringer," read this myth about an enormous flood that threatens to destroy all human life upon the earth.

When Zeus heard rumors that humans were wicked and corrupt, he went to see for himself. He wandered among the mortals in a human disguise to see their character firsthand. On his journey he visited the hall of a demented king, Lycaon, who offered him a dish prepared from human flesh. Appalled by this sacrilege, Zeus struck down the king's attendants with thunderbolts and transformed the king himself into a ravenous wolf. Returning hastily to Olympus, Zeus was convinced that mankind must be destroyed. The other gods were uneasy about this. Who would honor the gods if the humans were destroyed? But Zeus did not care. He would wipe them out. He knew he could not use his thunderbolts. The flames from so many of them would burn up the entire world, so he planned instead to drown the world in a divine deluge.

From where the titan Prometheus was imprisoned, he saw rain clouds covering the sky and sent word to his mortal son, Deucalion, to build a boat. The good man heeded his father's warning, and when Zeus opened the floodgates of heaven, Deucalion and his wife Pyrrha survived on their boat—riding the waves for nine days before finally landing upon the heights of Mount Parnassus. Seeing that the mortals had been completely wiped out, except for the kindly Deucalion and his wife, Zeus allowed the waters to go down.

Lamenting the loss of their race, Deucalion and Pyrrha called on the titaness Themis, known for her prophetic gifts, to ask her how they might repopulate the earth. She answered with a riddle: "Cover your heads and throw the bones of your mighty mother over your shoulder." Pyrrha believed that the titaness was speaking literally. Where would they find the bones of their mothers, and how could they dishonor them in that way? But Deucalion saw the hidden meaning of the riddle. Their "mighty mother" was not their earthly mothers, but Mother Earth herself, and, therefore, her "bones" meant rock. So covering their heads, they each took stones and tossed them over their shoulders. The rocks thrown by Deucalion became men, and those thrown by Pyrrha became women. So the human race was repopulated and given a second chance to live honorably.

DISCUSSION QUESTIONS

- Why does Zeus choose to turn Lycaon, the evil king, into a wolf, rather than killing him?
- Does Zeus have a good reason to destroy the entire human race? Explain.
- Almost every culture has an ancient story that involves the flooding of the world. Read the Biblical story of Noah found in Genesis 6:5-8:22. What are some similarities between the Greek myth and the story found in the Bible? What are some other flood stories from other cultures?

MOUNT OLYMPUS FIND·IT PUZZLE

CAN YOU FIND ALL OF THESE ITEMS HIDDEN IN THE PICTURE?

- 100-eyed Argus
- Anchor
- Ant
- Aphrodite
- Apollo
- Apples (3)
- Ares
- Artemis
- Athena
- Atlas
- Bee
- Bird in a nest
- Calendar
- Centaurs (2)
- Cow
- Cronus
- Demeter
- Dionysus
- Eagle
- Eros (Cupid)
- Flies (2)

- Fork
- Golden net
- Hades
- Hearts (5)
- Hebe
- Hephaestus
- Hera
- Hermes
- Hestia
- Horse bridle
- Hummingbird
- Iris
- Letter Ω
- Love letter
- Love potion
- Lyre
- Mechanical maiden
- Miniature Parthenon
- Mythology textbook
- Ode on a Grecian urn
- Giants (2)

- Owl
- Peacock
- Pegasus
- Persephone
- Poseidon
- Prometheus
- Satyrs (2)
- Scythe
- Sea monster
- Sea shell
- Skulls (2)
- Spider
- Staff of Hermes
- Stars (5)
- Stone hammer
- Thunderbolt
- Trident
- Turtle
- Vines (2)
- Word "Olympus"
- Zeus

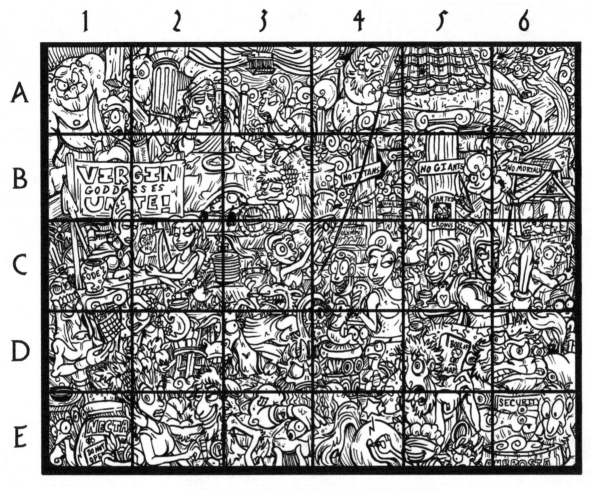

MOUNT OLYMPUS FIND-IT PUZZLE KEY

100-eyed Argus, **D6**

Anchor, **E3**

Ant, **C2-3**

Aphrodite, **C4**

Apollo, **A1-B1**

Apples (3), **D1, E2, E4-5**

Ares, **C5-6**

Artemis, **C2**

Athena, **B1-C1**

Atlas, **D5**

Bee, **E1**

Bird in a nest, **D2**

Calendar, **D1**

Centaurs (2), **D5-E5, D6-E6**

Cow, **B2-3**

Cronus, **B5-C5**

Demeter, **D2-E2**

Dionysus, **B3**

Eagle, **B5**

Eros (Cupid), **B5-6**

Flies (2), **D3, C3**

Fork, **B2**

Golden net, **A5**

Hades, **C1-D1**

Hearts (5), **A3, C5, C5, C5, C4-5**

Hebe, **C3-4**

Hephaestus, **A4**

Hera, **A3**

Hermes, **C5**

Hestia, **B5-C5**

Horse bridle, **D4**

Hummingbird, **C2**

Iris, **A6**

Letter Ω, **A6**

Love letter, **A3-B3**

Love potion, **C5**

Lyre, **E3**

Mechanical maiden, **C4**

Mini Parthenon, **A3**

Myth. textbook, **C1**

Ode…Grecian urn, **C1**

Giants (2), **A1, A2**

Owl, **E5**

Peacock, **E1**

Pegasus, **C6**

Persephone, **D2**

Poseidon, **D3-E3**

Prometheus, **C-6**

Satyrs (2), **C3-D3, E2-3**

Scythe, **A4**

Sea monster, **B5**

Sea shell, **D4**

Skulls (2), **C1, D4**

Spider, **A5**

Staff of Hermes, **C1**

Stars (5), **A4, A6, B6, D3, E4**

Stone hammer, **E2**

Thunderbolt, **A6**

Trident, **A5-6**

Turtle, **D4**

Vines (2), **A2, B4**

Word "Olympus", **C4**

Zeus, **A2**

TOURNAMENT OF THE GODS

Introduction: The Tournament of the Gods is a trading-card-style game. Players use their knowledge of mythology to design a trading card featuring a mythological character. Then players use the information on these cards to "fight" each other using a die.

TERMS TO KNOW	
HP (Hit Points)	This is the amount of "life" players have. When a player's HP reaches zero, that player loses the round. HP is regenerated each round of the tournament.
Die Roll	This game uses a single die to conduct the battle aspect of the tournament. *Die roll* refers to the number displayed on the die after a roll.

DESIGNING A CHARACTER

1. **Begin with the Character Card Template** (located on pg. 187) This template will guide you through the process of creating a character for the Tournament of the Gods.
2. **Decide which god or goddess you will be playing as.** This can be any god or goddess from a branch of mythology you have studied. Ask tournament directors about specific rules they might have concerning character choice: Can mortal heroes and monsters be included? Should your god or goddess come from a particular branch of mythology?
3. **Draw a colorful picture of your character in the top left box of the character card.** Also add color to the entire card to make it a complete composition.
4. **Write a description of your character in the top right box of the character card.** Example: "Athena is the Greek Goddess of Wisdom and a battle goddess."
5. **Distribute your character's attribute points using the box provided on the character card.** You have 20 attribute points to distribute among four categories: strength, stamina, agility, and speed. **Note:** Each attribute must have at least 1 point. For a breakdown of the four attributes your character has, see the table below.

ATTRIBUTES	ADVANTAGES
Strength This is the amount of strength your character has and will determine how much damage you inflict on your opponent each time you attack.	Raising this attribute increases the damage that your attacks do to opponents. Each time you attack, the number of your strength attribute is added to your die roll. (Strength + die roll = HP of damage to opponent)

Stamina This is your character's ability to sustain many blows.	This attribute determines the amount of HP or "life" you will have each round. Your stamina attribute will be multiplied by 10 at the beginning of each round to determine your HP. This number will reset after each round. (Stamina x 10 = HP)
Agility This is your character's ability to dodge an opponent's attack and deliver a sneak attack.	At the beginning of each round, you will examine your opponent's attributes. If your agility attribute is 3 points higher than your opponent's agility attribute, every attack you make will have an extra 5 HP of damage added to it. If your agility attribute is 5 points higher than your opponent's agility attribute, every attack you make will have an extra 10 HP of damage added to it.
Speed This is the speed at which your character battles.	Each round whichever character has the highest speed attribute gets to attack first. (If your speeds are the same, you will roll the die to determine who will go first.) If your speed attribute is 3 points higher than your opponent's speed attribute, you can take 1 extra turn any time during the round. If your speed attribute is 5 points higher than your opponent's speed attribute, you can take 2 extra turns any time during the round.

6. **Pick a godly attribute for your character.** This is a defensive power that your god or goddess has. You can choose from the following options:

Payback	When an opponent strikes you by rolling an *odd number*, you apply 5 HP of damage back to your opponent.
Holy Number	When an opponent rolls a certain number, you are impervious to the attack. (Example: Your opponent rolls a 3, but nothing happens because 3 is your holy number and cannot harm you.) This number must be chosen by you and indicated on your character card before the tournament begins. It *cannot* be changed at any point during the tournament.

Regeneration	When you roll an *even number* in an attack, 5 HP is added back onto your own life—up to 100% of HP. (You cannot have more than 100% HP.)
Mighty Smite	When you roll a certain number, it doubles the amount of HP damage done to your opponent. This number must be chosen by you and indicated on your character card before the tournament begins. It *cannot* be changed at any point during the tournament.
Godspeed	Every 4th time you attack, you are allowed to attack twice.

7. **Designate your character's special attacks.** Come up with names for three special attacks that your god or goddess will use. Make sure the attack names relate to your character. Be creative! (Example: Creating a "Shazam Lightning Attack" for Zeus.) While you do get to choose the names for your special attacks, they must have one of the following effects:

Offensive Special Attacks
+25 HP to your next attack
Double the HP of your next attack
Steal one of your opponent's special attacks and use it against him or her
Defensive Special Attacks
-25 HP from your opponent's next attack
Reduce your opponent's next attack by 50%
Your opponent loses his or her next turn
Be immune to a certain number for the rest of the round (Example: Attacks resulting from your opponent rolling a 3 do not hurt you.) This immunity expires at the end of the round. This number must be indicated on the character card at the beginning of the tournament.
Note: For each of your special attacks, you must choose a *different* effect.

8. **Designate two power objects that can each be used only once during the entire tournament.** Come up with objects that would be related to your character (examples: Zeus' thunderbolt, Athena's owl, Hermes' winged sandals). While you do get to choose the name of these power objects, they must have one of the following effects:

Power Object Effects
Fully restore your HP

Decrease your opponent's HP by half
Prevent your opponent from using any special attacks during your round
Permanently reduce all your opponent's attributes by 1 pt. (**Note:** No attribute can be reduced to 0, so this effect would not work on an opponent whose attributes were already reduced to 1.)
Permanently raise all your own attributes by 2 pts.
Note: Raising or lowering attributes stays in effect for the entire game. When affected, these numbers must be immediately changed on the character card.

PLAYING THE GAME

1. **Beginning a round**
   - At the beginning of each round, you will examine your opponent's character sheet.
   - On a scratch piece of paper, write out your hit points (HP) or "life." To determine HP, multiply your stamina by 10. (Example: A stamina attribute of 10 would result in 100 HP.)

2. **Check Speed Attribute**
   - At the beginning of each round, whichever character has the highest speed attribute gets to attack first. (If your speeds are the same, you will roll the die to determine who will go first.)
   - If your speed attribute is 3 points higher than your opponent's speed attribute, you can take 1 extra turn any time during the round. (See "Taking an Extra Turn" for more information.)
   - If your speed attribute is 5 points higher than your opponent's speed attribute, you can take 2 extra turns any time during the round.

3. **Check Agility Attribute**
   - If your agility attribute is 3 points higher than your opponent's agility attribute, every attack will have an extra 5 HP added to it. (Example: Strength attribute + die roll + 5 HP = amount of HP damage to opponent)
   - If your agility attribute is 5 points higher than your opponent's agility attribute, every attack will have an extra 10 HP added to it. (Example: Strength attribute + die roll + 10 HP = amount of HP damage to opponent)

4. **Attacking**
   - The player with the highest speed attribute attacks first.
   - Take turns attacking.
   - When the die is rolled, the resulting number is added to the attacking character's strength attribute to determine the amount of HP damage done to the opponent. (Example: A die roll of 3 is added to 10, the character's strength. This means 13 HP are deducted from the opponent's HP.)
   - HP damage must be deducted immediately after an attack.

- Rolling a 1 counts as a miss.
- After each attack, consult your godly attributes and apply any effects that apply. (Examples: Payback returns damage to attackers on some rolls, Holy Number makes players impervious to certain numbers, Regeneration adds HP on some rolls, Mighty Smite doubles amount of damage on some rolls, and Godspeed allows extra turns.)

5. **Using a special attack or power object**
   - Each time you use a special attack or power object, you *must* check a box to indicate that this special attack has been used. Each special attack can only be used three times during the *entire tournament*. Each power object can only be used once during the *entire tournament*.
   - If a special attack or power object affects the other player, these penalties must be applied immediately.
   - If your special attack involves using your opponent's special attack against him or her, the opponent must take the damage *and* mark this special attack off his or her character card as used.
   - If you wish to use an *offensive* special attack, you must play these on your turn and indicate this *before* the die is rolled. (Example: You cannot wait until you roll the die and then decide you want to increase your attack by 50%.)
   - If you wish to use a *defensive* special attack, you must play these on your opponent's turn and indicate this *before* the die is rolled. (Example: You cannot wait until your opponent rolls the die and then decide you want to decrease the attack by 50%.)
   - Power objects can be used at any time.

6. **Rolling a 1 while using a special attack or power object**
   - If you choose to use an offensive special attack and roll a 1, the effects are voided. You must still mark off the special attack as used. (Example: You chose to add +25 HP to your next attack, but you roll a 1. Your opponent loses no HP. In other words, you do *not* add 25 to 0 to make 25 HP of damage.)
   - Defensive special attacks and power objects *still* work if you roll a 1.

7. **Taking an extra turn**
   - You cannot take an extra turn when your opponent has the die. You must wait for your turn to come around again.
   - At the conclusion of your regular turn, indicate that you would like to take an extra turn.
   - If you have multiple turns coming to you, you may take them all at once.

8. **Dealing with Fractions** If the amount of HP to be added or deducted comes out to a fraction, round up to the nearest whole number. (Example: You add 50 % to your next attack, and you roll a 7. Instead of adding 3.5 HP to your attack, add 4 HP.)

9. **When one player's HP reaches zero, this means the round is over.** The winner will advance to the next round. (Depending on how the tournament director has set up the tournament bracket, the loser may play additional rounds.)

10. **As the rounds progress in the tournament, keep track of your number of wins and which characters you have defeated.** The tournament director will have a method for determining who has won the tournament.

DUTIES OF TEACHERS OR TOURNAMENT DIRECTORS

1. Be familiar with the game rules.
2. Thoroughly review the game rules with the players before the tournament begins. They are responsible for keeping track of their own HP, special attacks, power objects, etc.
3. Encourage players to be creative when designing their character cards, special attacks, and power objects.
4. Set up areas where players can battle one another. They will require a flat surface for their character cards and enough room to roll a die.
5. Provide the needed materials. Each pair of players will need a die, scratch paper for keeping track of HP, and writing utensils.
6. Determine how the tournament will be conducted. A double-elimination or round robin tournament bracket is recommended. For free, customizable brackets visit www.printyourbrackets.com
7. Monitor players as they battle. Make sure they are playing the game correctly and marking off special attacks and power objects as they are used.
8. Have fun!

TOURNAMENT OF THE GODS

CHARACTER DESCRIPTION:

ATTRIBUTES (20 PTS. TOTAL)

STRENGTH: **AGILITY:**

STAMINA: **SPEED:**

(MINIMUM FOR ANY ATTRIBUTE IS 1 PT.)

GODLY ATTRIBUTE (THIS IS A SPECIAL POWER THAT YOU HAVE FOR BEING A GOD.)

TITLE: _____

EFFECT: _____

SPECIAL ATTACKS (CHECK THE BOXES EACH TIME YOU USE THESE ATTACKS. THESE ARE ALL YOU RECEIVE FOR THE ENTIRE TOURNAMENT.)

☐ ☐ ☐   TITLE: _____   EFFECT: _____

☐ ☐ ☐   TITLE: _____   EFFECT: _____

☐ ☐ ☐   TITLE: _____   EFFECT: _____

POWER OBJECTS (CHECK THE BOXES EACH TIME YOU USE THESE OBJECTS. THESE ARE ALL YOU RECEIVE FOR THE ENTIRE TOURNAMENT.)

☐ TITLE: _____   EFFECT: _____

☐ TITLE: _____   EFFECT: _____

GLOSSARY OF IMPORTANT NAMES

Achilles Greatest Greek warrior in the Trojan War, son of Thetis the sea nymph, trained by Chiron the centaur, died by taking one of Paris' arrows in the heel

Aeneas Trojan son of Aphrodite, after the sack of Troy set out on his own quest to start a new city-state based on the legacy of Troy

Aeolus Lord of the winds

Agamemnon Ruler of Mycenae, brother of Menelaus, leader of the united Greek armies, slain by his wife, Clytemnestra

Ajax Greek chieftain who committed suicide during the Trojan War

Alecto (see "Furies")

Andromache Wife of Hector, taken into captivity after the Trojan War by Pyrrhus, the son of Achilles

Aphrodite (Roman name: Venus) Goddess of love and beauty, born from the foam of the sea, sister of Zeus, wife of Hephaestus, lover of Ares, mother of Eros and Aeneas

Apollo (Roman name: Phoebus Apollo) God of light and truth, twin brother to Artemis, son of Zeus, gifted in poetry and the playing of the lyre, his oracle in Delphi was the most popular in Greece

Arachne Weaver, transformed by Athena into the first spider

Ares (Roman name: Mars) God of war, son of Zeus

Argus One-hundred-eyed henchman of Hera

Ariadne Daughter of Minos, helper of Theseus

Artemis (Roman name: Diana) Goddess of wild things, goddess of the moon, twin sister to Apollo, daughter of Zeus, virgin goddess

Astyanax Infant son of Hector and Andromache, during the sack of Troy he was flung from the walls of the city to his death

Atalanta Heroine of ancient Greece, known for her nearly superhuman speed, helped to kill the giant boar of Calydon, joined Jason on his quest for the Golden Fleece

Athena (Roman name: Minerva) Goddess of wisdom, goddess of handicrafts, protector of the city, daughter of Zeus, inventor of the bridle, patroness of Athens, leader of the virgin goddesses

Atlas The titan who is forced to forever bear the weight of the sky

Bellerophon Hero of ancient Greece, tamer of Pegasus, slayer of the Chimaera

Calypso Sea nymph, lover of Odysseus

Cassandra Sister of Hector and Paris, prophetess, taken as a concubine by Agamemnon after the fall of Troy

Centaur Half-man, half-horse creature known for its wild and violent tendencies

Cerberus Three-headed hell-hound that prevents entrance into the Underworld

Charon Aged boatman who ferries souls across the River Styx in the Underworld

Charybdis Gigantic whirlpool, notorious for sucking ships down to their destruction

Chimaera Fearsome creature, part-lion, part-goat, part-snake, defeated by Bellerophon

Chiron Wise centaur who was renowned as a trainer of heroes, raised Jason up from a child, trainer of Achilles

Circe Famous witch who transforms the men of Odysseus into pigs

Cronus (Roman name: Saturn) Titan father of the first gods, devours his children to prevent them from overthrowing him

Cyclops (plural: Cyclopes) Large beings that have only one eye, said to be the sons of Poseidon

Daedalus Famous Athenian inventor, designer of the Labyrinth

Demeter (Roman name: Ceres) Goddess of the harvest and nature, mother of Persephone

Deucalion Mortal who along with his wife, Pyrrha, built a boat to escape the great flood

Dido Queen of Carthage, lover of Aeneas

Diomedes Famed warrior of the Greeks, during the Trojan War earned the distinction of physically harming two gods

Dionysus (Roman name: Bacchus) God of wine, the youngest of the gods

Dryad Tree nymph

Electra Daughter of Agamemnon and Clytemnestra

Eos (Roman name: Aurora) Goddess of the dawn

Epimetheus Titan, dimwitted brother of Prometheus

Eris Goddess of discord

Eros (Roman name: Cupid) Son of Aphrodite, shoots arrows that cause extreme infatuation

Fates Three ancient beings that control the lives of all living things, one spins out the thread of life, one measures out its length, one cuts the thread at the time of death

Furies Three foul spirits who torture those who commit offensive crimes

Gaea Spirit of the earth, "Mother Earth"

Giants Large monsters born from the blood of Uranus, attempt to climb to Olympus

Gorgon (see "Medusa")

Gray Women Three old hags who all share a single eyeball

Hades (Roman name: Pluto) Ruler of the Underworld and the dead

Harpy Evil creature, head of a woman, body of a bird, repugnant stench

Hebe Goddess of youth, cupbearer of the gods

Hector Greatest prince of Troy, defended his brother Paris against the Greeks

Hecuba Queen of Troy, wife of Priam, taken into slavery after the fall of Troy, stoned to death by the men of Odysseus

Helen Most beautiful woman in the world, daughter of Zeus, wife of Menelaus, given back to Menelaus after the fall of Troy

Helios God of the sun, drives a fiery chariot across the sky each day

Hephaestus (Roman name: Vulcan) God of fire and the forge, only ugly god, husband of Aphrodite, son of Zeus

Hera (Roman name: Juno) Queen of Olympus, protector of marriage, jealous wife of Zeus, busied herself making life miserable for Zeus' many mistresses and illegitimate children

Heracles (Roman name: Hercules) Mightiest Greek hero, endowed with superhuman strength, mortal enemy of Hera

Hermes (Roman name: Mercury) Messenger god of Olympus, god of commerce, guides souls down to the Underworld after death, master thief, inventor of the lyre, wears winged sandals upon his feet and a winged cap upon his head, carries a magical wand bearing the image of spread wings and intertwined serpents

Hippomenes Swift warrior, husband of Atalanta

Icarus Son of Daedalus, died while attempting human flight

Iphigenia Daughter of Agamemnon and Clytemnestra, offered as a human sacrifice to appease the anger of Artemis

Iris Goddess of the rainbow, secondary messenger of the gods

Iulus Young son of Aeneas

Jason Leader of the Argonauts, trained by Chiron, husband of Medea

Medea Witch, wife of Jason, murdered her young sons

Medusa Snake-haired gorgon, possessed the power to turn men into stone if they met her gaze

Meleager Famous warrior, admirer of Atalanta

Menelaus Brother of Agamemnon, ruler of Sparta, husband of Helen

Midas Foolish king who wished for everything he touched to turn to gold

Minos King of Crete, keeper of the Minotaur

Minotaur Half-man, half-bull creature, kept by King Minos in the Labyrinth

Mnemosyne Goddess of memory, mother of the nine muses

Muses Nine immortal beings who inspire every form of art

Myrmidons Fighting men of Achilles, their race is said to have been created from ants

Naiad Water nymph

Narcissus Handsome boy who falls in love with his own reflection

Nemesis Goddess of retribution

Nestor Oldest Greek chieftain who fought in the Trojan War, known for his great wisdom

Nymph Female nature spirit (see "Dryad" and "Naiad")

Ocean Punished titan, the body of water which surrounds the known world

Odysseus (Roman name: Ulysses) King of Ithaca, vowed to protect the honor of Helen with the other kings of Greece, formed the idea of the Trojan Horse, wandered ten years at sea to reach his home after the fall of Troy

Oedipus King of Thebes, murdered his father and married his mother

Olympus Home of the gods

Oracle One who speaks the wisdom of the gods, traditionally the priestess of a god or goddess' temple

Orestes Son of Agamemnon and Clytemnestra, avenges the murder of his father

Orpheus Famed musician, descended into the Underworld to rescue his lost love, accompanied Jason on his quest for the Golden Fleece

Pan Satyr, god of shepherds

Pandora First woman, opens a jar filled with evils sent to her by Zeus

Paris Exiled prince of Troy, lover of Helen, son of Priam, judged the beauty contest of the goddesses, killed by Prince Philoctetes in the Trojan War

Patroclus Beloved friend of Achilles, his death caused Achilles to re-enter the Trojan War

Pegasus Famed winged horse, ridden by Bellerophon

Penelope Queen of Ithaca, wife of Odysseus

Persephone (Roman name: Proserpine) Goddess of spring, queen of the Underworld

Perseus Hero, slayer of Medusa, founded the city-state Mycenae, married to the princess Andromeda

Phaethon Mortal son of Helios, asked to drive his father's chariot, causes natural disasters all across the world

Philoctetes Prince who bore the bow and arrows of Heracles, abandoned by the Greeks on the island of Lemnos for ten years

Phineus Prophet cursed by Zeus, plagued by the harpies, helps the Argonauts on their quest

Polyphemus Famous Cyclops, tricked by Odysseus (Ulysses) and blinded by his men

Poseidon (Roman name: Neptune) God of the sea, brother of Zeus, giver of the horse to man, carries a trident (a three-pronged spear)

Priam Elderly king of Troy, defended his son Paris against the Greeks, killed by the son of Achilles during the sack of Troy

Prometheus Titan who stole fire from the gods and gave it to man

Proteus Shape-shifting creature, known as "the old man of the sea"

Pyrrhus Red-haired son of Achilles, sired by Achilles during his stay at the court of Lycomedes, brought to Troy by Odysseus

Rhadamanthus Mortal king who judges the dead in the Underworld

Rhea Titan, mother of the first gods

Satyr Half-goat, half-man creature

Scylla Many-headed monster rooted to a rock in the middle of the ocean, notorious for sinking ships

Selene Goddess of the moon, drives her silvery chariot across the sky each night

Silenus Satyr, foster-father and tutor of Dionysus

Sisyphus Mortal king punished in the Underworld, must roll a boulder up a hill for eternity

Sphinx Creature with the head of a woman, the body of a lion, the wings of an eagle, and the tail of a snake, great teller of riddles, defeated by Oedipus

Tantalus Mortal king punished in the Underworld, cannot drink from the water at his feet or eat of the fruit that hangs just out of his reach

Tartarus The deepest part of the Underworld, where many of the titans were chained

Telemachus Prince of Ithaca, son of Odysseus

Thanatos God of death, releases mortal souls from their bodies

Theseus Famous Greek hero, slayer of the Minotaur

Thetis Sea nymph, mother of Achilles, wife of Peleus

Tiresias Blind prophet of Thebes, lived for seven generations of men

Troy City of legend, located on the shores of Asia Minor, destroyed by the Greeks

Uranus "Father Heaven," deity of the sky, castrated by his son Cronus

Zephyr The west wind

Zeus (Roman name: Jupiter, Jove) Ruler of the gods, wielder of the mighty thunderbolt, father of many heroes

PRONUNCIATION GUIDE

Achates	(UH-KAY-TEEZ)	Briseis	(BRIH-SEE-US)
Acheron	(ACK-UH-RUN)	Cadmus	(KAHD-MUS)
Achilles	(UH-KILL-EEZ)	Calchas	(KAL-KUS)
Acrisius	(UH-KRIH-SEE-US)	Calliope	(KUH-LY-O-PEE)
Actaeon	(ACT-EE-ON)	Calydon	(KAL-IH-DUN)
Æetes	(EE-UH-TEEZ)	Calypso	(KUH-LIP-SO)
Aegeus	(EE-GEE-US)	Carthage	(KAR-THIJ)
Aegina	(EE-JY-NUH)	Cassandra	(KUH-SAN-DRUH)
Aeneas	(EE-NEE-US)	Castor	(KAS-TER)
Aeneid	(EE-NEE-ID)	Caucasus	(KAW-KAY-SUS)
Aeolus	(EE-OH-LUS)	Centaur	(SIN-TAWR)
Aethra	(EE-THRUH)	Cerberus	(SER-BUH-RUS)
Agamemnon	(AG-UH-MEM-NON)	Charon	(KAH-RUN)
Alcema	(AL-SEE-MUH)	Charybdis	(KUH-RIB-DIS)
Alcinous	(AL-SIN-OO-US)	Chimaera	(KY-MEE-RUH)
Alcmene	(ALK-MEE-NEE)	Chiron	(KY-RUN)
Alecto	(UH-LEHK-TO)	Chryseis	(KRY-SEE-ISS)
Amata	(UH-MAY-TUH)	Circe	(SER-SEE)
Amphitryon	(AM-FIT-TREE-UN)	Clio	(KLEE-OH)
Anchises	(AN-KY-ZEEZ)	Clymene	(KLIH-MUH-NEE)
Androgeos	(AN-DRO-GEE-US)	Clytemnestra	(KLY-TIM-NESS-TRUH)
Andromache	(AN-DRAH-MUH-KEE)	Colchis	(KOL-KISS)
Andromeda	(AN-DRAH-MEE-DUH)	Corinth	(KOR-INTH)
Antigone	(AN-TIG-UH-NEE)	Creon	(KREE-ON)
Antinous	(AN-TEN-YOO-US)	Cronus	(KRO-NUS)
Aphrodite	(AF-RO-DY-TEE)	Cumae	(KOO-MEE)
Apollo	(UH-PAW-LO)	Cupid	(KEW-PID)
Arachne	(UH-RAK-NEE)	Cyclopes	(SY-KLOP-EEZ)
Arcadia	(AR-KAY-DEE-UH)	Cyclops	(SY-KLOPZ)
Ares	(AIR-EEZ)	Daedalus	(DAY-DUH-LUS)
Argos	(AR-GOS)	Danaë	(DUH-NAY-EE)
Argus	(AR-GUS)	Deidamia	(DEE-UH-DAH-MEE-UH)
Ariadne	(AIR-EE-AHD-NEE)	Delphi	(DEL-FY)
Artemis	(AR-TUH-MIS)	Demeter	(DEE-MEE-TER)
Asterion	(AS-TEER-EE-UN)	Deucalion	(DOO-KAY-LEE-UN)
Astyanax	(UH-STY-UH-NAX)	Dido	(DY-DO)
Atalanta	(AT-UH-LAN-TUH)	Diomedes	(DY-O-MEE-DEEZ)
Athena	(UH-THEE-NUH)	Dionysus	(DY-O-NY-SUS)
Atlas	(AT-LUS)	Dryad	(DRY-AD)
Atreus	(UH-TRAY-OOS)	Electra	(EE-LEK-TRUH)
Augeas	(AWG-EE-US)	Eos	(EE-AHS)
Aulis	(O-LIS)	Epaphus	(EH-PUH-FUS)
Bacchus	(BAHK-US)	Epeios	(EE-PAY-OS)
Battus	(BAT-US)	Ephialtes	(EH-FEE-UHL-TEEZ)
Bellerophon	(BEH-LEHR-UH-FUN)	Epimetheus	(EP-IH-MEE-THEE-US)
Bia	(BY-UH)	Eris	(EE-RUS)

Eros	(EE-ROS)	Latinus	(LUH-TY-NUS)
Eumaeus	(YOO-MAY-US)	Latium	(LAY-SHI-UM)
Europa	(YOO-RO-PUH)	Leda	(LEE-DUH)
Eurycleia	(YOOR-IH-KLEE-UH)	Lemnos	(LEM-NUS)
Eurydice	(YOO-RIH-DIH-SEE)	Lethe	(LEE-THEE)
Eurylochus	(YOO-RIL-UH-KUS)	Leto	(LEE-TOE)
Eurymachus	(YOO-RIM-UH-KUS)	Lycaon	(LY-KAY-UN)
Eurystheus	(YOO-RIS-THEE-US)	Lycomedes	(LY-KO-MEE-DEEZ)
Gaea	(GY-UH)	Lycus	(LY-KUS)
Geryon	(JEER-EE-UN)	Lyre	(LY-ER)
Gorgon	(GOR-GUN)	Maenad	(MEE-NAD)
Hades	(HAY-DEEZ)	Maron	(MAH-RUN)
Harpies	(HAR-PEEZ)	Medea	(MEE-DEE-UH)
Hebe	(HEE-BEE)	Medus	(MEE-DUS)
Hector	(HEK-TER)	Medusa	(MEH-DOO-SUH)
Hecuba	(HEK-YOO-BUH)	Meleager	(MEH-LEE-UH-JER)
Helenus	(HEL-UH-NUS)	Memnon	(MEM-NUN)
Helios	(HEE-LEE-OS)	Menelaus	(MEN-UH-LAY-US)
Hephaestus	(HEE-FES-TUS)	Mentes	(MEN-TEEZ)
Hera	(HEE-RUH) (HEH-RUH)	Mercury	(MER-KOO-REE)
Heracles	(HEER-UH-KLEEZ)	Midas	(MY-DUS)
Hercules	(HER-KYOO-LEEZ)	Minerva	(MIH-NER-VUH)
Hermes	(HER-MEEZ)	Minos	(MY-NUS)
Hermione	(HER-MY-O-NEE)	Minotaur	(MY-NO-TAR)
Hesperides	(HES-PER-IH-DEES)	Mnemosyne	(NEE-MAWZ-IH-NEE)
Hippolyta	(HIH-PAW-LIH-TUH)	Mycenae	(MY-SEE-NEE)
Hippomenes	(HIH-PAWM-UH-NEEZ)	Myrmidon	(MER-MIH-DON)
Iasus	(EYE-UH-SUS)	Naiad	(NY-AD)
Icarius	(IH-KAR-EE-US)	Narcissus	(NAR-SIS-US)
Icarus	(IH-KAR-US)	Nausicaa	(NAW-SEE-KUH)
Iliad	(IH-LEE-AD)	Nemean	(NEE-MEE-UN)
Ilium	(IH-LEE-UM)	Neoptolemus	(NEE-O-TOL-EE-MUS)
Io	(EYE-O)	Neptune	(NEP-TOON)
Iolaus	(EYE-O-LAY-US)	Niobe	(NY-O-BEE)
Iolcus	(EYE-UL-KUS)	Odysseus	(O-DIS-EE-US)
Iphigenia	(IF-UH-JUH-NY-UH)	Oedipus	(ED-IH-PUS)
Iris	(EYE-RIS)	Oeta	(EE-TUH)
Ithaca	(ITH-UH-KUH)	Ogygia	(O-JIH-JEE-UH)
Iulus	(YOO-LUSS)	Orestes	(O-RES-TEEZ)
Janus	(JAY-NUS)	Orpheus	(OR-FEE-US)
Jocasta	(YO-KAS-TUH)	Otus	(O-TUS)
Juno	(JOO-NO)	Ovid	(O-VID)
Jupiter	(JOO-PIH-TUR)	Palamedes	(PAL-UH-MEE-DEEZ)
Knossos	(NAW-SUS)	Pallas	(PAL-US)
Kratos	(KRAY-TOS)	Pandarus	(PAN-DARE-US)
Lacedaemon	(LAH-SEE-DEE-MUN)	Pandora	(PAN-DOR-UH)
Laertes	(LAY-ER-TEEZ)	Parnassus	(PAR-NAH-SUS)
Laius	(LAY-US)	Pasiphae	(PAS-IH-FAY-EE)
Laocoön	(LAY-O-KO-UN)	Patroclus	(PAH-TRO-KLUS)

Peleus	(PEE-LEE-US)	Rhea	(REE-UH)
Pelias	(PEE-LEE-US)	Romulus	(ROM-YOO-LUS)
Penelope	(PEH-NEL-O-PEE)	Satyr	(SAY-TER)
Penthesilea	(PEN-THUS-SIH-LEE-UH)	Sciron	(SKY-RUN)
Perigune	(PER-IH-GOO-NEE)	Scorpio	(SKOR-PEE-O)
Persephone	(PER-SEF-UH-NEE)	Scylla	(SIHL-UH)
Perseus	(PER-SEE-US)	Scyros	(SKY-RUS)
Phaeacia	(FAY-EE-SHUH)	Selene	(SEE-LEE-NEE)
Phaethon	(FAY-UH-THUN)	Silenus	(SUH-LY-NUS)
Philoctetes	(FIL-OK-TEE-TEEZ)	Sinis	(SY-NUS)
Phineus	(FIN-EE-US)	Sinon	(SY-NON)
Phoebe	(FEE-BEE)	Sisyphus	(SIH-SIH-FUS)
Phoebus	(FEE-BUS)	Styx	(STIKS)
Phrygia	(FRIH-GEE-UH)	Tantalus	(TAN-TUH-LUS)
Pisistratus	(PIH-SIH-STRAH-TUS)	Tartarus	(TAR-TUH-RUS)
Pittheus	(PITH-EE-US)	Taurus	(TAW-RUS)
Plautus	(PLAW-TUS)	Telemachus	(TUH-LEM-UH-KUS)
Pluto	(PLEW-TO)	Thalia	(THUH-LY-UH)
Polites	(PO-LY-TEEZ)	Thanatos	(THAN-UH-TOS)
Polyphemus	(PO-LEE-FEE-MUS)	Thebes	(THEEBZ)
Polyxena	(POL-EK-ZEE-NUH)	Themis	(THEE-MUS)
Poseidon	(PO-SY-DUN)	Theseus	(THEE-SEE-US)
Priam	(PRY-UM)	Thessaly	(THEHS-UH-LEE)
Procrustes	(PRO-KRUS-TEEZ)	Thetis	(THEE-TIS)
Prometheus	(PRO-MEE-THEE-US)	Tiresias	(TY-REE-SEE-US)
Proserpine	(PRO-SER-PEEN-UH)	Tiryns	(TEER-UNZ)
Proteus	(PRO-TEE-US)	Troezen	(TREE-ZUN)
Pylos	(PY-LOS)	Troilus	(TROY-LUS)
Pyrrha	(PEER-UH)	Tyndareus	(TIN-DARE-EE-US)
Pyrrhus	(PEER-US)	Uranus	(YOO-RUN-US)
Remus	(REE-MUS)	Zeus	(ZOOS)

ABOUT THE AUTHOR

Zachary Hamby is a teacher of English in rural Missouri, where he has taught mythology for many years. He has seen how ancient myths can still capture the imaginations of young people today. For this reason he has created a variety of teaching materials (including textbooks, posters, and websites) that focus specifically on the teaching of mythology to young audiences. He is the author of two book series, the *Reaching Olympus* series and the *Mythology for Teens* series. He is also a professional illustrator. He resides in the Ozarks with his wife, Rachel, and children.

For more information and products (including textbooks, posters, and electronic content)
visit his website
www.mythologyteacher.com

Contact him by email at **mr.mythology@gmail.com**

CPSIA information can be obtained
at www.ICGtesting.com
Printed in the USA
BVHW012315310722
643479BV00006B/44

9 780982 704936